"There is plenty of action in *Bino*. But more: Gray writes with a pen dipped in hemlock. Repulsive fat cats, unscrupulous politicians and shameless hypocrites are taken for a lovely ride."
—*The New York Times Book Review*

"SANDPAPER TOUGH!" —*Booklist*

"Lots of action, and in all the right places."
—*Rave Reviews*

"CAPTURES THE READER FROM THE VERY FIRST LINE . . . This is a brilliant new writer to watch."
—*Publishers Weekly*

"GREAT DIALOGUE, propelled by sardonic wit . . . with hard-nosed polish from first corpse to last."
—*Kirkus Reviews*

A. W. Gray

PUBLISHER'S NOTE

This book is a work of fiction. Names, characters, places, and incidents either are the product of the author's imagination or are used fictitiously, and any resemblance to actual persons, living or dead, events, or locales is entirely coincidental.

NAL BOOKS ARE AVAILABLE AT QUANTITY DISCOUNTS WHEN USED TO PROMOTE PRODUCTS OR SERVICES. FOR INFORMATION PLEASE WRITE TO PREMIUM MARKETING DIVISION, NEW AMERICAN LIBRARY, 1633 BROADWAY, NEW YORK, NEW YORK 10019.

This is an authorized reprint of a hardcover edition published by E. P. Dutton. The hardcover edition was published simultaneously in Canada by Fitzhenry and Whiteside Limited, Toronto.

ONYX TRADEMARK REG. U.S. PAT. OFF. AND FOREIGN COUNTRIES
REGISTERED TRADEMARK—MARCA REGISTRADA
HECHO EN DRESDEN, TN, USA

SIGNET, SIGNET CLASSIC, MENTOR, ONYX, PLUME, MERIDIAN and NAL BOOKS are published by NAL PENGUIN INC., 1633 Broadway, New York, New York 10019

First Onyx Printing, May, 1989

1 2 3 4 5 6 7 8 9

PRINTED IN THE UNITED STATES OF AMERICA

For Marvelous Martha
and the Juniper Jumping Beans,
a chin-up bunch
that's headed down the homestretch

Sonny Starr blew whatever chance he might have had about two seconds after he walked into the room. Prancy little dipshit. Wearing those brown, polished leather, pointy-toed shoes and press-creased tan slacks, a loud flower-patterned shirt open to the third button, dark hair on his scrawny chest acting as a cushion for the round gold medallion that dangled there. All that Sonny had to do was say, "Hey, Buster, howsa man?" Kind of nice and casual, set down the brown paper sack he was carrying, take one of those dark green wine bottles that Buster could see in the bag, uncork it, and pour a drink for the two of them. All he had to do. But Sonny didn't. Instead he took one look at Buster, Buster sitting in the beat-up green cloth easy chair with a leg draped over the arm, squawked like a chicken, and tried to bolt back out into the hallway.

Buster watched big John-boy step out from where he'd been hiding, back against the wall just inside the door, and block Sonny's path. Big John-boy, huge biceps pumped up doing four flat years on Darrington Prison Farm. John-boy, massive chest straining against a pink muscle shirt, half-bald, what hair he did have, straight and black. *John-boy! John-boy Driggers! King of the Wild Frontier.* Standing there, legs apart, corded arms folded like Punjab.

Sonny froze in his tracks, his black-eyed gaze darting back and forth from John-boy to Buster like that of a trapped roadrunner. Then Sonny grinned. "Hiya, John-boy. Buster. Say, where you men been keeping yourselves?"

Buster thought, too late, Son. Should have started the pals-forever bullshit about three seconds ago. Buster's right arm was over the chairback, hand out of sight. Now he brought it into view, feeling the heft of the Winchester .45 revolver he was holding. He gripped the gun loosely, holding it in his lap pointed off to the side as he said, "Why we was going to ask you the same thing, Son. Like how come you moved off without giving no new address to your old buddies? S'matter, Son, ain't got time for old cons no more?"

"Well . . ." Sonny took short, almost-mincing steps in the pointy shoes, went over to the table in the breakfast nook. The white paint on the table was chipped and yellowed with age. The waterfall-patterned wallpaper was faded and cracking, bare Sheetrock peeping through. Sonny put the bag down on the table. "Well, I was going to. You know, soon as I got situated, first thing. Well how you guys been? Yeah, hey, how 'bout a drink?" He was playacting now, trying not to look at the Winchester, but glancing at it anyway, a grin frozen on his skinny face.

Buster bent to the side and spat a brown shower of tobacco juice into the wastebasket. It splattered on some newspapers in the bottom. Buster had red kinky hair and a full scraggly beard; his cheek puffed over the massive chaw in his mouth. "Naw, Sonny, me and John-boy don't want nothing to drink. This ain't no fucking social call. You hard to find, boy. We hunted North Dallas, shit, West Dallas, all over. What you doin' in Oak Cliff, Sonny? Shitty neighborhood, Son, for the kind of money you ought to be packing." He looked with a half sneer around him at the raggedy furniture, the old-timey wood venetian blinds on the windows. There was a faint odor of grease-cooked meat hanging in the air.

Sonny gave a nervous giggle. "Oh, you know. Kind of livin' low style, stringing the money out far as it'll go. You two made the same as I did on the deal. Say. How you guys find me, anyway?"

Buster eyed John-boy, who shrugged massive shoulders and chuckled deep in his throat. Buster said, "We had sort of a guide. Didn't we, John-boy?" He leveled the .45 at the wall to his left, squinting down the barrel. "Clarice. Your main squeeze, Son. She brought us."

A fleeting look of panic. "Clarice? She's here?"

"Why sure, Sonny. Only you might not want to squeeze her no more. John-boy, he got a little carried away with her." Buster jerked his head in the direction of the bedroom. He was wearing a grimy white T-shirt. His skin was pale and freckled.

Sonny looked toward the bedroom. "Naw, you didn't—Jesus fucking Christ, Buster! Not the broad, not Clarice. She don't know nothing." It was a begging whine.

John-boy took a step toward Sonny. He dropped his muscled arms to his sides. "She goddamn sure don't know nothing now, Son. But you know something. Don't you?"

It was beginning to dawn on Sonny, Buster could tell it from the look about him. The shifty, darting glances. First the shock of seeing them there, then the faint hope that, hey, maybe he could jive-talk his way out of it. Kidding around. But now he knew for certain. Sonny spat out, "You fucks."

Buster climbed slowly to his feet. He was big and

beefy, no pretty-boy muscles like John-boy. But just as dangerous. The pistol hung in Buster's limp hand, barrel pointing down. "Sit down, Sonny. We going to talk."

Sonny looked unsure of himself, hesitant. John-boy grabbed a rickety wooden kitchen chair. He set it on the floor behind Sonny, put a hand on Sonny's shoulder, and pushed him down into the seat. Then John-boy and Buster stood shoulder to shoulder, Sonny in the chair looking up at them. The kitchen table was at Sonny's back. The linoleum on the floor had age wrinkles in it. Buster lazily aimed the pistol between Sonny Starr's eyes.

"You should have told us, Sonny," Buster said, almost sadly. "See, if we'd of known you was out selling coke and weed and got yourself busted we might have helped. But you never said a word. Man gets arrested and don't tell his friends about it—well, it means they ain't his friends no more. So what's happened, Sonny? You making some kind of deal with the Feds? Like to give me and John-boy up, get your own ass off? Shit, maybe scot-free, from your chickenshit dope beef and the other deal as well. That it, Son? We think maybe it is, particularly since you ain't keeping in touch like you used to."

Sonny's lip curled. "Keeping in touch? With you dumb shits? Naw, I ain't gave you up. But I might. I got a lawyer, man. He's got a file I give him, all about the—you know, the deal. How you two fucks like that, hey? Anything happens to me you go to Huntsville Death Row. Whoosh, needle in your arm. So don't fuck with me."

Buster looked at John-boy and shrugged. "See, I told you. He ain't going to give any straight answers. Whatcha think we ought to do?"

His bushy, dark brows knitted, John-boy said, "Up

to you, Bus. Don't make no difference to me." He needed a shave.

Buster looked thoughtful. Then, half-smiling, spittle brown against stained teeth, he steadied the pistol. He shot Sonny Starr twice. The .45 jerked hard in Buster's hand. *Blam! Blam!* The first slug blew the point of Sonny's shoulder away. The second tore into the left side of his chest. Sonny flew backward, head over heels, the chair crashing and splintering on the floor. On thc table behind him, one of the bottles in the sack exploded. The odor of cheap wine blended with the burning smell of gunpowder. One of Sonny's arms and one of his legs twitched in unison. Then he went limp.

John-boy scratched his head. "Might should have waited, Bus. He might have told us—shit, you think he was telling straight? About the lawyer?"

"Could be," Buster said. He spat tobacco juice on the floor. "Who's this dudc's lawyer, John-boy? You got any idea?"

Winston Bennett Anspacher III, short to begin with, but looking like a dwarf to Bino Phillips from across Anspacher's dark wood, handball-court-sized desk, took a file folder out of his top drawer and opened it with soft, pink hands. There were two pieces of paper in the folder. Bino recognized the district court letterhead on one of them. The other was a bar association buck slip, a form that got passed around by mail from one member to another so that each could make a comment like "Off with his head" or "This lawyer is a prick," then put his initials on it and send it on to the next guy.

"I've got a matter to bring up with you, Bino," Anspacher said. "Not a major issue, but a rather touchy one at that."

So here it comes. The phone call this morning. Drop on up to the sixty-eighth floor of InterFirst Tower today, Bino. You know, we haven't talked in like eighteen years and we love to have a lot of criminal lawyers hanging around up at Anspacher, Anspacher, and Mortarhouse. Makes it look good when the Chrysler V.P.'s or the boys from Washington come in. Then the buildup, Bino drinking coffee while listening to

"Glad you're doing great" and "Remember the time over at the Phi Delt house when we had the big dinner and a guy got drunk and took a piss in the bowl of mashed potatoes?" Yeah, only Winston Bennett Anspacher III had been *eating* the meal. Bino Phillips had been serving it, trying to make a couple of extra bucks to supplement the ten dollars a month that the athletic department furnished, calling it laundry money.

Bino crossed his legs, shifting a little in his chair, looking at Anspacher maybe a mile away across the desk. "Oh? What is it, Winnie?"

"Well—maybe I'd better just let you read it." He held out the district court's letter. Bino stretched his full six feet six out of the chair, bending from the waist over the desk, reaching out and barely getting the letter with his fingertips. He sat and read it. Judge Hazel Burke Sanderson didn't like Bino Phillips for shit.

"Now, Bino," said Winnie Anspacher, the Mercantile Bank looking like a miniature toy through the picture window behind him, "you know very well that the bar association would rather get its teeth pulled than to get involved in something like this. The members know that you and I are old frat brothers, and have asked me to chat with you about this and see if we can't get it informally handled without ruffling any feathers." Meaning, oh, we got you, Bino, and it just tickles us to death to get to jump on somebody.

Bino's gaze shifted away from Winston Bennett Anspacher III to Bino's right, and he stared straight into the eyes of Winston Bennett Anspacher I. It was one of those pictures that photographers warn against, with the subject looking directly into the camera instead of at a bird that the guy taking the picture was waving around, and old Winnie I seemed to be putting the whammy on anybody sitting anywhere in the room. Bino had heard the stories about Winnie I defending a man who'd allegedly robbed the old Lakewood Post Office and winning an acquittal; the Anspacher firm hadn't needed to buy postage for a year after that. Old Winnie I, if anybody crossed him, didn't give a shit *whose* feathers he ruffled. Bino looked back at Winston Bennett Anspacher III.

"Well, Winnie, I did win the case, you know," he said.

Anspacher got up. He walked around the edge of his desk to a rolling, hand-carved wood server and poured himself a goblet of ice water from a silver pitcher, the top of his head on a level with the bottom of his grandpappy's photo. Winnie III had on silver wire-framed glasses and was bald, the fringe around his ears and the back of his head trimmed short. Next to the massive desk, and with the rolling server waist high to him, Winnie looked like The Incredible Shrinking Man, around the middle of the picture when the guy had lost about two feet. Winnie carried the glass of water back behind his desk and sat down.

"Yes, you did," said Winnie, "that's something that nobody can argue with. Nothing succeeds like success, and all that. But really, Bino"—he took off his glasses, huffed a fog onto the lenses, and cleaned them with a spotless handkerchief—"let's face it. Vince Lombardi didn't practice law. Winning *isn't* everything. The old girl herself says that you ate the government's case alive; it says that right in the letter. But criminey, making remarks about the judge carrying the trial on one day past the scheduled adjournment, and doing so right in front of her staff, why that's—"

Bino Phillips said, "He was eavesdropping."

"Huh?" Winnie put the handkerchief away and put on his glasses, blinking at Bino like a short owl. "Who was eavesdropping?"

"The bailiff. When I said that the old heifer sure was fucking up my tee time, Half-a-Point and I were in the john, taking a leak. The bailiff must have been in the water closet on the crapper. Is this a grievance?"

Anspacher laughed. Sort of strained, come to think about it. He put his fingertips together, tapping them lightly on one another. "Well, really it isn't. She hasn't said that you've done anything *unethical*, just that—well, it's the whole picture, Bino. She says you're using a bookmaker as an investigator—"

"That's Half-a-Point," said Bino. "Horace Harrison. He's been to trial, Winnie. A jury acquitted him."

"Everybody in town knows about that, Bino. You defended him, and the government witness couldn't distinguish between his voice on the phone and the prosecutor, Marvin Goldman's voice. You-all recorded Goldman placing a bet. The case is legend. But having your secretary eat lunch next to a tableful of jurors . . ."

Bino's neck was getting warm. "Look, Winnie. Dodie eats at the Bluefront four days out of five. It wasn't planned. And Goldman is the one that told the judge about it. How the hell do you think *he* knew about it? He was buying the fucking lunch, Winnie, sitting between two of the jurors." Bino got up and began to pace back and forth. "There's a lot you don't know about criminal cases, Winnie, particularly ones in federal court. If you beat the Feds, they all get pissed off—the judge, the prosecutor, even the bailiff. And suddenly they all want to brand you as a pain in the ass in court."

Anspacher took a swallow of the ice water. "Well, really, Bino, I told you to begin with that we really didn't want to stick our noses into this. Look, we all have to work together and around each other. Now, you're in a different ball game than us civil lawyers, that's for sure. But when a federal judge gets down on one of us, she's down on us all. And none of us can afford that. So now I've given you the message, straight from the bar. No action is going to be taken on this, but in the future please don't upset old Hazel. It'll help us all. After all, most of us went to the same law school."

"*You* went to the same law school, Winnie, you and most of the other lawyers in this town. Not me. When my basketball scholarship ran out, I couldn't afford S.M.U. anymore. I went to night school, South Texas C. of L., worked during the day."

"I'd forgotten that, Bino. We've all been practicing around here for so long now, one tends to forget everybody's launching pad. Well, anyway, just watch it with the old girl from now on, would you please?" Winnie grinned. "A bookmaker? On your staff? Oh, that's rich, buddy boy."

Bino said, "Can I use your phone?"

"Certainly, certainly. The one out front, if you would, by the elevators. I'm sorry, but I've got a couple of people waiting. Don't stay away for so long next time, huh?" They shook hands, meaning audience over, get out. Bino left.

He used the phone at the receptionist's desk while she was pressing switchboard buttons and routing calls. He watched her breathing as he punch-dialed. He sat down in a little chair while the other line was ringing, his knees nearly hitting him in the chin. Everybody in this frigging office, along with all the clients, must be the same size as Winnie Anspacher.

On the line, Dodie said, "Atttt-orrrr-ney's office."

He winced. "Let's go back to plain old 'Lawyer's office,' Dode."

"Oh! Bino! Wow, I'm glad you called. Sonny Starr got killed." Dodie got right to the point.

Bino didn't feel any tears forming, but he said, "That's terrible, Dode. What happened?"

"Well, I don't know. Mr. Goldman called and said the trial is off because Sonny Starr is dead. Says for you to call him."

"Are you sure he said that, Dodie? I mean, that Sonny himself is dead, and not that my case is dead, or something like that?" She said no, she was sure, and Bino could see her round blue eyes batting. "Get Sonny's file, will you?" he said.

"Sure. Hold on."

Now she'd be propelling her rolling secretary's chair across the office to the file cabinet, her spike-heeled feet moving like petite ferryboat paddles. In a few minutes she said, "Got it."

"Are there any phone numbers in there, like for friends or relatives?"

"Nope. I already checked. Only the rooming house where he lived."

Picturing Sonny Starr, feet propped up on Bino's desk, arrogant look on his face, Bino wasn't surprised that he didn't have any friends. Sonny Starr might not even have a mother. Did Winnie have any clients who lived in a rooming house? Or took their calls at a pay phone? The receptionist was watching him.

"Well, Dodie, try to get in touch with somebody that can fill us in. I don't want to talk to Goldman until I know the score. Oh, and Dodie. I won't be back in today. I have another appointment."

"Oh. Does that mean you won't be seeing Barney Dalton? He called and said you were meeting him at Joe Miller's Bar."

"Well, Dode, it means—well, I'll take care of Barney, okay? See you tomorrow."

"Okay, boss. Keep your chin up." She was gone. Wonder what she meant by that? Dodie made the office seem enchanted.

The receptionist said, from behind harlequin glasses, "Is your hair bleached?"

"No," said Bino as the elevator door opened. "I was scared as a kid. It just turned this way."

His stomach churned up in the vicinity of his eyeballs on the ride down. Express car, sixty-eight floors. He went to the parking garage, ducking slightly as he went into the cashier's booth, paid the check, and picked up the Lincoln Town Car. White. To go with his hair.

He went north out of downtown on Akard Street until it merged with McKinney Avenue, taking the short winding hop on Harry Hines Boulevard to the tollway entrance, thinking, Winnie Anspacher must not have had much else to do today. Never had had much to do, at least to *have* to do, growing up in Highland Park. A far cry from where Bino and Half-a-Point Harrison came from.

Not far at all in miles, just the next city limit sign east from Dallas. Mesquite, pronounced Mess-*keet* by the folks who ran out of gas there on the way to Big D from Tyler, Wills Point, Greenville, and Texarkana, put up white-framed houses, and fixed cars and ran convenience stores on wide, dusty street corners or made book and played poker like Half-a-Point and his dad, just to get a bankroll started so they could move on into town. Most of them never made it.

Bino was one of them who did, on the strength of a soft, rafter-scraping hook shot and a fallaway baseline jumper that hit nothing but cord most of the time. They won him a scholarship to S.M.U., the rich kids' school, where he made the grades and got married. To Annabelle Bradley, pleated cheerleader skirt swirling around her slender legs, campus sweetheart and daughter of a rootin', tootin' oil-well millionaire. Her dad wanted Bino in the oil business with him, but Bino wanted to be a lawyer and made that, also. Worked his way through. Lost Annabelle somewhere in the process.

What Bino would really have liked to do was take Winnie Anspacher out to Mesquite and separate him from his bankroll, playing on a honky-tonk pool table.

* * *

Joe Miller's Bar was on Lemmon Avenue, a shady old street in a shady old neighborhood. It was dimly lit and served good bar whiskey. Bino Phillips went to Joe Miller's early and stayed late.

Early in the evening, Barney Dalton said, "You should grow a mustache, Bino. Your beard's white, just like your hair, and it would look striking on you. A thin one, like Half's." The ice tinkled in his near-empty Scotch as he gestured it, toast-fashion, at Half-a-Point Harrison, sitting skinny across the small round table.

"I've thought about it, Barney," said Bino. He was sitting at the same table, with Barney on his left and Half-a-Point Harrison on his right, drinking drawn Michelob. "But I've got to be careful. You're a golf pro, can go around any way you want to. But even today there's some people around who resent mustaches. I've got to be careful how I come across to a jury."

"You don't come across too good now, Bino." Half-a-Point Harrison had a thin hawk face to go with the skinny rest of him. He looked like an undertaker who had accidentally embalmed himself. He was drinking plain soda and lime. "You owe me seventeen hundred bucks. Seventeen ten, with last night's juice."

Bino said, "That can't be, Half. The Redskins were ahead, twenty-one-ten, after three quarters."

"That's why they got four quarters, Bino. Marino went crazy in the fourth. Miami won it, thirty-one–twenty-one." Half sipped some of the soda through a tiny stir straw. "Seventeen ten."

Bino thought, Jesus Christ. He felt in his pocket. "Well, I don't have it right now, Half. Tell you what. Just deduct it from the part of the office rent and phone bill that you're paying."

"I did that last month," said Half-a-Point. "Now we're getting into next month."

Bino snapped his fingers. "Terrible news, Half. Dodie says that Sonny Starr got killed."

"Why's that terrible?" said Half-a-Point. "Did he owe us?"

Later at the bar, with Half-a-Point gone, the deeply tanned-by-sunlamp brunette said, even white teeth flashing against her walnut skin, "What does the Cecil-fish eat?"

Bino thought, what the hell is this? He said, "His *name* is Cecil. Oscar is what he is. Oscar fish. He eats minnows, snaps them up like good cake. You should see him—I'm sorry, I don't remember your name."

"It's Syl. You mean Oscar is a *cannibal*?"

It's Cecil, thought Bino. Oscar is—shit.

The peppy redhead sitting next to Syl, both girls between Barney and Bino, said, "Are you guys writers?"

"Nope," said Bino. "I'm a poor country lawyer, and Barney is the golf pro out at Crooked River. He qualified for the open, three years running. Huh, Barn?" Barney shrugged nothing-to-it, the alligator on his pocket going up and down.

"Come on, Syl," said the redhead. "Let's sit at a table where we might meet some writers." She picked up her drink and moved.

The brunette got her purse off the bar. "Sorry. But Polly is freakso for writers. Nice talking to you—I'm sorry, I can't remember your name."

"It's Bino. Short for albino."

At fifteen minutes after one, Bino Phillips paid his tab, left Barney at the bar talking to a girl in leopard pants, and went into the parking lot. He was listing some. The fall night had scared up a wind with some teeth in it. He flopped into the Linc's soft velour seat, put a Bob Dylan cassette on the wraparound stereo, and drove away. As he wheeled out of the lot, he lit a filtered Camel and cracked the window open to let the smoke out.

At the corner of Lemmon and Wycliff he signaled left, waiting for the light to change. Headlights glared at him in the rearview mirror like cat's eyes. He looked closely for bubble gum flashing lights on the car's roof in the mirror, popping a Cert from the glove compartment as he did. It didn't *look* like a cop car. Nevertheless, when the light changed, he eased around the corner very slowly.

The cat's eyes followed.

The lights stayed close to his bumper, tailgating, as he went south on Wycliff. Bino slowed and carefully moved the Linc's nose far to the right. He flashed his left-turn signal, indicating go ahead and pass.

The cat's eyes slowed, moved to the right, and stayed behind him.

Bino gunned the Lincoln as he went downhill, bouncing, bumper going up and down as he took the on ramp to the Dallas North Tollway. The lights stayed on his tail, bouncing up and down behind him. He had a quarter and dime ready, tossed them into the basket at the tollgate, and shot the speedometer needle up to seventy as he whipped onto the freeway. The cat's eyes came through the same tollgate and caught up with him. Tall freeway lights illuminated the other car. It was a two-toned Cadillac Seville.

Slowly, carefully, keeping one eye on the road and the other on the rearview, Bino fished the Mauser pistol out of the glove compartment. Two shells were in it, the best he could remember. The gun was a fee from a burglar doing ten years and wishing that he had it back.

Bino thought, Half-a-Point? Naw, Half wouldn't—

As he sped under the overpass at I-635, Bino hit the brakes, giving no signal, and veered across two right-hand lanes onto Dallas North Parkway, tires squealing. Then he braked again, turned hard right, and bounced into his apartment complex lot. The complex had a brook winding in and out and big trees dotting the courtyards. The Caddy's radials whined loudly as it followed.

Bino wheeled into his numbered slot and cut the engine. The Seville's passenger-side window was sliding down as the car pulled up on his left. Bino opened his door, thumbed back the Mauser's hammer, and held it in plain sight, ready.

There was a sharp intake of breath from within the Seville. Even white teeth showed against deeply tanned skin.

"My goodness," said Syl. "I *just* wanted to meet *Cecil.*"

If there was one thing that Buster Longley had learned doing both federal and state time, it was his way around the courthouse. Nothing to it. If a big dumbo sat around in his cell and wrote letters to the judge, they'd never get read. The dumbo could write until he was blue in the face.

But clerks, now, particularly young girls with little brothers, who had getting knocked up and married on their minds, they'd listen. Like the time in the federal joint up at Danbury trying to get a five-year beef reduced, when Buster wrote the following note, attached to a letter to the judge:

Dear Clerk,

Will you please give me some hep. I know the Judge is real, real bizy. I don't read and rite so good, but my mom needs me at home awful bad to make her living for her, and I shure need for the Judge to see this. Please put it where he will.

Then he made certain that the note had a few coffee stains on it and mailed it off, putting the stamp on the envelope upside down. In two weeks his sentence was reduced from five to three years. Buster bet that the judge would have thrown the letter away if a young girl hadn't been shoving it under his nose and keeping an eye on him.

Keeping this in mind, and figuring that any dumbo with sense enough to read a sign could find the clerk's office, he left big John-boy running the vacuum and making the beds and went down to the federal courthouse. He had put on a clean checkered shirt, had left his Days Work in a dresser drawer, and stood behind the counter looking dumb and country.

A girl with just enough lip gloss on to make a pinkish shine and a thin blue blouse covering just over a handful of boob, said, "Yes, may I help you?"

"Well, yes, ma'am, I expect that you could. I come up here from Corsicana today to try and help a poor lady from our church out. Poor woman, she raised a boy with a real wild streak in him that went and got himself in a lot of trouble. The boy got killed yesterday, and his mama's beside herself in grief. I told her I'd try to find his lawyer to see if maybe the boy'd left anything with him that she could have. Now, I'm no good at things like this, but I think the young fella had some charges on him, and if he did you folks might have the name of his lawyer down here. Could you—well, I hate to put you out any, but his name's Andrew Starr. With two *R*s."

The girl said, "Oh. Well I can certainly look for you," writing Sonny's name on a piece of paper. She had short brown hair that bounced around when she moved her head.

Buster leaned on the counter and read the equal employment opportunity signs on the bulletin board, glancing at the way the girl's ass and legs moved as she stooped and went through the files. She came back with a thick folder.

She chuckled as she wrote. "*Wendell A.?* I didn't

know that was Bino Phillips's real name. There you are." She tore off the top slip from a notepad, the one she'd been writing on, and gave it to Buster.

Buster's red mustache, combed neat, moved up and down as he said, "Oh, I'm beholden to you for helpin' me out, miss. Could I have your name? So if Andrew's mama wants to know anything about his case down here, she'll know who to call?"

"It's Andrea. Andrea Morton."

Buster left, wondering how Andrea Morton would look with John-boy tying her wrists to the bedpost. Scared, probably. Made it better.

When the vault drawer rumbled out and the shroud was pulled back, Bino thought that Sonny Starr actually looked better than the last time Bino'd seen him. But Bino couldn't figure out *why* Sonny looked better, and it took a few seconds of looking for it to dawn on him. Sonny wasn't sneering or smirking.

Finally, after he, Assistant Coroner Shoesole Traynor, and Assistant U.S. Attorney Marvin Goldman had stood for several minutes looking down at Sonny like three men watching a flea circus in a box, Bino said, "Yeah, it's him."

Shoesole Traynor, not as tall as Bino but tall enough, with thick graying hair and a pot on him that strained against the fabric of his white knee-length smock, was smoking a pipe. It was a briar, Sherlock Holmes style, that he kept clenched between his teeth, so that only his lips moved when he talked. He was burning a sweet-scented tobacco.

Traynor said, as he shoved the vault closed like a giant file drawer, "That's three for three. According to Mr. Goldman, the landlady says it's Sonny Starr. Mr. Goldman says it's Sonny Starr. And now *you* say it's Sonny Starr. But it still ain't Sonny Starr until somebody signs this fucking form that I've got in my office. How about it, Bino? You sign it?"

Bino's gaze flicked at Goldman, who was studying the label on Sonny's sliding coffin with sudden interest. Bino said, "Well, yeah, Shoesole, I don't see why not. If nobody else will."

Traynor sighed. "Well, finally. Right this way, gents."

Traynor led the way out the double swinging doors, smoke from the pipe trailing behind him. Bino motioned for Goldman to go ahead, then brought up the rear, watching the way Goldman's back tapered down to his waist under his tailored black suit coat. Goldman worked out quite a bit. Bino reminded himself—for the fifth time this year—to join a health club.

Shoesole Traynor's office was in County Medical's basement, behind a door with a frosted glass panel in it. Goldman waited in the hallway while Bino went in and sat across the desk from Traynor and signed a form with his name next to the words "Identified by." After "Relationship," Bino wrote "None—Attorney," then thought a minute and added "Friend" in parentheses. Even Sonny Starr should have at least one.

Traynor got his nickname from a preoccupation with feet, claiming that there were more clues in a corpse's foot than anywhere else. Claimed he could tell if a victim was sitting or standing when he got it, and everywhere they'd been in the last week, just by examining feet. His theory wasn't proven; Traynor's foot evidence had been ruled inadmissible in the last four trials in which he'd testified. A lot of people, Bino Phillips included, thought that Shoesole just had a foot fetish.

Bino said, "Actually, Goldman knew Sonny just as well as I did. He could have signed this." Bino thought about Goldman, calling at seven this morning, just as Syl was talking about showing Bino a trick she knew with an ice cube in her mouth. Bino wondered if

Goldman had known what he was interrupting. Naw—if he had, he'd have called even earlier.

Traynor said, "This whole thing's peculiar, Bino. I can understand why the landlady would be reluctant to give us a make. Sonny Starr paid his rent in cash, and she didn't even know if Andrew Starr was his real name or not. But Goldman's position on this is really funny. Goldman himself called the report in, from his office. In fifteen years, this is the first time a homicide report's come through the Feds, unless it was the Feds that did the killing. Normally the report comes from the local police, or whoever finds the body." He tapped the spent tobacco out of his pipe and refilled the bowl from a pouch. His certificates of education, in black frames, were visible over his shoulder. "You got any idea who the gal with Sonny might have been?"

Bino shook his head. "Nope. But I wouldn't start trying to find out by checking the membership roster of the Junior League."

When Bino left Traynor's office, he found Marvin Goldman leaning against a corridor wall with his arms folded. Goldman's curly black hair had little threads of silver in it. He said, "Well, I guess that's that, Bino. I'll have a dismissal motion fixed up and bucked over to you. You can sign it and send it over to Judge Sanderson's court—or take it over to old Hazel yourself." Goldman's lip twitch said that he knew about Judge Sanderson's letter to the bar.

Bino said, "How'd you know that somebody offed Sonny, Marv? Who called you on it?"

Goldman smiled. He had thin lips and wore a clipped goatee. Not looking directly at Bino, he said, "Oh, I got the message from one of the girls in the office—I'm not sure who phoned it in."

Bino thought, Yeah, and I'm not sure that the Dolphins beat Washington. Half-a-Point just told me.

He said, "That's funny, Marv. Shoesole's report says that you told *him* that the landlady called you."

Goldman checked the thin gold watch that stood out in contrast to his pale blue cuff. "Well, maybe she did. Look, Bino, I've got to run. Thanks for coming down, buddy. I could have I.D.'d Sonny, but I didn't think it would look right for the prosecutor to put his name on the morgue sheet. Be better if his own lawyer did."

Suddenly, Bino got it.

"Who found the bodies, Marv?"

Goldman looked like a shoplifter searching for the nearest exit. "Huh?"

"The landlady didn't call, did she, Marv? Come to think about it, Sonny Starr said that the manager of his building was a faggot. Let me guess. The F.B.I. found the bodies, didn't they?"

Goldman said, "I'm really late, Bino. I've got to—"

"And the only way the F.B.I. could find the bodies would be if they were inside Sonny's place, isn't it, Marv?"

Goldman shrugged, adjusting the knot in his tie. "Sounds reasonable," he said.

Bino grinned. Chuckling, he said, "So the boys went in to shake down old Sonny's pad, huh? Without a warrant, of course, and thinking that nobody's home. And what do they find but poor Sonny, only Sonny's missing part of himself here and there. So what does the F.B.I. do? Why, they can't report the killing, 'cause then they'd have to explain what they were doing there in the first place. So they think it over and say, 'Hey, we'll just call old Marv—he sent us over here to begin with. Let Marv handle it.' "

Goldman squared his shoulders and looked up at Bino, his forehead on a level with Bino's chin. He said, "So sue us, Bino."

Bino thought it over, then finally decided to say,

"*Sue* you? Sue the Feds? In federal court, yet? Don't make me laugh. Land of the free, huh, Marv?"

Goldman said, defiantly, "You heard me, Bino. If you don't like it, or think we're doing something illegal, the courtroom door is open to you. Now, if you'll excuse me, I've got to go. I'll send the dismissal papers over, just as I said."

With that, Goldman spun around and walked away, his back rigid and his polished black shoes clicking on County Medical's basement tile.

Bino thought, What an asshole.

Bino took the Linc on the short hop from County Medical, on Harry Hines Boulevard, down Inwood Road to Stemmons Freeway doing a slow burn, and very nearly sideswiping a Merchants' Fast Motor Freight bobtail as he whipped the Lincoln onto the entrance ramp to Stemmons Freeway, going south. The truck's driver, wearing a baseball cap, his cheeks puffy and red as he chewed on a soggy cigar, shot Bino the finger.

The day was overcast and windless, the temperature in the fifties, the cloud cover gray, mountainous, and unmoving. The black wisps rising from the factory smokestacks east of Stemmons hung like painted pictures.

Bino thought, the Constitution is dead as the dodo bird, guys like Marvin Goldman are flattening it like runaway trains. Sure, Sonny Starr was a turd. Go ahead and bust in and search his pad without a warrant. Take away Sonny's rights, and three cheers for Marv. But what happened when they figured out that if they could do it to Sonny, the guy with a mortgage, wife, and kids wasn't far behind? It was already coming to that, but America wasn't waking up to it. Probably wouldn't until it was too late to do anything about it.

By the time he'd parked in a lot on the south side of Main Street and gotten a receipt for the Linc, Bino had cooled off. He crossed the street with the light at the Akard Street intersection, horn honks echoing, buses chugging, their exhausts atomizers for the acrid downtown perfume. He watched the way a tall brunette's hips moved as she crossed the street ahead of him, her purse suspended by a strap from her arm and swinging from side to side.

The Davis Building was old, a bank thirty or forty years ago, now cheap downtown rent hanging on between modern skyscrapers. Bino liked it. It still employed elevator operators who sat on stools that were bolted into the cars' walls, and who cranked handles that made the doors open and close and the cars go up and down.

Teresa Valdez smiled and nodded to Bino, twirled the handle, and the car rose to the sixth floor. Teresa was under five feet, less than breastbone height to Bino, her dark hair short, her cheeks round and rosy. Teresa's mom ran the elevator next to hers, her grandmother the car next to that. Bino grinned down at Teresa as he got off.

His feet were noiseless on the carpet. He flicked a speck of dust from the lapel of his dark brown suit as he went to the door marked W. A. PHILLIPS, ATTORNEY in plain gold letters, then opened the door and looked at Dodie's butt. To say that Dodie had a butt was like saying that Laurence Olivier was an actor. Or that Lee Trevino played golf. She was bent over a bottom file drawer, her back to the door.

Bino said, "Lookin' good, Dode."

She sniffed, didn't look up. "I got a ticket. It's on the desk."

And it was, a long carbon-copy slip from a traffic cop's booklet. Bino read that Dora Annette Peterson, five feet, four inches tall, weighing a hundred and twenty-one pounds, hair blond, eyes blue, driving a red 1983 Trans Am, had made a right-hand turn from Southwestern Boulevard onto Skillman Street at 8:17 this morning. From the left-hand lane.

She was due in the office at 8:30. The intersection was a block from her apartment.

Bino said, "Running a little late, weren't you, Dode?"

Dodie slid the file drawer closed, bounced to her feet, and jiggled over to sit behind her desk. She was wearing a green fall knit that clung. "Wow, that was the problem. I went to Skillman, thinking I'd go left on it to Northwest Highway. But the traffic was all cloggy going that way."

"So you turned right?"

She nodded, smiling, her face lighting up. Her eyes sparkled. They hadn't always.

Bino remembered the dull, lifeless, drugged-out eyes, dark circles under them, looking helplessly through the bars in the attorney's visiting booth, County Jail. Nineteen going on thirty-five. Lush curves straining against a coarse jailhouse smock.

He remembered a quick talk with the narcotics cop. "See 'em every day. They'll sell dope, sell their ass, too, if it'll get 'em enough money to get high on."

But there was something else in the way Dodie moved and talked. Something about the way she said things, straight-out, no-nonsense.

Probation suited the D.A., probably all a jury would have given Dodie anyway. At first, she just worked for Bino to earn out her fee, doing some filing, running some errands. Wanting to learn.

Fresh air in the country straightened her out. Half-a-Point Harrison was to be thanked for that—him and Pop and the farm. College at night. The look on her face when the A's and B's came rolling in. Sixty-two hours of three-point-four credit, Bino and Half-a-Point cheering her on, Half not knowing what it was she was reading a lot of the time. Now a one-girl office who knew her way around the courthouse and ran a typewriter like a berserk machine gun. And a sparkle in her eyes.

Marvin Goldman had wanted to put Half-a-Point Harrison in the penitentiary for taking bets on football games—some of them from Marvin Goldman.

Bino held the ticket out to her, saying, "Not this time, Dodie. You'll have to take your medicine, pay the fine, whatever. You could solve the problem if you'd just start getting up a little earlier. This is your third ticket in a month, all of them on your way to work."

Dodie's pink tongue tip flashed as she licked her full lower lip. She was wearing a light blush makeup. "It's the alarm clock, Bino. Sometimes it works, sometimes it doesn't."

"Well, get yourself a new one. Get one of those nifty digital clock radios. Throw your old alarm away."

"But—" She folded her hands, her long lashes down. Well, Bino, you know that's the clock that you got for me."

Bino put his hands in his pockets and looked at his shoes.

There'd been one night. Two years ago, Dodie's birthday, her twenty-third. Dinner. Bino gave her the cheap drugstore alarm more as a joke than anything else—get to work on time. She held the big brass clock in both hands and grinned at him like a sexy Tinker Bell, soft candlelight shadows doing a tom-tom dance across her cheeks and nose. Then she giggled like a munchkin as she set the old clanger and let it rip, right there in the pomp of Old Warsaw Restaurant. Dodie *ohh*hed at herself as she fumbled, trying to turn the damn thing off, pressing buttons that wouldn't press and turning knobs that wouldn't turn. Finally, two jacketed waiters hustled from the shadowy corners to the rescue, while Bino pretended not to notice the down-the-nose looks from nearby tables.

They made a few more spots, Dodie dragging the sappy old clock into every one of them, telling bored waitresses, "Looky. My boss gave it to me. It rings." Then setting it off again while her laughter tinkled and drunks at the bar looked around for the raiding cops or the fire trucks, whichever it was.

Sometime later, a little daiquiri-giddy, she leaned her head against his shoulder in a booth at Joe Miller's, the faint scent of Carnival in her soft hair. Suddenly there were warm, yielding lips against his, a small hand on his arm, nails digging in. The cheap old clock blasted him awake the next morning in her apartment, her smooth bare thigh firm against his leg.

Bino picked up the ticket and folded it in half. He put it in his pocket. "I'll fix it, Dode."

The door to Half-a-Point Harrison's cubbyhole of an office, marked INVESTIGATOR, was ajar. Bino went in. Half's desk was old, but Dodie had painted it for him, dark brown. There were two phones on the desk. One was a pale-green three-line rotary, tied in to the office lines. The other, plain black, was sitting off to one side. Half-a-Point, in a plaid vest and black bow tie, was reared back in his wooden swivel chair with his feet propped up on the corner of the desk. The receiver from the black phone was flattening his ear, held in place by his jaw and chin. His brown hair was thinning and combed straight back. He was holding a ruled pad in his lap, writing on it.

Half was saying, "Okay, Gil, readin' it back to you. Cincy four. Jets two and a half. Philly ten—Jesus, that's a steal, bettin' on Indianapolis. New England one, L.A. three and a half . . ."

Xerox copies of the inside pages of *Cosmo's Football News* were in an inch-high stack on the front of the desk. Bino took one and sat down. The Cowboys were giving six points to Cleveland, playing at Cleveland. Silly.

Half banged the receiver into the cradle, saying, "Where the hell is Dartmouth?"

"Uh, I don't know, Half," said Bino. "Up north, somewhere. Why?"

"Why?" roared Half. "Because the whole fucking town is taking Dartmouth and giving up six against Brown, that's why. And not even knowing where the hell the place is."

Bino said, crossing his legs, "Say, old buddy. I thought the deal was that the bookstore didn't open until after the office closes. Goldman would have a field day, saying we're down here running a sportsbook."

Half-a-Point had a calendar on the wall that was a month behind. He tore October off. "I ain't open for business. Just freshing the line up is all. Got a guy that copies the numbers down from the board at the Stardust every morning, then waits in a booth out on the Strip for a call."

Bino's jaw slacked. "You're calling interstate? On this phone?"

Half snorted, saying, "This is Half, Bino, not some hayseed off a turnip load. Naw—I call Pop. He's got a three-way setup, calls the guy so we can both get the info at the same time."

Bino pictured Pop Harrison, Half-a-Point's mirror image in twenty or thirty years, phone resting on his shoulder, notebook in his hand. And another picture, Pop buying Half and Bino Grapette soda in a bottle, and licorice sticks from a jar in an old drive-in grocery in Mesquite that smelled of fresh cold cuts and cheese.

Bino said, "You-all having Thanksgiving?"

"Don't we always? Mom's makin' dressing from scratch. Detroit–Oakland at eleven, Dallas–Washington at two. You comin'?"

Bino's mother had been killed by a trucker coming off I-30 when Bino was a junior; an empty pint was found in the truck. His dad had waited around to see Bino get his sheepskin before joining her.

Bino said, "Wouldn't miss it, Half. You want to investigate something?"

"Sure, that's what I'm here for."

"It has to do with Sonny Starr."

"I'll wear gloves," said Half. "And a clothespin on my nose."

"I want to get a statement from the manager of Sonny's place. Just whether or not he was the one that found Sonny's body. Or if he wasn't, when and how he found out that Sonny was dead."

Half-a-Point stood up, putting the stack of *Football News* copies away in his bottom drawer, going over the top one and marking a couple of line changes as he did. "What's that for? Sonny's case is closed, ain't it? I mean, I got a lot to do, Bino."

"I'm trying to catch Goldman with his finger in the pie."

"I'm on my way. My little girl got the address?" Half called Dodie his little girl. Bino nodded.

On the way out, Bino stopped at the door and turned around. "Oh, Half. About the seventeen hundred."

Half waved his hand like he was batting at a mosquito. "Forget it. I've straightened it out with the rent. Your credit's still good, Bino."

As Bino went across the twelve-foot stretch of carpet between Half's office and his own, Dodie said to him, "Wow. That was the weirdest call." She'd just hung up, and her hand still rested on the receiver. She was wrinkling her nose.

Bino said, "What do you mean?"

Dodie rolled her chair back from her desk and folded her arms, a yellow pencil in her hand. Her legs were crossed. "It was this guy. He wanted to know if we had an envelope that belonged to Sonny Starr."

Bino rested a hip on the corner of her desk. "Maybe he thought Sonny mailed *him* something that got in the wrong envelope—you know, went to the wrong place."

She shook her head. "That wasn't it. He straight-out asked if Sonny gave you something, Bino. He talked a lot like some of yours and Half's friends do, the ones that live in Mesquite."

"What's wrong with that?"

"Oh, nothing, but there's more to it. He—well, he just sounded weird, that's all. Sort of creepy."

Bino shrugged. "So Sonny Starr had some weird friends. Sonny was weird. Why shouldn't his friends be?"

Bino spent the day in the office signing up two new clients and turning one down. An elderly black woman in a print dress, wringing her hands and dabbing at her eyes with a lace hankie, turned a Social Security check in the amount of $267.80 over and signed it on the back. It was to be a down payment on Bino's thousand-dollar fee for representing her grandbaby. A burglary. Bino looked at it for a moment, then fished in his pocket and handed her five twenties.

"You can pay me a little at a time," he said.

Dodie found two quarters in her purse and bought a Coke, giving it to the old woman and hugging her around the shoulders.

A white North Dallas heroin dealer, wearing a gold chain around his neck and with his shirt unbuttoned to his navel, counted twenty-five one-hundred dollar bills out on Bino's desk and checked the Rolex watch on his wrist.

"Here's half down," said the dealer, "and I'll finish

makin' you smile on Friday. Shipment comin' in. Go ahead and spring the bimbo, man."

Bino counted the money, put it in his pocket, and eyed the dealer. He said, "Write him a receipt, Dode. We'll post bond on Friday, when he brings the rest."

A few minutes later, Dodie made the arrangements with the bondsman over the phone. Bail would be up by three o'clock today. Then she carried the Rolex next door to the Metropolitan Savings and Loan, putting it in the safe-deposit box. The dealer muttered, "Cheap, Easter-bunny-haired son of a bitch."

Just after lunch, a man in a white, open-necked dress shirt who had a five o'clock shadow lit a Camel short and nervously set it in an ashtray on Bino's desk. His hands were stained with printer's ink.

He said, "It was a goddamn miracle. If I'd made the light at Ross and Carroll, I'd have already been at the shop. But I didn't. By the time I got there, they had Tony in cuffs and were takin' him out to the car. I just kept on truckin', came straight down here." The man had yellow teeth.

Bino took a tiny, battery-operated fan out of a drawer and turned it on, blowing the smoke in the direction of the door. "So what do you want to do?"

The man shrugged. "Make a deal. I've got the plates, tucked away nice. I can put Tony in a lot of places, selling a lot of twenty-dollar bills. I figure I can cop to a two-year beef, do it in a camp without a fence around it. Call the Feds."

Bino thought it over a minute, then reached behind him. He picked up the Yellow Pages and tossed them on the desk in front of the man with a solid thump.

The man said, "What's that for?"

"It's to help you find a lawyer. I don't represent snitches, pal. There's a book full of lawyers right there that do, but not me. Snitches make me sick."

The man left.

Sometime during the afternoon, Bino decided to get the bar association off his ass. He made an appointment through Judge Hazel Burke Sanderson's secretary to see the judge the next morning at eleven.

The secretary said, "I win the pot."

Bino said, "Huh?"

The secretary said, "I picked closest to the day and time that you'd call."

Dodie came and stood in Bino's open door at a few minutes after three. She was giggling. She held her nose, saying, "Mrs. Satterwhite is on the line."

Bino looked up from the *Football News*. "Have you heard from Half?"

Dodie nodded. "He called. He won't be back today. He had me forward the calls on the black phone over to Pop's. Do you want to talk to Mrs. Satterwhite?"

"Who's she?"

"She's that Mr. Anspacher's secretary—the one you went to see yesterday." Dodie giggled again. "She sounds like she's talking through her nose."

Winnie Anspacher? Maybe Bino'd been disbarred. The little fan was still on, its battery running down, the blades slowing. Bino turned it off, saying, "I'll take it, Dode." He punched the flashing button and picked up the phone.

"Hold for Mr. Anspacher, please." Mrs. Satterwhite sounded like she was talking through her nose.

In a minute, Winnie Anspacher's voice said, "Bino? Hi, big fella. Small world. It's the second time I've gotten to call you in two days."

Bino tried to remember whether Winnie's nose was higher than his desktop when he was sitting down. He said, "Hi, Winnie. I'm going to talk to the judge. Has a grievance been filed?"

Winnie laughed. "No, nothing like that. Say, Bino, did you know that Art Stammer is running for Richard Bigelow's old congressional seat?"

Bino hesitated, picturing Art Stammer as a skinny kid with a freshman beanie on. And Richard Bigelow, a fine old man, rolling in a gutter with his guts blown out. He said, "I've heard that he is."

"Good. I'm sponsoring a fund-raiser for him. I happened to mention to Art that I'd seen you, and he *insisted* that I ask you to come. It's tonight. At my place."

Bino thought, Why'd he insist? He hasn't seen me in eighteen years, either. He said, "I don't know, Winnie. I've got a lot of work piling up." Dodie cupped her hands at her mouth, pantomiming, "Liar."

Winnie said, "All work, Bino. Makes Jack a dull boy. Come on, it'll be like old home week. You'll know over half the people there."

Used to know. Bino thought about the bar association and seeing the judge tomorrow.

Winnie gave him his phone number in Highland Park.

Winnie said, "Now don't lose it, Bino. The number's unlisted. Anytime after eight, huh? Ciao, buddy."

Bino thought it over some more and decided to go. For just a little while.

Buster waited until John-boy was doing his stomach crunches and three-quarter sit-ups before he gave John-boy a ration of shit about the phone call. Anybody started to give John-boy a ration of shit when he was eating dinner or just sitting around scratching his nuts, John-boy was subject to put the hurt on them. But when he was working out, John-boy was too busy counting his reps to think about fucking with anybody.

"That wasn't no way to find out anything, John-boy, not just coming right out and asking about it."

Buster was spraddle-legged on the hassock, finishing off a Coors. He crushed the can, deciding not to get another one until he finished giving John-boy a ration of shit. Buster was in Jockey briefs, his gut sticking out, red hair on his stomach and chest.

John-boy said, ". . .forty-three, forty-four, forty-five—How's that, Bus? Forty-eight, forty-nine . . ." He had on blue jogging shorts. The laterals on his belly rippled, showing big muscle cuts when he straightened out at the bottom.

"Well, shit, John-boy, we don't know any more'n we knew before. Maybe Sonny was bullshitting, maybe he wasn't. But they weren't *telling* you. Maybe that's what they're waiting for, for some dumbo to call up and say, 'Hey, you got Sonny's shit, huh?' "

John-boy didn't say anything, just counted. He was slowing down, beginning to breathe harder.

Buster said, "I'm thinking about calling the man, see what he wants to do."

"The man—(puff)—told us not to call anymore, not till we find out about Sonny's lawyer, what he knows."

Buster thought, You ain't thinking, and said, "It's the man's ass, same as it is ours—more his, prob'ly. The man might just put some bread on us, you know, tell us to split." John-boy was really straining.

Buster thought, Shit, John-boy's getting outta shape. This little workout didn't used to be nothing.

Buster remembered Cinderella at Darrington, cute little punk that shaved his legs and had an ass just like Tina Turner's. Cinderella, eyes dancing, leaning forward on the bottom bunk, wearing short-shorts, his legs crossed, egging John-boy and the Drooper on.

"Come on, big John-boy, go. Drooper's catchin' up to you; come on, John, you want Cinderella milk it dry, don'tcha honey? Work out, John."

John-boy and rangy black Drooper, sweat pouring on both, really glistening on Drooper's chocolate hide. Buster counting for John-Boy, four ninety-eight, four ninety-nine; Little Fletch, eyes bugging, counting for Drooper. Blacks on one side, giving Drooper hell; honkies behind Buster, yelling for John-boy. Cinderella in the middle. Gorgeous punk. Dangerous. Doing the goddamndest time—man, you wouldn't be*lieve* what for. Throwing down on a Houston vice cop, making him drive Cinderella to Galveston, blowing the cop, and leaving him hand-cuffed naked to a pier on the beach.

Drooper wearing down around number six hundred, slowing, slowing. Blacks yelling, "Goddamn yo' rotten ass, Droop. You move it, you heah? Ain't no white boy gonna win that punk's ass offen you." Drooper giving up finally, John-boy still moving strong. Cinderella grinning, jacking off John-boy right there, him hard as a nail, Cindy's lips forming an *O* going down, whites cheering and hollering.

Yeah, John-boy had shape then. But now—

"Ninety-nine—(puff)—hunnerd. Shit!" John-boy relaxed, flat on his back. Then he got up and began to flex his stomach in front of the mirror. This was the part of the workout Buster thought was pretty dumb.

John-boy said, "Let's have a go at the dude's office, first. If that don't work, then maybe we call the man, huh?" He pounded a clenched fist on his midsection.

Buster thought that over, going into the kitchen to pop another Coors, the shag carpet coarse under his bare feet. It didn't make any sense to Buster, doing it the hard way, when all they had to do was tell the man to come up with some bread. Shit, the man'd do it. When Buster got back to the living room, John-boy was flexing his biceps with his back to the mirror, looking over his shoulder. Jesus, what a pain in the ass.

Buster said, "What you got against splittin', huh, maybe goin' to California and layin' around with some surfer-girl wool?"

John-boy lowered his arms, turned one wrist around so it pointed his hand away from his waist, and flexed his triceps. "Look, Buster, we're okay now, huh? Got us a little bread left, a North Dallas pad with a pool, get laid good and strong ever once in a while. Now, all that's gonna end it is if somebody gets us for the you-know-what, and they'd get us in California same as they would right here. Nobody knows about it 'cept us two and the man. Sonny don't know it no more, but maybe his lawyer does. I think we got to know if the lawyer knows or not. If he does, then maybe we talk to the man."

Buster had to admit, it wasn't bad thinking.

Teresa Valdez sat on a high stool behind the podium and watched it get dark. The traffic on Main Street was bumper to bumper at five and stayed that way until after six. Teresa passed the time counting the cars, three hundred between 5:00 and 5:05, a hundred and eighty-seven in a five-minute stretch an hour later. The count was down to fifty-two from seven until five after, and getting smaller. At 6:15 a pickup went by with its lights on; a Buick Riviera passed a few minutes later with dull parking lights glowing. By the seven o'clock count, every car was casting a low beam on the pavement in front of it.

She got bored and stood up and leaned on the podium. For a while, she pretended that she was John Houseman in *The Paper Chase,* her mother's favorite T.V. program, and posed a lot of legal questions to a class that never satisfied her with its answers. Someday when she got her nerve up, she was going to ask Mr. Phillips if law school was like *The Paper Chase.*

Then she was a preacher for a while, deciding on John 3:16 for that day's sermon. "He so loved you, brethren, that he gave his only begotten son." She didn't think she'd like being a priest—a lot of responsibility without much credit, and hearing a lot of people's confessions and wondering who it was on the other side of the screen. But she watched Jimmy Swaggart and Oral Roberts on Sunday while she stayed with the little ones and Mama and Grandmama went to mass. It would be glorious to be a preacher like that.

Teresa didn't go to mass anymore, hadn't since she'd turned eighteen last year, and Mama didn't like it a bit. The mass was in Spanish, and Mama and Grandmama liked to go. They were both born in Monterrey, and said they could go to mass and feel right at home. But Teresa wouldn't speak Spanish. After all, she was a born and raised Texan, wasn't she? Even at home, when they'd say, *"Por qué tú no hablas en Español, Teresa?"* she'd answer right back, "'Cause I'm an American, that's why. Americans speak English."

She looked at the lobby clock, crawling laboriously toward eight. She'd only signed two people in and out since she'd locked the front door at six. Mrs. Jeffers on four had left some roses on her desk; Teresa ferried her up and down in the elevator and got a sweet, damp whiff of the flowers. The other in-and-out was Mr. Tanner, the C.P.A. who had the only office on eight and weighed too much; he came huffing and puffing in late from an appointment, and dropped his briefcase off upstairs before calling it quits for the night.

Security would be in at ten, the uniformed, white-haired old man who always smelled a little of bourbon and had a granddaughter Teresa's age. He would walk her the half block to the bus stop like he always did, waiting until she was safely aboard. "Downtown's no place for a young girl to be walking alone at night," he'd say, as if old Security would be much help if trouble did happen to start. But Teresa liked him anyway and appreciated the thought.

She decided to pass the time by thinking about being pretty, like Miss Peterson who worked for Mr. Phillips, and imagined herself riding in—well, riding in a car like Mr. Phillips's white Lincoln, with a man who looked like Beau Bridges, only a little more distinguished, who opened the door for her and took her to dinner. Teresa thought, I'm not *ugly*, or anything—just ask Bobby, the day manager at Bek's Hamburgers in the underground tunnel. He's got his eye on me right enough. But nobody's any prettier than that Miss

Peterson. Teresa turned to a blank page in the sign-in register and began to draw a picture of herself with long blond hair, like Dodie.

There was a tapping on the street door, and Teresa looked up. A stocky man, with a red beard and mustache, stood there smiling. He showed Teresa a wrapped package, mouthing "Delivery" at her through the glass. She knew she really should send him away, tell him to come back during business hours. But she was bored, and he looked friendly.

Starting the last fifteen minutes of her life, Teresa Valdez smiled back at the friendly man with the red beard and went to let him in.

The first two times around the block, Buster thought that the little Mex gal was some kind of loony or something. It looked like a loony place, okay, a loony, drippy old building where a dumbo like Sonny Starr would go to try to find himself a lawyer. Not Buster. If Buster wanted a lawyer, he'd go to one of the swanky buildings with mirrored glass going up fifty or sixty floors, get him a lawyer with some clout. Not like the dirtbag who took his money, fed him a line of shit, and gave him up, leaving Buster to plead to the ten-year beef in Darrington. Maybe he'd even go to One Main Place, a block up the street from the funky old dog of a building with the Mex gal guarding the door, One Main Place with stone pillars in front. Buster and John craned their necks and saw the escalators and banks in the lobby of One Main Place as they went by it, circling around to check the Davis Building out again. Yep, bet you could find you a helluva mouthpiece in One Main Place.

The little Mex gal was something else. The first time they went by in John-boy's supercab, she was just sitting there on a stool, looking out into the street from behind a tall lecture table with a slanted top—what'd you call it? Podium? Yeah.

But then another time they went by, she was standing up with her hands on both sides of the podium, talking into thin air like she was giving a speech or something. Not bad looking, round, rosy cheeks, little-bitty thing. Couldn't tell if she had any tits or not, 'cause she was behind the podium and had this shapeless tan uniform on, like a bellhop or an elevator operator. But weirdo. Standing there making a speech to fucking nobody. Another time they went around, she was letting a fat old dude with a briefcase in. She locked the door behind her.

John-boy said, "Whaddya think?" He was wearing a fur-lined leather jacket, black, his shoulders filling it out.

Buster checked for cops, opened his door, and spat a chaw of Days Work into the street. "We're gonna need the gal to get in, I guess. Delivery ought to do it. Let's go find us a package to deliver." They cruised by a jewelry store with a clock in the window. Seven. Traffic was thinning. John-boy tooled around a couple of blocks east of Sonny's lawyer's building, looking for a place to park.

As he watched John-boy drive and look, Buster thought, Shit, it ain't that the supercab isn't nice. It's plumb boss, no doubt about it. But John-boy didn't have any sense about his money. They got the payoff for icing the old man, what'd John-boy go and do? Paid three hundred bucks the next day for a fucking *bench*, no less, just to do his presses on, then bought the supercab right after that. Didn't shop or nothing, just hauled Buster down to the G.M.C. place, sat up high on the cushioned leather seats, listened to a Michael Jackson tape on the stereo, fucked with the a/c and the padded steering wheel for a minute, then said, "How much is it?" The salesman thought that John-boy was a dumb hick with an oil well, Buster could see it in the salesman's eyes as John-boy skinned the sixteen grand off of a roll. Damn near half of John-boy's cut. No brains, man. Good thing old Sonny was a tightwad. Buster and John-boy'd had another bundle to split up after they'd gone over Sonny's pad. Otherwise, Buster was fixing to have to start loaning to John-boy, and John-boy was a bitch to have to collect off of.

They parked and walked, giving downtown a quick once-over. November was crawling on—it would be Thanksgiving in a couple of weeks—the night air was beginning to get good and nippy. Buster put his hands deep in his jeans pockets. His plaid shirt was flannel; that helped some. The beard kept his face warm.

Package. All of the stores seemed to be closed. They passed a stand-up hot dog joint, chili smell drifting out. An old guy in an army jacket asked for a dollar. Buster said, "Get lost, asshole." Fucking beggars. Never catch Buster Longley begging. The buck knife's handle, cold when he first strapped it on in the supercab, was warming against the calf of his right leg.

John-boy was being about a half pain in the ass, stopping and gawking in department store windows, looking at his own reflection, and sticking his chest out. Buster thought, Next score we make, I'm putting a fucking mirror on his ceiling. He can watch himself beat his meat, if he wants to.

Buster said, "This ain't getting us anywhere, John-boy. Where we gonna get a package this time of night, everybody going home?"

John-boy glanced at himself sideways in Neiman's window. "Easy, Bus. Hell, I thought you just wanted to sightsee. Hotels, man. They got a million of 'em downtown."

Buster, feeling dumb, thought, Now why didn't I think of that?

Buster felt even dumber when he was standing inside the lobby gift shop in the Adolphus Hotel, just a block up the street from the lawyer's office. Shit, walking around to hell and gone all over downtown, buck knife strapped to his leg; all it would take would be for some lazy cop, with nothing to do, to walk up and say, "Hey, what you two doin' just walkin' around here lookin' in all them store windows?" Dumb as shit, to get busted on a silly weapon beef, when all they'd had to do was park and come in this hotel to begin with.

The shop was lit brightly, and had rows of greeting cards on display. Buster picked one up, a big stiff card, bright green, that read, YOU KNOW WHAT I'D LIKE TO GIVE YOU FOR OUR ANNIVERSARY? in gold on the front; there was a picture of a baboon in a bonnet inside, with its hairy lips puckered up. The hotel lobby, long counter with REGISTRATION in big lit-up letters overhead, was visible through the gift shop door. Clerks in gold blazers were signing folks in. Lot of strange poontang got in here, betcha.

John-boy was taking his sweet fucking time. *Any* book. Jesus. John-boy should have stood in front, let Buster do the buying. John-boy's half-bald head was way in the back of the store, neck bent as he looked through, seemed like, every damn book on the shelf. They weren't gonna *read* it, fer Christ's sake, just fake out one dumb little Mex broad that made speeches into thin air.

John-boy finally came to the front, half walking, half strutting, grinning, a big nine-by-twelve paperback in his hand, pictures on the cover of a sawed-off dago-lookin' dude in his Jockey shorts, chest stuck out, big pectorals flexed, fireplug legs. Dr. Franco Columbo.

John-boy said, "New ab routine, I been looking for this."

Buster thought, Jesus Christ, I'm running up and down the street with a fucking lunatic. John-boy should sit in front of the podium, listen to the Mex broad's nutty speeches and give her a hand.

At the checkout counter, the heavy, gray-haired lady in the brown dress, eyeglasses on a chain around her neck, hit the keys, $10.95 showing on the register readout, then raised her plucked eyebrows, saying, "Anything else?"

"Well, yes, ma'am, the book's for my nephew," said Buster. He sure as hell didn't want anybody thinking it was for *him*. "It's for his birthday, and I'm wanting to mail it off. You maybe got wrapping paper? And some tape?"

Easy as pie, she led them to a big table in the shop's storeroom, where Buster wrapped the book up good in brown paper, then taped the edges down. He wrote W. A. PHILLIPS, ATTORNEY on the package with a red marker, even spelling it right, checking the slip of paper that he'd copied it out of the phone book on, his tongue curling against the inside of his cheek as he did. Instant delivery boy, Buster.

A few minutes later, Buster and John-boy stood in the shadows next to the lit-up Davis Building entrance. A few cars drifted up and down the street. Somewhere a horn honked, echoing.

Buster said, "When I get inside, I'll knock twice on the glass. Cover me." John-boy, leaning his back against the red-brick wall, his black eyebrows smudges on his stark-white face, nodded.

Buster squared his shoulders, put on a grin like an encyclopedia salesman, and stepped into the light, holding the wrapped-up book in front of him. The goofy Mex broad was writing or doodling. He tapped once on the glass. She looked up. Round, rosy cheeks, little boobs pressing against the front of her starched uniform. Kinda cute.

Buster grinned wider, his mustache tickling his lips, and said, "Delivery," pretty loud, but he doubted she could hear him through the glass.

She got up and came around the podium, hesitant, taking small, halting steps. She put her hand in the uniform's pocket and took out a steel ring, maybe twenty keys on it. There were two swinging glass doors at the entrance where Buster was standing, one on either side. She peered at Buster through the door on his left. Her eyes were dark green.

She glanced at the package and said, "Who's it for?" No accent, her voice muffled by the door.

Buster thought, anything, say anything, man, just get her to open the fucking door. A movement flickered in the corner of his eye. John-boy, edging away from the building. Buster said, "It's for Attorney W. A. Phillips, ma'am." He held the package so that she could read the writing on it.

She put a key in the door, the ring jingling as the bolt slid, smooth, and half-opened the door. She said, "I'll take it."

Buster handed her Dr. Franco Columbo's book, then bent down, raising his pants cuff, glancing up and down the block. Only one set of headlights, maybe two blocks away. He said, "Thanks. Now if you'll just sign for it, please."

She stood there with the package in her hands, looking at Buster funny, probably wondering, What am I gonna sign? Where's his book? Who carries a pen in his pants leg? Before she could ask, Buster had the buck knife out.

He straightened and yanked the door. Her eyes wide, she saw the knife and pulled on the door handle from her side, but she wasn't strong enough to keep him out. He grabbed her short, dark hair, yanking, hearing her soft baby whimper, spinning her around. She struggled, strained, his arm around her neck, her buttocks round and firm against his thighs. He put the knife point to her throat, and she stopped fighting him; her wide, dark-lashed eyes looked at him over her shoulder. The ring of keys clattered to the floor, the book fell with a bang.

Keeping pinprick tension on her throat with the knife, he took his other hand away from her neck, reached behind him, and knocked twice on the glass door. Then he grabbed her shoulder with his free hand, guiding her sideways, stepping carefully, until they were flattened against the inside wall, out of street view from the doors.

John-boy sauntered in, grinning, his beard beginning to darken. He hadn't shaved since last night. His big shoulders stretched the leather of his jacket tight as he stooped, picked up the keys and the book, came over, and stood in front of them. The top of Teresa's head reached to the point of his chin; John-boy and Buster were eye to eye.

Buster said, "Anybody see us?"

John-boy twirled the ring of keys on his index finger. "Naw. All clear."

Buster put his chin on her shoulder, his lips against her ear. She smelled nice. Violet. She gasped.

He said, "Now, we're going travelin', little lady." He looked up. "Lock the door, John-boy." As John-boy did, Buster said in her ear, "Now John-boy's gonna lead, you're gonna follow. And I'm following you, right into that open elevator over there. Got it?"

Nothing. He squeezed her shoulder hard. She nodded.

Inside the elevator, John-boy took two pairs of soft cotton workman's gloves out of his pocket, handed one of the pairs to Buster, then stood with his legs spread apart and yanked his gloves onto his hands. Buster put his on, then dangled the ring of keys in front of Teresa, saying, "Now, you're gonna take us to

Lawyer Phillips's floor, tell us which key opens his door. Ain'tcha?"

She had her back to the wall, eyes wide, breath coming fast, small breasts rising and falling. She said nothing.

Buster shrugged, glancing at John-boy. "She ain't talking to us, brother. Here, I'll try to drive this thing."

As Buster spun the handle and the elevator door closed, John-boy doubled up his fist and drove it into Teresa's midsection. Pain shot through her, unbelievable agony. She gagged, tried to scream.

No one heard her except Buster and John-boy.

The gloves made the going pretty clumsy, and after a little while Buster quit trying to be careful, thinking, what's the difference? They're gonna know *somebody* was up here. Ain't no way to keep them from it. Wasn't anything in Sonny's folder—they'd found that right away, right there under the S's, where it ought to be. But there was nothing in the folder except a sheet saying that Sonny'd paid his lawyer ten grand (Jesus, Son, they paying that much for lawyers in *this* dumpy old building?) and some court papers about this trial Sonny'd been supposed to have. Buster thought the lawyer should thank him and John-boy for seeing to it that the lawyer didn't have to fuck with no trial.

Buster was sitting behind Bino Phillips's desk. The little brass lock hadn't been any problem, but Buster'd splintered some wood on the top drawer when he was prying it open. That was probably when he'd decided to quit being careful, pulling all kinds of paper and shit out, going through it, and tossing it on the floor. Nothing about Sonny, though.

The problem was, when Buster was thinking straight he could see that this trip wasn't really going to tell them anything. If they found something, something where Sonny'd written down all about the deal, then they'd know for sure what all the lawyer was savvy to, have to figure a way to get the lawyer alone and put the cooler to him. Only this time the bozo was going to be tied down where he couldn't do anything dumb like Sonny did, making a no-chance play. No, the lawyer was going to tell Buster everything, who knew, who didn't, before the lawyer went bye-bye, catch ya later.

But what if they *didn't* find anything? Wouldn't mean shit, wouldn't mean that the lawyer *didn't* know. For all Buster knew, a plainclothes cop was walking around right now, saying, You ever seen this pair? then showing photos of Buster and John-boy, probably the ones taken when they were released from Darrington. Find something, or not find something, it looked like Buster was going to have to take John-boy and visit this dude. And why couldn't the man think of all this, the smart-ass man with all those black-framed diplomas he had, talking Buster and John-boy into shaking this office down.

Buster had found a picture tucked off in a corner of a drawer and looked at it for a while before putting it in his pocket. Yeah, it was this lawyer, even though nothing was written on the picture. Buster knew it was him, okay. Didn't know *how* he knew, but he did. Tall, rangy ape, snow-white hair, clear eyes. It was a full-length shot, color, with a golf green in the background, the lawyer holding a putter like he was going to hit a stroke. Grinning, but something behind the grin. A gaze to him, a set about his jaw. A lot like Grady Brewster, one con in Darrington that you didn't want to fuck with, no way. The look made Buster just a little nervous, like maybe this was a dude that didn't shake down too easy, and if you put some shit on him you'd better make sure he was dead when you got through with him. Otherwise, you could count on hearing from him.

Jesus Christ, John-boy was making a racket in the outer offices, storming around like a lunatic, throwing shit around. John-boy probably wouldn't know what he'd found if he found something, hard as John-boy was thinking about knocking off a piece of that little Mex girl in there, snug away in the closet with the copying machine and coffeepot and shit.

It had been the push that did it. She'd opened up pretty fast after John-boy let her have the old one-two—dumbass had to bust her one in the mouth, bringing blood and puffing her lip. Another body punch would have done it and not marked her up any. But Buster didn't think John-boy would have ever thought about sticking it to her if she hadn't fallen just the way she did.

It was when Buster had shoved her into the closet, saying, "Keep your mouth quiet in there." She'd sprawled, the stiff uniform skirt flying, showing pink panties tight around her legs and ass, brown legs, good solid shape, about an inch of cheek showing. As Buster closed the door, John-boy'd seen her legs and ass and got that look about him. That little Mex gal was going to get herself busted tonight for sure.

Buster found the little smoke fan in Bino's desk and turned it on; liking it, he put it in his pocket along with the picture. Might as well. Couldn't find anything else, at least not what they were looking for.

Teresa Valdez kept her eyes shut tight and stayed on the floor, listening to the crash and slam of file drawers and the cursing from the two men outside the closet. Over and over she thought, Hail, Mary, full of grace, the Lord is with thee: Blessed art thou among women. *Madre mía, donde tú vas, yo voy también*—Whither thou goest I go also.

Her upper lip was numb and swollen, with blood caking where the big man (the strongest one—oh, my

God, they're both so big) had smashed his fist into her mouth, Teresa finally saying, "Oh, sir, please, I'll take you where you want, please, my God, just don't—"

She opened her eyes and rolled over, pain now roaring in her chest. Oh, God, her rib must be broken. Please, Mama, please, if they'll go away I'll go to mass, I promise, Mama, and I'll speak the old language, too, Mama, just like you and Grandmama do.

Suddenly, the door opened. They were there—oh, God—both of them. The big one, the one who hit her, came to her—Hail Mary, full of grace, the Lord—He stood above her, looked her over—is with you, blessed art thou—

John-boy said, "You got any tits to go with that ass of yours?"

His strong hands went to the front of her uniform, pulling, yanking, the fabric ripping. Cool air hardened her bare nipples.

John-boy grinned. "She's got some tits, Bus."

Later, John-boy held Dr. Franco Columbo's book in his hands as they left. The wrapping paper was gone. Buster was cleaning the buck knife with it.

Bino didn't really need the gathering of Cadillacs and Mercedeses strung out on both sides of the street for a block or so to tell him that this was where Winnie Anspacher lived. Fund-raiser, huh? Well, there were plenty of funds on hand.

As Bino'd wound on wide, curvy streets between stately old oaks and sycamores, homes built in the days when if you paid a lot you got a lot, with lawns the size of polo fields on both sides of him, and made the turn onto Drexel Drive, things had begun to look familiar. He'd been here once. The Winnie Anspacher III's of the world never really moved anywhere, they just hung around and waited for the Winnie Anspacher II's to pass on, or even just to get too old to keep the big place up, rent a condo in the mountains, and let Junior take over.

It was a lot of water under the bridge ago when a couple of new-convertible-driving Phi Delts had said, "There's a seat open; Winnie's old man is out of town and he's having a game. Come on by, Bino." Then a knowing look passed between the Phi Delts, hidden grins that said, well, we did our duty, inviting the hayseed, knowing that there'd be more on the table in one pot than Mr. Basketball could scrape up in a month of waiting tables.

Then Bino'd made a phone call to Pop Harrison, Pop dropping everything, leaving nineteen-year-old Half handling the phones. Pop drove all the way in from Mesquite and handed Bino a roll of bills, saying, "It ain't like a loan, son, I'm in fifty-fifty, you hear? Now you go on over and put East Texas poker on them silk-stocking Highland Park boys' asses." Bino had, too, not remembering how much he'd won nearly so much as he remembered the downcast look on those two Phi Delts' faces when they'd had to owe Bino until their allowances rolled in.

Bino pulled to the curb behind a Rolls, a silver one. He got out, the soreness already stiffening his chest, arms, and shoulders, thinking, Jesus, be a bitch tomorrow.

It wasn't really Marvin Goldman's fault, but Bino liked to think that it was. Just as Bino had been about to shower and change, he'd remembered Goldman's muscular, wedge-shaped back as the prosecutor had walked away from him at County Medical.

He'd stopped and looked at Cecil, eye to eye. Cecil was floating there, fins waving, probably thinking about the tanned, naked lady who had dropped a minnow in his bowl around three in the morning, and thinking that being a fish that belonged to a nut wasn't all bad. Cecil's coal black body was motionless between the waving fins, his bulldog mouth opening and closing.

Bino said, "You think I can't? Old Push-up Phillips can get down there and give you fifty any time he wants to."

Cecil didn't look like he believed it.

So Bino'd given Cecil a quick fifty (well, thirty-five, really), grunting, straining, finally collapsing. When Bino was able to get on his feet, Cecil had turned around and flicked his tail in disgust. Bino'd said, "Fuck you, Cecil. What's a fish know, anyway?"

Jesus, but he'd feel it in the morning.

The Anspacher home was like he remembered it—raised, rolling lawn, exposed aggregate circular drive climbing gently away from the street and passing in front of huge stone steps. There was a fountain full of goldfish at the foot of the steps and a stone cherub holding a seashell in front of him, circulating water pouring out of the shell and splashing back into the pond. Bino edged around behind the cherub. Yep. From just the right angle, it still looked like the statue was pissing in the pond.

At the top of the steps, Bino stood in the semicircle of red brick that was flush on the surface of the concrete porch and pressed the button. Before the chimes could bong their second bong, Mrs. Winston Bennett Anspacher III opened the massive door and said, "Yes?" Had to be. She went with Winnie like a bow with a fiddle.

She was tall and razor thin, her hair short and curried and combed into a perfect forward sweep, just the right thing for your delicate features, Mrs. A., which is what the high-priced stylist would call a hawk nose between jutting cheekbones. The hair was auburn, no gray. She wore a blue knee-length cocktail dress with frilly sleeves and stood in her navy spike pumps like she'd been born in them. Probably not far from it, thought Bino, at least from around the age of ten at Miss Merrill's Studio, Highland Park Shopping Village.

Bino said, "Mrs. Anspacher? Hello, I'm Bino Phillips." Her nose was on a level with his Adam's apple, which made her about five-ten, over six with the heels on.

He was about to offer her his hand. But before he could, she said, "Well, of course you are." Then she raised her right arm, bent her wrist so that her palm faced the top of her head, and did a little jump-step to her right, somehow doing it in those shoes without looking awkward about it.

Bino thought, it's the Highland fling, those people are doing the Highland fling in there. Do I raise my right arm and go the opposite direction from her? Or my left and—? Oh. It dawned on him. The hook shot.

He thought pretty fast. "I never looked that graceful shooting the hook, Mrs. Anspacher. Did you go to S.M.U. with us? You sure don't look old enough to've."

Now she shook hands, a bony grip but good and firm. Nice. "Flattery will get you everywhere, Bino. I'm Sarah Anspacher—was Sarah Gilbert. We had Freshman Bio together under Dean Longnecker. Remember?"

No, he didn't. "Sure," he said. "Sarah. My, I could kick myself for not recognizing you."

She offered her arm. He took it, and she patted his hand warmly as she led him into the interior of the house. The entry hall had a stained-glass partition on the left.

"It's sweet of you to say so," she said, "even if you don't. I was Wanda Wallflower, I'm afraid. Come on, join the powers behind the politicos. Dreadful people, don't you think?" Bino decided that he liked her a lot more than he did Winnie. They went by a round mirror in a gold frame, and Bino checked his own navy suit out. Looked okay.

Sarah led Bino into a massive den, where a four-piece combo was playing a mellow "Misty" at one end. There was a piano, a grand that belonged there, a sax, trombone, and muted drums, played by musicians in tuxes. At the other end of the room, probably sixty feet from the music, a tall, red-jacketed black was mixing something in silver cocktail shakers behind a fully stocked wet bar. He poured a green, frothy something-or-other that exactly filled a stemmed champagne glass.

Between the bartender and the band, the room was wall-to-wall people, men in business suits and some even done up all the way in black tie and tuxes. Bino recognized a silver-haired woman he'd seen on the cover of *Dallas Life*, the Sunday newspaper supplement. There'd been a feature article about her home.

Sarah steered him over in front of the bar. "Now, you'll have to name your own poison, Bino, and do your own circulating. Most of the conversations will bore you to death, but if it doesn't kill you, Winnie will be doing the intro for Art Stammer later on. Then Art will tell a hundred reasons why he should be your congressman, ninety-nine of them bullshit. That should really finish you off. But there is an unattached or two about, if you're into that sort of thing." She winked. "You're single, aren't you?"

He nodded.

She said, "Well, you'll do all right. I've got to circulate now. Oh, Bino, just so you'll know, it's not an accident that I'm not doing the hostessy thing and mingling you in with somebody. I don't want you to hate me because I've stuck you with a bore."

With that, Sarah left Bino and mixed, laughing at a whispered joke here, squeezing a hand there, moving expertly through the crowd. Bino grinned to himself. Boffo lady. He turned and got a Scotch, neat.

Bino knew a lot more of the faces than he did the names, and a lot more of them knew him than he did them. He made small talk with a group or two. He caught a glimpse of Winnie's bald head across the room as Winnie fondled a highball and talked up to a guy in a charcoal suit. The guy—well, Bino knew him from somewhere, and he rattled his memory bank. Nothing. About six feet, iron gray hair, black horn-rims, fifty or so. Bino'd have to think about it. Something told him that it was important to remember the guy.

A beefy, red-faced man named Bob was saying, "No way. It wasn't goaltending. I was sitting right behind the bucket. The ball started down, was below rim level. Best I remember, Bino never even left his feet."

Charley (Gerber? Gervan?) nodded and sipped. "Hell they gave the Aggies too much time, anyway. Wasn't but two seconds left on the clock when they threw it in bounds, and the guy dribbles all the way to the center before he puts it up. I think a movie film showed a full four seconds worth of frames before the shot. Slow clock and a bum call cost us the conference. Huh, Bino?"

Bino'd been looking at the guy with Winnie Anspacher. "Wha—I'm sorry, Charley. What did you say?"

"We were talking about the Aggie game—the goaltending call, you know. Give us a firsthand report. Was it goaltending, or wasn't it?"

Bino thought, Tell them that you have to go take a piss.

He said, "Well, the ref said it was. I guess that makes it that way."

Bob's puffy throat quivered as he said, "*Ref?* Aggie blind asshole, I say! He must have rode up on the team bus from College Station with 'em."

Bino caught a man's eye across the room, waved. The guy looked puzzled. Bino'd never seen him before.

Bino said, "Excuse me, guys. I see an old client of mine over there. I've got to talk to him."

Charley looked around. "You mean there's a *convict* at this party?"

"No," said Bino. "Civil matter. I do some of that, too. Talk to you later, huh, guys?"

As Bino walked away, Bob said, "Hang around,

Bino. There's a couple of old Texas Longhorns around that we can give hell to."

Bino had made it about halfway across the room to the puzzled guy, wondering what he'd say when he got there, when a warm female hand touched his arm. There was a gold bracelet around the slim wrist and a sapphire ring on the hand's middle finger.

A husky, soft voice said, "I'll race you to the door, mister."

He didn't turn his head at first. "Bet you would, with this cast on my leg." Then he looked. She had the same laughing hazel eyes.

He said, "Hello, Annabelle."

How long? Ten years? Eleven? Heard about her every once in a while, of course, a dropped remark that he was always careful not to pick up on. In the long run, what had happened between them was probably for the best—she came from her world, he from his. Besides, by now she'd be about six axhandles across the backside.

Wrong.

She sighed, and tossed her head the same way as ever. "Well, Bino Phillips, are you just going to stand there gawking at me, or do I get a hug?" She rocked forward, bending her knee and lifting one shapely ankle as she gave him a sisterly peck on the cheek, holding her drink away to one side, and balancing herself with her other hand on his arm. Annabelle still wore Estée Lauder. She had on a belted green dress that hugged her waist and hips.

He said, "You look great. Like you could still cartwheel from the fifty to the goal line." She did look great. She probably could.

"Well, I don't know about that." A half smile. Still one slightly crooked front tooth. "But I do jog, do some aerobics. Your hair is even whiter. Or looks like it is. But how could it be? My drink's empty, Bino."

She handed him her glass. It was cool and damp, ice still in the bottom.

As he escorted her to the bar, sidestepping bunches of people, she said, "Does your ankle still bother you?"

Bino thought, Honeymoon on crutches, grats of Jabbar—Lew Alcindor, then. For months, Annabelle on top, never seeming to get enough. Frenzied joy, coupled with shooting pain. "When it rains, gets damp sometimes. Mostly not, though."

She slowed, nodded to a couple she knew; the man, in a blue silk suit and wearing a pinkie ring, lifted his glass to her as they went by. Her hair was permed at the ends and frosted. She said. "I've seen your name in the paper some. What—won more cases than any defense lawyer, something like that?" She turned her head to face him with a questioning half smile, her glossy lower lip reflecting a tiny ray of light. "You fooled Dad, good and proper. He said you'd never make it, be on your butt."

Bino said, "How is your father?"

"Oh—Dad passed on, Bino. What is it, three years? I thought you'd know." She said it with a slight head drop, a tiny, almost unnoticeable quiver in her voice. They were nearly to the bar.

Suddenly, Art Stammer came into their path, facing them. He was leaner than Bino remembered. His dark blond hair was razored, and he was smiling. Perfectly capped white teeth. Trim waist showing where the coat to his Woolf Brothers suit hung open. Bino thought about the push-ups and winced.

Stammer didn't even look at Bino. To Annabelle, he said, "Aha! The disappearing Mrs. Tirelli. Dante's looking all over for you, Annabelle."

Dante Tirelli. Sure. The guy Winnie was talking to. Annabelle turned her head to look at Bino, her expression one of—guilt? He hoped so. She had one bang of chestnut hair that she'd never been able to train, and it still was slightly out of place.

Annabelle laughed nervously, saying, "Well, he hasn't been looking very hard. I've been right here. Art, you remember my"—now she looked panicked—"you remember Bino Phillips, don't you?"

Bino started to say, Yeah, Art, thanks for having Winnie invite me over. But before he could, Stammer held out his hand and said, "Sure, Bino. Long time no see. Glad you could make it. Always glad to see an old S.M.U. Mustang." He shook hands, a short, firm grip.

Bino closed his mouth.

Annabelle said, quickly, "I was just telling Bino a few ins and outs of the campaign. Bino's an old Richard Bigelow man."

Bino thought, How did she know that?

Art Stammer half-smiled, his eyes sad. Lot of charisma. "Nobody's ever going to fill Richard's shoes, Bino," he said. "But nobody. But we're going to die trying. Stick around, buddy, listen to what we have to say. I don't think we're going to be far away from your ideas, if you were for Bigelow."

"Well, I was," said Bino. "Hundred percent. Somebody dealt a helluva blow to these parts—whoever hides out with rifles and shoots down wonderful old men that those somebodies can't beat at the polls." Annabelle was giving him a funny look, her head cocked to one side. Maybe she'd been just trying to think up something to say, maybe she didn't know Bino really was one of Richard's backers. Bino could write a book on why he was for Bigelow.

Stammer said, "I really hate to cut this short, Annabelle, but Dante really does need to see you. Stick around, Bino. We'll have to visit."

Stammer led Annabelle away, his hand on her elbow, and Bino thought, Sure, Art. Right after Bob and I give hell to the old Longhorns. Annabelle looked over her shoulder and gave a helpless little shrug that said—something, he wasn't sure. Goddamn, she was beautiful.

A different female voice, lower pitched than Annabelle's, evener, more cultured, said, at Bino's elbow, "I'll substitute for her, if you'll get me a clean glass. And won't blow my cover. Or cross-examine me."

She was tall and cool as a rum daiquiri, brown hair clipped close and razored into a perfect line at the back of her head where it joined her swan neck. Her modest brown skirt flowed loose at her hips; a couple of Bino's clients said that she filled jeans like they were painted on, snapped her fingers, and talked hip as they come. Right up until she pulled her badge.

She didn't have a glass. Bino raised his arm and pointed his fingers to the bar, palm up. She led. He followed.

As the bartender stirred her a vodka martini and colored Bino's Scotch, she said, "Your lady friend married well."

Bino thought, Which time? He said, "Lady friend? Who's that, Karen?"

She smiled and nodded at the bartender as she reached for the 'tini. On the rocks. She lifted it and wet her lips. "You didn't know? Maybe you didn't. Dante Tirelli's a lot of rungs above your clients. The lady you were just hustling. It's his wife. What brings you here, Bino? I thought that all these Repubs would be a little far to the right for you."

Bino took his drink and fished in his pocket. The smallest he had was a five, so he flipped a couple of quarters in the tip glass. The bartender didn't look thrilled. Bino said, winking at Karen Allen, "Me? Naw. Conservative through and through. How 'bout you, Karen? I didn't think that the bureau was supposed to go to the right *or* the left. Straight down the middle of the road. Lock 'em both up, hey?"

She glanced around, giving a gentle eyebrow arch. "Shh. My cover. For real, Bino. Don't blow it." Her skin was dark. Natural, this one, no sunlamps. Soft, smooth cheeks.

Bino thought that one over, then said, "Okay. What do we talk about?" Charley and Bob went by, probably looking for the old Longhorn. Charley glanced at Karen, then gave Bino the thumbs-up sign. Bino nodded to him.

Karen said, "Well, we could start with How're you, where are you from, like that. Sort of go over backgrounds, get acquainted. Leave out business, you know. Maybe I'll ask if your hair and eyebrows have always been white."

She was standing with one hip higher than the other. Bino wondered how she'd look in jeans. He said, "How are you, Karen Allen? I'm fine. I'm Bino from Mesquite. Where you from?"

"St. Louis. Webster Groves High. K State. Dad had a hemorrhage over it—he went to Mizzou, is a C.P.A. How'd you get into representing criminals? Like Sonny Starr?"

"Now you're blowing *my* cover. I thought you didn't want to talk business." I represented Dodie, too, he thought. How about that? "How'd you know about Sonny, Karen? You into his case?"

She dodged the question, saying, "To each his own, I guess. Like, some people will do anything for money, smuggle dope, rob banks, anything. But I suppose it's a lot smarter to represent them. That way you get all the money, don't have to go to jail for it."

Bino thought, How'd we get to talking about this? I'm from Mesquite—

He hitched up his coattail and put his hand in his pants pocket. "Well, that's one way to look at it,

Karen. But there's another, too. Like everybody's entitled to have their rights protected. You didn't answer my question."

She held the martini up, sipping, looking at him over the rim of the rock glass. Her eyes were big and round, no mascara. Long, natural lashes. Irises deep brown. She swallowed. "What question?"

"About Sonny Starr. You're not the investigating agent on Sonny's dope case. Is that why you're having a drink with me, to find out something about Sonny Starr? Go to the morgue. Ask Shoesole Traynor. Maybe you can look at Sonny's feet. Or better yet, ask Goldman. Your boys found Sonny. Without a warrant."

She looked away from Bino, didn't seem to be watching anything. Maybe just thinking. She had on little round gold earrings. Nice lobes. She said, "Were you familiar with Richard Bigelow? Not his killing, of course, everybody knows about that. I mean, what he stood for. Politically."

"Well, that's a relief," said Bino.

"What's a relief?"

"That you aren't investigating me. Then you'd already know that Richard Bigelow gave me my start practicing law. Do you know where his office was? The glassfront, catty-cornered from the County Courthouse? His old office, before he got elected."

She thought a minute. "I think so. There's several law offices along there, with signs in the windows. Used to be pawnshops, they look like, or maybe finance companies."

He nodded, taking a drink. It was Chivas, warm in his throat and sending a little burn up his nose as it went down. "Well, you know the area, anyway. I went to law school in Houston, South Texas C. of L. after I finished at S.M.U. Came back to Dallas on the seat of my pants, figured I'd have to go to work for the D.A. or a big firm, handling rich clients' traffic tickets and dog leash violations. Anyway, I ran into Richard down at the courthouse one day. Never had met him; knew who he was, sure. Never lost a client to the electric chair and all that. Anyway, he says to me, 'Don't screw around with the big firms or the government. Come see me.' So I did. He set me up in a back office, handling his overflow. Now, you wouldn't believe this, but Richard had over a *thousand clients.* A thousand, standing in line to pay on their bills with tens and twenties in their hands. Never saw anything like it. How's your drink, Karen?"

She made a face, but still looked cool doing it. "It's awful, but I'm faking it. Anything but water is awful to me. Diet pepsi, sometimes. So you knew Bigelow well. Any ideas on who might have wanted him out of the way?"

"Not the specifics, just the type. It was a paid hit, I don't guess you have to be Miss Marple to figure that out. It was somebody that's making a lot of money out of being conservative—if conservative is what you want to call it."

Karen said, "Well, what do *you* call it?"

"It's all votes, Karen. Right now it's chic to be conservative. Nifty platform. Put away the criminals, get more votes. Only there's not any publicity to be gained in fighting old-fashioned crime, rapes, and murders and whatnot. So they've got you folks running around inventing new crimes, hitting some high-profile people. Abscam, stuff like that. Now they can say, 'Look what we've done. Look at all the new guys we've put in the pen. Ain't we wonderful?' Richard Bigelow was against that kind of bullshit. He was changing a lot of minds about the justice system, and I think he got killed for it."

She looked thoughtful. "I've got to talk to you, Bino. I've got some pictures—"

Winnie Anspacher's voice interrupted, amplified. He

was where the band had been playing, standing on a dais of chairs. He still looked short. He said into a mike, "Gather round, folks, it's time to hear what this little get-together is all about. Come on. Your attention, please."

There was a low sound that grew into a muted rumble as people pressed toward the platform, Winnie asking for quiet two more times. Bino turned to Karen.

"What was that? Pictures?"

She looked a little nervous all of a sudden, not quite as cool. She put her hand lightly on his arm. "Not now—I can't. Tomorrow. Maybe the next day. I'll get in touch. I have to go now, Bino."

Just like for Annabelle, there was a guy waiting for Karen Allen. Youngish, around thirty, in a dark suit, with black curly hair. Bino didn't know him, and the guy didn't seem to want to change that. He stood about six feet away with his arms folded. Karen went to him, and he turned and walked to the dais with her. Bino watched her slim back and waist. And wondered about her hips, picturing her in low-slung jeans.

Art Stammer wowed 'em. He spoke in a full baritone, sounding over the mike a lot like Pat Summerall, just folksy enough for Texas, just uppity enough for Highland Park. He talked about Richard Bigelow, the country's loss, how nobody'd ever fill Richard's shoes. Bino liked that part. He stayed far to the rear, even managed to sneak in a Scotch refill, noticing a little buzz and thinking, what the hell.

Stammer was saying, ". . . and though Richard's terrible tragedy makes us all heartsick, it's time to pull our heads up and go on.

"Now, tonight, we're going to be brief. We invited you-all over here for a good time"—smiling, winking at the crowd—"and besides, we don't want anybody to be asleep at donation time." That drew a small titter.

Perfect. Not too funny, but getting the real purpose across.

He let the laughter subside and went on. "And since we're being brief, I'm only touching on one issue out of several—there's a little pamphlet"—holding it up, his own picture on the front of it, just a few pages—"available at the door, that outlines our platform on most of the major issues.

"But tonight, we're going to talk about one. Crime control. What's being done about crime right now in Congress, and what we're going to accomplish if—no, friends, *when*—I'm elected. I think we all agree that we need to get tougher on it, for ours and our families' protection. Now, we've got a real expert on the subject among us, who I'm going to ask to help me out. So, without further ado—this man needs no introduction to most of you—come on up here, Bino Phillips."

Bino thought, Huh?

Stammer, even white teeth flashing, was pointing his finger straight at him. People were turning, staring. There was a hesitant smatter of applause.

Bino was standing there with a full Scotch and a buzz on. Sarah caught his eye from the front row of spectators, gestured with her head toward the platform of chairs. Annabelle was doing a little clapping, standing next to Dante Tirelli. He was trapped. No way out. He shrugged, tried to grin, and headed to the platform.

The crowd parted in front of him, little by little, most of them smiling, some looking a little puzzled. Charley and Bob stood back to let him through, Bob clapping him on the shoulder, saying, "Go get 'em, you big Al*bino*!" Bino grinned at Bob, nodding, thinking, Hell, this isn't a *jump ball*, for Christ's sake. Sarah's face crinkled as she winked at him. Winnie was next to her, his bald head on a level with her shoulder. There were a lot of diamond necklaces in the crowd.

Stammer was up on one of four side-by-side straight chairs that had their backs flush against the wall. Winnie Anspacher I was over his right shoulder, and Bino wasn't sure if it was the same picture that hung in Winnie III's office or not. Stammer offered his hand, and Bino used it as a crutch to boost himself up on the makeshift platform. He wouldn't want to arm-wrestle Art Stammer. He took a pull from the Scotch, remembering that Stammer was somehow related to Judge Hazel Burke Sanderson.

Stammer, standing next to Bino, took a long look up at him. The skin on Stammer's face didn't have a wrinkle, and he had a straight Roman nose. Bino wondered if he used a sunlamp. Stammer grinned, putting his lips close to the handheld mike, saying, "Well, folks, it looks like we're giving up a little height to the opposition."

Laughter, Bino thinking, Opposition? Stammer went on. "Bino"—one eye on Bino, the other on the crowd—"I want to talk some about the Comprehensive Crime Control Act of 1984. The bail bond portion of the act is already in force, and I believe the rest of the provisions become law—what, first of next year?" A pause, questioning look. Bino nodded.

Stammer said, "I thought so. As some of you good folks may know, the act, and we'll brag a little here, it was a Republican Congress that put it over. But under the new law, criminals no longer roam the streets on bond, to commit more crimes. The Bail Bond Reform Act keeps them where they belong. Right, Bino?"

Bino thought, Richard Bigelow sure as hell wasn't for it. Stammer was pointing the mike at him. Bino's tongue was getting a little bit thick. He said, "Well, it's made it a lot harder to get bail for my federal clients than it used to be, but—"

"Yes—your clients," interrupted Stammer, rolling his eyes. "So now the criminal's mouthpiece can't spring him so easily—that's part of the new law. And when the rest of it goes into force, they'll have to stay in jail a lot longer for their crimes. Now, Bino, even a liberal like yourself will have to agree that it's a good law. Won't you?" He shoved the mike at Bino again.

Looking slowly down, then back up, Bino eyed Stammer. He said, "Yeah. Unless you happen to believe in the Constitution." In the far reaches of the back row, Karen Allen was looking at him, a half smile on her face.

"The Constitution is what it's all about," said Stammer. "And that's what my platform is all about, too—to see that Americans get their rights, the right to have a safe place to live. And one way to make America safe is to stop coddling all of these criminals."

Someone in the crowd shouted, "Say it, Art, say it!" Bino wasn't sure, but he thought it was Dante Tirelli who yelled. Tirelli was smiling, his arm around Annabelle's waist. He looked like anybody's banker or broker, standing there in horn-rim glasses, a thin gold watch gleaming on his wrist where it showed through the bend in Annabelle's delicate arm. Bino wondered what it took to get to wear a cement overcoat these days.

Bino said, "Well, if you don't want the criminals to be coddled, then quit coddling them."

Stammer had his mouth open, ready to interrupt again, but he wasn't prepared for what Bino'd just said. Bino took a healthy slug of the Scotch as Stammer finally said, "I beg your pardon?"

In the front row, Sarah looked like she was having a good time. Winnie didn't; he was looking puzzled, like Stammer. Bino swallowed the liquor, then said, "The Crime Control Act is nothing but a façade. It's a trick to make the voter think that the conservatives are doing something about crime, when in fact they're not. The rapists and murderers can still get bond, no problem. Those are state crimes, and they can be out raping and murdering again in no time. Plus, even when those people do go to prison, the federal court orders about overcrowding force the states to let them out before the water gets hot. The Crime Control Act only affects people that are charged with federal crimes—bank fraud, drugs, mostly nonviolent types. The Feds are making the taxpayer bear the cost of housing white-collar criminals for long prison stretches, while the violent offenders are still out on the streets. Richard Bigelow wouldn't—"

Now Stammer cut in, but fast. "And it's just this sort of bleeding-heart liberalism that we're fighting, Mr. Voter. Here we have a typical criminal lawyer, a man who makes his living off of the fruits of crime, who employs a known bookmaker as an investigator—"

So Stammer'd read the judge's letter, too. Bino cut back in. "Now wait a minute, Art. Wait just a minute. Let's see, you're a banker, I guess your family still owns North Dallas Bank. Now, I've got a client who banks there—Piggy Bratton. Piggy's a nice enough guy, owns a few massage parlors, runs a few whores. But basically, a real nice guy. And do you know who old Piggy goes to see when he wants a loan? Why—"

"And that's to be expected, folks. Slurs. The liberals can't fight us with facts, so they turn to slurs." Stammer was really excited now, his eyes flashing. "That's right, Bino. Stand in there and slur it out. Put up a front, and keep the sleazy bookmaker on the phone in the back, making the money. If—"

It wasn't at all like the gossip columnist wrote in the next morning's paper, a "roundhouse punch that put the candidate on the seat of his platform." There wasn't any doubt that the whiskey had a lot to do with it, but it was the crack about Half-a-Point that finally tore it, where Bino was concerned.

No, it wasn't a roundhouse at all, but a straight, short, hard right that jarred Bino all the way to his shoulder. It felt good. His fist made contact with Stammer's jaw just as Stammer was turning his head to the left, probably to stare a few more daggers at Bino. The punch landed right on the button, with Stammer's head moving in one direction and Bino's fist in the other. The sound was like that of a bat hitting a soft melon.

First, Stammer's head snapped to the right and hung there for an instant. Then he looked at Bino like a man who'd just been slipped a Mickey, his eyes glazed, sagging all over, his knees buckling in slow motion.

Through the alcohol haze, Bino thought, Oh, shit. He reached forward, dropping his half-full Scotch to thump on and wet the thick carpet, and put both hands under Stammer's armpits, holding him up. As he stood there looking like he was going to dance with Art Stammer, Bino said, "I'm sorry, folks, I—" His voice didn't carry, the microphone was on the floor where Stammer had dropped it.

Everyone was staring, some of them openmouthed. There was dead silence.

Finally, Sarah said, "Well for goodness' sake, let him down carefully. He's our candidate." She was grinning and her shoulders were heaving.

Slowly, carefully, Bino put one foot on the floor, then the other, his arms around Stammer's chest in a dead man's carry. By the time Bino had Stammer in a sitting position in one of the chairs, his eyelids were fluttering, and Stammer was beginning to moan softly. There was the barest trace of blood on the corner of his mouth.

At Bino's left elbow, Winnie said, "Well, I hope you're satisfied."

Bino straightened up, his head nearly clear now. His right hand throbbed, would probably swell. There was a cut on the knuckle, and it was beginning to sting. "Hey, look, Winnie. I'm sorry, okay. I don't know what got into me."

A slim blond woman came and sat down by Stammer. She was wearing a dark print and a diamond bracelet. She held Stammer's head between her hands, glared at Bino, hissed, "Beast!"

Winnie said, "I think you'd better be going, friend. And not returning. You'll be hearing from us, Bino."

"Oh, pipe down, Winnie!" said Sarah. "The man was invited over here on the pretext of having a good time, and you-all proceeded to roast him." Winnie stared at her with his mouth open. She went on. "Yes, roast him. Deliberately. I felt like punching Art myself. Come on, Bino. I'll see you to the door."

She took his arm, and he let himself be led. The crowd parted again. Karen Allen and the guy with her were the last two people they passed on the way out. Karen started to say something, then changed her mind.

At the door, Sarah said, "Don't pay any attention to Winnie. You're welcome here anytime." She winked. "A man who packs that kind of a wallop is good to have as a friend." He still liked her.

As he left, Bino wondered exactly how close Art Stammer was to Judge Sanderson. At the foot of the stone steps, he found a pebble in a flower bed and tossed it. It ricocheted off the cherub and splashed down among the goldfish.

Barney Dalton twisted halfway around in the Linc's front seat so that he was facing Bino, put the cool red-and-white Budweiser can against his forehead, and said, "Shit, Bino, have you lost your mind? It's bound to be fixed after all this time, and I didn't drop everything and charge over here in the middle of the night just so's you could get me arrested."

Bino thought that over. "I'm betting it isn't fixed, Barn. And what if it is? We just go up there, rattle the window, and if it won't open we'll just turn around and come back. Nobody's gonna get arrested."

The nose of the Lincoln was straight-on to the south wall of Moody Coliseum, about fifty feet of manicured lawn and a ribbon of sidewalk between it and the row of ground-level windows that opened into the visiting team's dressing room. The three-quarter November moon painted some dark shadows here and there, one from a nearby telephone pole cutting the Lincoln's stark white hood nearly in half. Parked right beside the Lincoln, Barney's dark blue Monte Carlo looked pitch black.

Barney craned his neck and looked past Bino to the Cyclone fence that surrounded the football practice field, then peered in the opposite direction over some red-brick apartments, where the lights along North Central Expressway made a dull glow on the black skyline. He said, "Do the campus cops still patrol around here?" Barney's thick, rust-colored mustache made a shadow across his lower lip.

Bino grinned and picked up the six-pack from the Lincoln's floorboard. Two cans were gone. Bino's coat and tie were in the backseat, and the collar of his white shirt was open at the neck. "How the hell would I know, Barney? Besides, what are they gonna do? Turn us over to the dean of men?" He opened the door, the interior lights suddenly illuminating Barney's sky blue windbreaker, "Crooked River" on the breast, a golf green with a flag on it underneath the words.

Barney shook his head. "I'm stone nuts. I mean, I gotta be. This is a young, healthy chick I'm talking to, and she's got just enough Joe Miller's tequila sunrise in her to make for a strong night in the saddle. I thought about it all the way to the phone when you called. So what do I do? My old buddy calls, I leave the chick dangling, and don't even get a phone number, much less a rain check. And for what? To help a broken-down old basketball player break into a gym, that's what. I've gone bananas. I've got to have." He opened his door.

A few minutes later, Bino stood in front of the center window in the ground-level row, the six-pack in his left hand, Barney behind him with his shoulders hunched over. Bino said, "I think this is the right one." Then he slipped the fingers of his right hand between the edge of the window and the frame, pulling. It came open an inch. Bino drew his hand back; it was throbbing, and he shook it in the air.

"What's wrong with your hand?" said Barney.

Bino didn't say anything for a second, thinking. Then, "Aw, nothing, Barn. I slipped in the shower, banged it on the tile. You try it." He pointed at the window.

Barney shrugged, muttering to himself, then went past Bino and tugged. The window creaked, then swiveled open, sticking out from the wall at a forty-five-degree angle. "Sonofabitch," said Barney. "They've never fixed it. Eighteen years. Sonofabitch."

Bino said, "Hold the beer, Barney." He gave Barney the six-pack, wiggled through the opening, and dropped to the cement floor inside. Pain razored through his hand where it had grabbed the windowsill. Barney tossed the beer inside—it clattered and echoed off the hollow metal lockers—then came through the window himself. As he dropped to the floor next to Bino, feet thudding, Barney muttered, "Two crazy fucking lunatics." He fumbled around and picked up the beer.

Bino used his Bic lighter as a torch, flame turned up high, to light the way down the long corridor that led from the dressing room to the coliseum floor. He'd flick it, making light shoot out and dance against the brick tunnel walls, then they'd walk ten or fifteen feet and he'd flick it again.

It took a few minutes of standing inside the huge arena for Bino's eyes to adjust to the near dark. Finally, he could make out the glass backboard at the near end, the hoop, and the net hanging from it like a spider's web.

Bino walked to the wall just outside the center-court boundary line. He sat down on the floor, his back against the folded-up students' section bleachers, and locked his hands in front of him, arms hugging his knees. Barney got down next to him and popped a beer. The shook-up suds fizzed and spewed; Barney put his mouth over the opening in the top to catch the beer.

As his eyes got more accustomed to the dark, Bino looked up into the cavernous stands across from him. His gaze lingered on one section of seats in particular, in the high right corner. He pictured a lot of folks from Mesquite who never quite made it into town, sitting up there in boots, jeans, and western hats and having the time of their lives, pounding on seat backs and chanting, "Go, you big Albino, go." And Bino's dad and Pop Harrison, a gambler and a Baptist deacon who kept his nose to the grindstone and wouldn't bet that fat meat was greasy, jumping up and down and hugging each other every time the big, soft hook swished home.

Bino said, "The law's a pile of shit, Barney. The whole justice system is like the biggest, festering stack of dog crap you ever saw, laying in the middle of the road with a bunch of flies buzzing around it. And us lawyers are the flies, carrying off our own little pieces of shit, back to the nest. I'd have a more honest way of making a living being a pimp."

Barney opened another beer, this one not fizzing quite as much. He handed it to Bino, saying, "Now, that's a helluvan observation at this late date, Bino. After all this time. You sound like a brain surgeon that I'm giving golf lessons to. He's decided he wants to be a golf hustler."

Bino shrugged. "Any of his patients died lately? A client of mine died yesterday, a horse's ass named Sonny Starr. So you know what? Today I signed up two more. I don't think I want to be a lawyer anymore." He sipped the beer. "I saw Annabelle tonight, Barney."

Barney was silent. Then he said, "Yeah. She's married to Dante Tirelli."

Bino's eyes widened. "You knew?"

"A couple of Tirelli's associates, or whatever you want to call 'em, play golf at the club. When one's not looking, the other one improves his lie in the rough. Then vice versa. It evens out. Anyway, Tirelli brought her out, had dinner with them."

"She's still gorgeous, isn't she, Barn?"

"Yeah."

Bino pointed his finger down the court, away from them. "Right there, Barney. She used to jump around right there. *S—M——U! Go, Mustangs*, all that. Now she's gone and married into the mob."

Barney thumped an imaginary speck of dust off his pants. "Well, at least she married the top, not the bottom."

"And you know what?" said Bino. "Her second husband's really no different than her first. I mean, both of us stay in the background, live off of somebody else's crime. Don't we?"

Barney didn't answer.

They sat there awhile, drinking beer, not talking. Then Bino pointed again, this time at the goal at the far end of the court. He said, "Whatcha think, Barney? Was it goaltending, or wasn't it?"

Barney chuckled. "The Aggie game? I swear, Bino, I don't know. I was too busy trying to block the shot, made a lunge for it. By the time I got turned around, there you were, standing there with the ball, and the ref was giving the two-point sign." He swigged. "After all this time, Bino, I still don't know."

Bino got up. "Let's go home, Barn."

Barney looked up at him for a minute, then stood. "About fucking time."

"And in the black corner"—Sarah Anspacher was the announcer, in a yellow cocktail dress—"at eight-feet-five, wearing transparent briefs—theeee *challenger—Lucky-Punch Phillips!"*

Gong!

Art Stammer came out fast, dancing, in good shape, gloves up, classic pose. Bino felt like his feet were moving in quicksand. He looked down. He was naked, except for black hightop shoes.

Stammer threw a jab. It missed, but Bino felt the air whistle under his chin.

Bino said, "Look, Art! Over there! Voters!"

Stammer turned his head to stare, still dancing. Bino let him have it.

Gong! Gong! Gong!

Buzzzzz!

" . . . and it's a windy day over the Metroplex, folks, just windy enough to blow the fourth lucky caller a *whole pile* of K.V.I.L. cash, while we listen to the sounds of Stevie Nicks, doing—"

Bino rolled over, reached, and pressed the clock radio button. The buzzer quit buzzing and Ron Chapman quit talking, cut off in midsentence.

Bino blinked. There was a growing crack in the ceiling, bigger than yesterday, had to be. He turned his head. The glowing digital readout said 8:15. New health kick, up before noon, fifty-yard trudge. His shoulders and pectorals were sore as boils. His right hand throbbed. His mouth tasted like a dried-up horse turd. He groaned out of bed, standing in Jockey briefs.

By the time he'd showered, steamy water pulsing through the massager nozzle, and dried with a fluffy beach towel, he'd decided that he was going to live. He hand-rubbed a clear spot in the frosty mirror and checked himself out. Long nose, slight bump. Thin, white eyebrows. Slight overbite, a little jut-jawed. Blue eyes not too bloodshot. A couple of drops of Murine fixed that in a hurry. He blew his hair dry. Natural look. Or as natural as short, snow white hair *can* look.

He stopped for a minute in the walk-in closet, holding a white shirt in one hand, tie in the other. He didn't feel like it. He hung them up and slipped on a gray-striped rugby shirt instead, and dark green slacks. Then he stood in front of the bedroom full-length mirror and stuck his chest out. Pain roared in his pectorals, and he rubbed them.

Between the breakfast nook and the living room, Cecil goggle-eyed him from the round aquarium. Bino fished a minnow out of a bucket with a tea strainer and plopped him in; the little bugger darted to and fro. Cecil closed his eyes, pretended to be asleep, and waited for the minnow to swim closer. Bino said, "Cagey fucker," then poured himself a cup of coffee. He got the newspaper from the patio and spread it out on the breakfast table.

It was on the front page of Section B, State and Local News, in the lower-right-hand corner. Bino thought, Jesus Christ.

The small headline said, LAWYER DECKS CANDIDATE. Bino thought about Judge Sanderson, this morning's meeting. He'd just read the first paragraph, containing his name and Stammer's, when the phone rang.

It was Dodie. Her small, frightened voice made the warning bell go off in his brain even before he understood what she was saying.

"Bino? Oh, my God, Bino, it's Teresa! She's in the—the supply room, and she's—"

He stiffened. "Teresa? The little elevator girl? Dodie—?"

Her voice rose an octave, nearly hysterical. "Yes, Teresa! She's *dead*, Bino! And the office is torn up, it's like—oh, God—"

"Dodie! Dodie, you listen. You get out of there, right now. Get somebody, anybody! Call the police. I'm on my way."

By the time Bino had herded the Linc into the parking lot and hustled across the street on foot, jaywalking and dodging traffic, there were three squad cars at the curb in front of the building, motors running and rooflights flashing. As he jogged abreast of the squad cars, an ambulance careened into sight, its siren wailing full blast, and screeched to a halt behind them. Bino did a running column left and ducked into the lobby.

Teresa's mom and grandmother were there, two women, one old, the other older and more wrinkled, hugging each other, burying their faces in each other's shoulders, each sobbing heart-broken sobs and consoling the other in their native tongue. Bino slowed and walked past them with his head down. He slipped quietly into an open elevator, cranked the handle, and drove himself up.

Bob Denton, the slim, brown-suited building manager, was in the hall outside Bino's office, talking animatedly to a woman in a gray dress. Denton stopped Bino.

"Nasty business, Bino. Jeez, I hope there won't be any press on this. For your sake *and* ours."

Bino didn't say anything for a moment, then said, "Where's Dodie, Bob?" Denton pointed at the door, and Bino shouldered around him and went in.

She was behind her desk in a frizzy pink sweater, her hands trembling as she held a cup of coffee, the black surface of the liquid making ripples. A blue-skirted policewoman was talking to her and taking notes on a spiral pad. Dodie set the cup down and rushed to Bino, throwing her arms around his neck, standing on her tiptoes, and crying into his shoulder.

"Oh, it's so awful! Poor Teresa—and she—" She looked up at him, her blue eyes wide and round. "She just happened to get in the way, Bino. They were after you. Oh, I know they were." She was slurring her words. She began to sob again.

Bino said, "Try to relax, Dode. They give you something?"

She nodded. "A big white pill. Dr. Traynor—he's in—in there." She pointed, not looking at the supply room door. "Half-a-Point is in his office, talking to a policeman."

Bino spoke to the policewoman. "Can you get her home?" The woman put down her pad. She had short, mouse-colored hair and wore glasses. She said, "Yes, sir. I'll take her myself."

Dodie said, sniffing, "No, Bino, I'm all right. The phone—it might ring, and—" The pill, whatever it was, had made her dopey. She blinked.

"Don't worry about the phone, Dode," said Bino. "It'll take care of itself. You get some rest." He kissed her gently on the forehead. Then he walked out in the hall with them and made sure that the woman had Dodie's address. Dodie was still sobbing as they left.

Shoesole Traynor, wearing a white doctor's coat and smoking his Sherlock Holmes–style pipe, was taking notes. Two plainclothesmen were dusting the supply room for prints, paying particular attention to the top of the Xerox. Something was huddled on the floor in a zip-up plastic bag. Bino didn't want to see it.

Traynor said, "It sucks, Bino, the works. Seminal fluid all over her, in every orifice. There were two of 'em."

"How do you know?"

Traynor jerked his head toward a file cabinet. There were several square glass lab slides on top. He said, "Pubic hair. Some black, some red, none of it hers. Shit, Bino, they gutted her." He shook his head. "Like she was a fish or something. The downstairs night guard said that she was gone when he came to work. He thought she'd gone home. Detective work's not in my line, and there'll be somebody else to question you about it. But these are two mean bastards, Bino. They got a hard-on for you?"

Bino scratched his chin. "I don't know, Shoesole. Who they might be, anything. I'll swear I don't."

A slim, short-haired, hard-eyed guy was behind Bino's desk. He had gloves on and was scraping residue from an ashtray into a sterile Baggie. Papers were all over the floor and on the desk-top. The guy said, "I'm Detective Earlson. You Mr. Phillips?"

There was an open copy of the *Football News* on the desk, with the point spreads written next to the teams. Bino started to reach for it, to stick it in his pocket. He changed his mind, nodding. Earlson went on.

"Well, Mr. Phillips, somebody has gone over your office with a fine-tooth comb. Every room, every file. We figure that the little girl just happened to be here, maybe stumbled onto 'em, so they—well, went to work on her. Any idea what they were looking for?"

Bino sat down across from Earlson. "None. Any prints?"

Earlson had on a gray checkerboard sport coat and

a blue tie. He said, "No, sir, not one that we can find. Probably wore gloves. You got any clients that might be pissed off at you?"

Bino shrugged. "A lot of my clients are in jail. The ones that are are pissed off. But not *this* pissed off."

Earlson stroked his slim cheeks with a thumb and forefinger. He had a pencil mustache, a lot like Half-a-Point's. Earlson said, "Well, somebody is. Listen, I'm going to ask you to give me a few more minutes in here to check things over. My partner's in the next office, interviewing your—investigator? He'll have a few questions for you, too." He tossed a printed business card over in front of Bino. "That's my number. I'm going to ask you to make an inventory, list what's missing, and give me a call in the next couple of days."

Bino said okay, tucked the card in his pocket, and started to leave. He had his hand on the doorknob when Earlson said, "Oh. Mr. Phillips."

Bino turned around.

Earlson had the *Football News*; he was holding it out, grinning. "I'd put this away if I were you. Someone might get the wrong idea." Bino took the paper and left.

Two uniformed cops were lugging the body bag out on a stretcher, with Shoesole Traynor behind them, puffing away on his briar. Bino averted his eyes from them and went into Half's office.

Earlson's partner was too fat, older, his puffy neck sticking out over his starched white collar in folds. He had a bulbous nose and was frowning, looking through the stack of *Football Newses* from Half-a-Point's desk.

Half-a-Point sounded a little choked up as he said, "And so a lot of us, you know, like to call each other, pretend we're betting on the games. We pass those out, try to see how our old pickers are doing against the line. Sort of like the sports-writer—Bayless, yeah, that's it—just fooling around, seeing how we'd do if we was to bet for real." He chuckled nervously.

The chubby cop didn't say anything; he was eyeing the black phone. Bino sat down next to him.

Bino said, "Detective Earlson told me to come in and talk to you, answer a few questions. I'm Bino Phillips." Half-a-Point squirmed, crossing his arms on his desk.

The fat detective regarded Bino through thick, half-closed lids. "Yeah, well, I'm Detective Garrett. I've been talking to Mr. Harrison here"—jerking his head at Half—"to see if we can't come up with some sort of motive for all of this. Robbery doesn't seem to be it. We're thinking about the usual stuff, but nobody's being blackmailed here—and I don't guess there's any gambling going on is there?" He glanced at the black phone again.

It rang.

The bell was echoing, hanging in the room. Half-a-Point seemed to shrink. Bino crossed one leg over the other.

It rang again.

Garrett said, "Want me to answer it?"

Bino grabbed it fast, saying, "Hello."

There was a throaty female chuckle. Then a cultured voice, familiar, said, "Goodness, are you answering the secret line yourself?"

Garrett was watching with interest. Bino said, "Well, yeah, sometimes. Who is this?"

She laughed again. "So soon we forget. I want to show you some pictures." It was Karen Allen.

Bino said, "How did you—" He stopped in midsentence. Of course. Goldman. He put his hand over the mouthpiece, and said to Garrett, "It's the F.B.I."

Half-a-Point looked like he was about to crawl under his desk.

Bino spoke into the phone, saying, "Well, yes, Agent

Allen, it's good that you called. We've had a tragedy here, an apparent homicide. Someone broke into the office. I was just visiting with Detective Garrett from the City. What's this about pictures?"

There was a pause, Bino thinking about the way she stood last night, one hip higher than the other. Then she said, "Be careful what you say in front of the local police, Bino. Was your office searched?"

Bino's gaze flicked at Garrett for the barest instant. "Why, yes, Agent. That's right."

"Bino, I've called on this line because I don't want any of your staff, secretaries, whatnot, to know I'm talking to you. Now, I'm going to tell you that you might not be safe. Can you come by? Over here, to the office?"

Bino leaned back in the chair and propped his elbow up on its arm, holding the receiver against his ear. His tricep was sore, like his pectorals. "Well, I don't see why not. My secretary—well, she's gone for the day, but I think my investigator will hang around, answer the phone." Garrett was putting his notepad in a briefcase, folding up his tent.

She said, "You mean the bookmaker?"

"Horace. Horace Harrison. I'll be there in a half hour or so."

"Okay. One more thing, Bino. It's about Sonny Starr. Don't mention that to anybody." She hung up.

Garrett said, somewhat subdued, "Well, I guess we've done about all we can for right now. You'll call us if anything comes up, huh?"

Bino said that he would, and Garrett and Earlson left. Half-a-Point brightened.

Bino remembered what he and Half had talked about yesterday. "Did you go out to Sonny Starr's?"

"Yeah. That manager's a real queen. Says no, he never found no body. Didn't even know what happened, not till a couple of Feds talked to him." He shook his head. "This is the shits, Bino. That poor little gal, having that happen up here. And the law, all they want to know about is whether we're doing a little booking. The drizzlies, that's what it is."

Bino nodded, thinking. Then he said, "I've got to go see a lady about some pictures. The manager tell you anything else?"

"Naw—but he did ask about the rent. Says Sonny always had a lot of cash, liked to flash it around. Wanted to know if he could make some kind of claim on it."

"Nobody's told me that they found any cash at Sonny's place," said Bino. "Not the cops or the Feds."

Half fitted a cigarette into a plastic holder. "Something's weird about all this, Bino. I mean, Sonny Starr was a two-bit dope bust. Shit, they sent enough F.B.I.'s over there to investigate the killin' of the president or something."

Bino said, "You're gonna be around, aren't you? To answer the phone?"

"I'll be here," said Half. He reached into his bottom drawer and brought out a slim Beretta, laying it on his desk. "Me and this equalizer. Staying here alone gives me the creeps, after what's happened."

Bino crossed his legs and read the sign that said anyone who entered this office was subject to being searched. Then he went over it again. You'd think that there would be some magazines to read or something, not just a sliding window in the wall through which you gave your name and stated your business to a bored receptionist who looked like a mouse, then a sign about getting searched for you to read while you waited.

Karen Allen came into the reception room looking different. Same face, same high cheekbones, nearly olive skin, natural eyes. Dressed differently, sure, now in business gray wool, skirt right at the knee; black, medium-heeled shoes, squared toes. The walk was different, straight-on, one foot in front of the other, no hip sway. Here in this F.B.I. office, plain, no-nonsense furniture, no pictures on the wall, a single tall potted fern in the corner that looked like an afterthought, she belonged. And last night, too, band playing, cocktail shakers shaking, loose flowing skirt, little hip cock when she stood—well, she'd belonged there, too. *Chick snaps her fingers, talks right in there, man. All the way up till she flashes down with the shield.*

Bino stood.

Karen checked her watch, a modest Lady Bulova. "You're prompt, Bino. I like that." A different kind of smile, more impersonal. "Follow me, right this way."

She led him down a narrow hallway, her back straight as a board, no come-on to this walk. Nearly all the rooms that they passed had the doors open, cubbyhole offices, some with men or women behind the small desks, most of them on the phone. They went into a conference room, curtains drawn, with a slide projector on the table and a small screen set up in front of it. She had a yellow ruled pad laid out, ballpoint laying next to it and ready. She sat; Bino took the chair next to her, noticing her thigh line as she crossed her legs.

She licked her upper lip and picked up the ballpoint. "Someone was killed in your office?"

He nodded. "Little elevator girl. Pretty gruesome stuff. The F.B.I. using a lot of women agents these days?"

She shifted enough so he'd know she didn't like the question, drew a doodling circle on the pad, and said, "A few. The police find anything they can use?"

"Said they didn't. It was a ransack, every file pulled

out, stuff thrown all over the floor. I couldn't tell them anything 'cause I don't know. For real. Do you?"

She wrote something down; Bino made the effort not to turn his head sideways and read it. She said, "I might. I need to tell you a few things, Bino. About federal investigations. The kind I'm doing."

"You mean, like, undercover stuff? Buying dope, all that?"

"I've—I've graduated from that, Bino. I'm working on Richard Bigelow, as if you didn't already know. It's a hot item, a top-priority case, just like if a judge were assassinated. Now, I think you've got some things that could help us. I need to talk to you about Sonny Starr."

Bino put his elbow on the table and rested his chin on his fist. The window line was visible where daylight hit the back of the closed drapes. "I had an attorney-client relationship with Sonny, Karen. I'm not sure whether his death ends that or not." The nails on her hand that held the ballpoint gleamed dully with a clear lacquer polish. One had been broken and mended.

She said, "Attorney-client privilege doesn't work anymore, Bino, not in a case like this. You know that, too. We can make you tell us, if we want to."

Bino thought, She's right. I've seen the new cases. Another smashup of the Constitution. A guy's not even safe telling his lawyer anything anymore.

She went on. "But I don't think I'll have to after I show you these. Get the lights, will you, Bino?" She breathed a little sigh, chest rising and falling, and flicked on the projector. The sudden white light on the screen made him blink. He got up and switched off the lights. She reached forward, the artificial light from the projector bulb illuminating her hand and reflecting from her gold watchband. The projector whirred and turned, and a picture appeared. It was a mug shot, front and side views next to each other.

Bino said, "I've seen Sonny look prettier than that, Karen." Her neck and head were in darkness; he had just a view of her shoulders, chest, and narrow waist. Good body.

With a short, dry chuckle, she said, "Oh, really? When—at the morgue? Since he's so pretty, let's see some more of him."

She hit the button. Sonny's scrawny neck and hawk face disappeared, to be replaced by a zoom-in shot, side view. The whiskers on his jawbone stood out like cactus thorns, and the bottom of his earlobe looked like a satellite photo of the South Pole, upside down. She said, "These were taken on Sonny's release from Darrington, state pen. What do you see?"

Bino looked closer, narrowing his eyes. Judging from the size of the blown-up earlobe, the thing would have been close to an inch long, with a wingspread of nearly twice that. The detail was amazing, right down to weblike veins in the wings. "Well, I'll be damned," said Bino. "It's a fly." Funny, he'd never noticed it before. Surely he would have, a tattoo like that. It was on the cord of Sonny's neck, just a little behind and below the earlobe.

Karen Allen's head turn was barely visible in the dark, the moving of her lips totally unseen by Bino as she said, "This next one is the same angle, close-up taken by the marshals when he was arraigned on the federal drug charges."

Click. Whirrr. Bino looked, then shrugged. "So he had a tattoo removed. Lots of people do it. Maybe Sonny wanted to change his life-style, clean up his act."

"Probably reformed by you, Bino. No, he's our man—one of them. The thirty-thirty rifle was easy to find, quick. It was on the rooftop across the street from where Richard Bigelow went down. Its registration was fake, phony driver's license, the works. But the gun dealer that sold it remembered the tattoo. On the guy—there were three of them—that did the talking, and paid for the gun. Our computers came up with nine fly tattoos on necks—would you believe there were nine of them? Sonny's the only one that had his removed—see the little scar there? Now, Sonny got out of Darrington on the nineteenth of June, thirteen days before Mr. Bigelow was killed. And for some reason had the tattoo cut off between his release and the drug bust. So we took photos to the gun dealer, and bingo. Sonny's one of our men, Bino. No doubt about it." Her voice was even, all business, but still soft and feminine.

Bino thought about Sonny, arrogant little bastard, strutting, talking big. If Bino'd known about this, he might have killed Sonny himself. Would at least have turned his own client in, relationship as a lawyer or no. He said, "Three of them? Any ideas on the others?"

She turned off the projector and regarded him a moment in near darkness. Then she scooted back her chair, stood, and turned the lights on. "You really don't know anything? Sonny never mentioned it, huh?"

He shook his head. "Square Injun, Karen. After last night, what I told you about Richard and me, I think you know I'd tell you."

She sat back down. "Yes, I think you would. The other two, well, we've got some vague descriptions from the gun dealer. Not much to go on. Maybe somebody he knew in jail; we're checking it out. Somebody thinks you know, Bino, the way your office was broken into last night. Probably the other two, probably them that killed Sonny."

Bino felt some little goose bumps, like cold pinpricks. He said, "Last night, Karen, did that have something to do with Sonny? Why you went to the party?"

She looked thoughtful, then smiled, changing again,

back to the girl he'd seen at Anspacher's. "Why, no. I wanted to see some live fisticuffs. Good right, Bino."

"Uh, let's forget about that, okay? Really, is that why you were there?" He mentally snapped his fingers, looking at the watch on her arm, next to him on the chair. He'd missed his appointment with the judge.

"Well—not directly, Bino, and I've told you all that I can for now."

She said it with a little eye movement and jaw set that meant subject closed. There wasn't any point in asking her any more, so Bino said, "So. What do you want me to do?"

She took a business card from between the pages of the ruled notepad, turned it over, wrote on the back, and gave it to him. "It's my home address and number, office on the front. You find out anything, anything at all, that might help us, day or night, call me. It's that big, Bino. That important."

Bino read both sides of the card, studying the handwritten back closely. She didn't live too far from Dodie. Swinging singles area. He looked up. She was watching him, her lips parted, expectant.

He said, "What if you're not there?"

"I usually am. Leave a message on the machine otherwise. I've got a remote, get the messages every hour or so. I'll get back to you." There was a little softening around her eyes. "I'd be careful, Bino."

Bino used the pay phone in the lobby. When the secretary answered, he said, "May I speak to the judge, please? This is Bino Phillips."

She was silent for three heartbeats, finally saying, "You've got guts, I'll say that for you." The line clicked. He was on hold.

In a few minutes, Judge Hazel Burke Sanderson's gravelly voice said, "I'm waiting, Mr. Phillips."

Bino pictured her, iron gray hair in a severe bun,

Martha Washington glasses that usually perched on the end of her nose, lips set in a deadpan no-smile, no-frown. He swallowed hard. "I've had some unexpected things come up, Your Honor. I'm sorry to keep you waiting. Can I make another appointment?"

"Unexpected? What, practicing your roadwork, working out on the heavy bag?" She'd read the paper.

Bino thought, What do I do now? Tell her? He said, "I assure you it was unavoidablc, Judge. Please, another appointment?"

Papers rustled, like static on the phone. "The rest of the week is full, Mr. Phillips. Normally I only make one appointment, but I really want to hear what *you* have to say. Monday at one, sir. Don't be late."

She hung up.

Bino made one stop on the way to his office, in a small pawn-broker-gun shop. He came out with a box of shells. They fit the Mauser pistol in his glove compartment.

Buster thought about it a minute, then went ahead and took a toke off of the fat, machine-rolled joint that the girl who worked in Keller's Drive-In was offering. He drew it down fast, breath whistling, held it, and got a pretty good rush. He gave it back. She took a drag off the joint herself as she went back to the couch where John-boy was sitting. The flesh on the inside of her thighs quivered under her flowered bikini panties; then she sat down and brought one leg up under her, resting her knee on John-boy's lap. John-boy took a hit off the grass himself. The girl pulled the hem of her T-shirt down to cover her panties, then noticed where Buster was looking and scootched so it'd ride back up again.

John-boy clapped a beefy hand down on her thigh, saying, "You better go ahead and get some of this, Bus. It's prime choice." She giggled and smoked some more.

Buster shifted his weight on the hassock and swigged some beer. "Naw, John-boy. You go ahead. My mind's on something else." He thought, Jesus Christ, isn't no way that I could think about getting laid right now, not after what we done to the little Mex last night.

Buster couldn't even tell you why he'd gone ahead and done it, and, shit, it *bothered* him. John-boy, he just woke up as horny as ever, called down to Keller's, and told this gal to bring herself over after work. Wasn't no problem in getting her to, as long as John-boy had something to smoke. Buster wanted to talk to John-boy about what they were going to tell the man, but he couldn't so long as the broad was there, so he'd have to make up his mind about what to say to the man on his own. Couldn't wait no longer, had to talk to him.

They were going to have to get something done about the lawyer pretty quick, so Buster could leave town, probably go to California. Both Buster and John-boy ought to haul ass, sure they should. But whatever direction that John-boy was going in, Buster wanted to go the other way. The way John-boy threw money around, flashing a bankroll and talking like a lunatic, pretty soon somebody would start wondering where he got it. That, or he'd spill all the beans, bragging and popping off to some bimbo like that one on the couch there, just 'cause she'd smoke a joint and give him a little pussy.

John-boy put the girl's hand in his lap, saying, "Feel how hard my heart's beating for you, darlin'?"

She snickered again, scratching her head, her brown-rooted bleached blond hair wiggling. John-boy kept hold of her hand, getting up, leading her off into the bedroom. Buster thought, that's sure okay with me. So long as she don't yell so loud a man can't hear himself think.

Buster went over and stood at the window, looking down at the courtyard and deserted pool. He was in jeans without a shirt. The pool was okay in summer, but kind of dingy looking in fall and winter, with nobody swimming or playing volleyball in it. The net whipped lonesome in the breeze.

Buster needed to get his thoughts together, figure out how much bread he'd have to get the man to come up with. If he'd known how rich the man was, and who he was, when the boss on Darrington who called Buster "Old Thaing" too often had put the man in touch with him, if Buster'd known all that to begin with, the price of killing the old dude would have been a lot higher.

When Boss Whitten, that was his name, had first come to Buster, all that skinny boss had wanted to talk about was parole. Boss Whitten wasn't really no bad boss. He looked the other way while Buster drove the tractor and swigged the Old Crow whiskey that Little Fletch's niece threw over the fence. But Whitten knew that Buster didn't like being called "Old Thaing," even though all the bosses called the men that. They'd only called Buster that once before he'd asked them polite not to, and most of them wouldn't call him that anymore. Boss Whitten just called Buster "Old Thaing" because he knew that it pissed Buster off.

Buster had the tractor parked under a shade tree, one eye completely closed and the other one getting that way. It was July, around one in the afternoon, sun beating down, and just about the time of day when the bosses gathered up at the tractor barn to shoot the shit. Buster had line-drug two or three rows in a hurry, killing off a bunch of the cotton, getting through so he could park the tractor and catch a few Z's.

Right over Buster's left shoulder, Boss Whitten's high, whiny voice said, "Whatcha doin' out here, Old Thaing? Fuckin' off, I reckon."

Buster jumped and banged his knee on the steering wheel. The pint fell out of the tractor and thudded on the soft ground. While Buster cussed, bent over, and rubbed his knee, Boss Whitten picked the whiskey up, held the bottle to the light, and squinted at it. It was a little under half full.

Boss Whitten said, "Some old thaings don't think too good, Old Thaing. If tractor drivin' don't set too good with you, boy, we can put your ass back to swingin' one of them hoes." His Adam's apple stood out like he'd swallowed a rabbit. He was wearing mirror shades under his wide-brimmed western hat.

Buster stuck a freckled hand underneath his white prison workshirt and rubbed his belly. Doing his best to look pitiful, he said, "Ain't feelin' too good, boss. Had to park in the shade a spell. I might puke up from all this heat."

Whitten reached under his blue collar and scratched the back of his neck. "Puke up? You might puke up from sittin' out here drinkin' this Old Crow whiskey, that's all you'd puke up from, Old Thaing. Listen here, Longley, I ain't got but jus' a minute. You goin' to the board in August, ain'tcha?"

"Well, yeah, boss. First time up on this little beef here. You know, first time with my track record, I ain't really spectin' much. But I'm goin' right enough." Nearby, some grasshoppers started a loud, high-pitched buzz.

Boss Whitten leaned an elbow on the tractor, propped a foot up on the tread of a big rear tire, and rested a forearm on his skinny thigh. The bottle hung loose in his hand. The shine was worn off of his western boot, and the leather was scarred. "Fella wants to talk to you on the outside, Longley. Says a Mr. Bradley Peach tole him to talk to you."

Buster narrowed his eyes in the shade. He couldn't see Whitten's expression behind the mirrors, and the boss's lips were set in a thin line. Buster thought, Peach the Leach, hey? Old cellie, Peach, doing him a big two-oh right now in the Fed. Marion, Illinois. Solid lockdown.

Buster said, "Who's Bradley Peach, boss?"

Boss Whitten snorted through his nose. "Say, looky here, Old Thaing. Ain't no nevermind to me. Fella on the outside wants a job done, says to get word to you." He leaned closer. "Big shot fella, Old Thaing. Big *so's* you can get paroled, he gives the word."

Buster glanced down, reached, took the bottle. He unscrewed the cap and nipped. The whiskey burned his gullet. "What work this fella talkin' about, boss?"

"Well, you'd know that better'n me, Longley, 'Course, you might not, bein' as you don't know no Bradley Peach, huh? Listen, Old Thaing. I can't be jawin' here, an' soon's I walk off I want you to go to drivin' this tractor. Fella wants three men, you an' two others, your pick. You can get word who's the others through me. Now, when you go, parole board's gonna ask you what you'll do iffen you get out. You want this job, you say you're goin' to Dallas, do construction. Don't want the job, you say you're going up to Foat Wuth, hear me?" He stood away from the tractor, walked off about ten feet. Then he stopped and looked at Buster over his shoulder. "Wanna get paroled, you go to Dallas, Old Thaing. Now, git yo' *ass* to drivin', boy. You heah?"

Buster thought that over. A few days later, sweat pouring off his forehead, he plunked a forty-pound bag of horse manure on top of a stack in the shed, saying, "How come this fella wants me, boss? I mean, I ain't no name. I done a few stickups, maybe a poker game here and there. But for what you're talkin' about, they's dudes around got a track record in it."

Boss Whitten was chewing on a long piece of straw, counting the sacks, tapping each one with a yellow pencil. He wrote the number down on a list that he was keeping on a clipboard, talking as he wrote. "I guess it's why he wants you, Old Thaing. Something comes down like what he wants, the name boys is who gets looked up first." He took off his mirror shades and rubbed his eyes. "Mr. Bradley Peach, he gave the word. Says you're okay for it."

"Well, let's say I go for it. How's this man get ahold of me?"

Boss Whitten put the shades back on. "Easy as pie, Old Thaing. You just tell me where you're gonna be. The man, he'll get in touch." He turned his head, looking at the wagonload of horse manure sitting outside the door to the shed. "Now get yo' *ass* to unloadin', boy."

Buster had more sense than to talk about it in the joint. Too many cons around, looking for a cut in their time, who'd just walk up to a boss and say, "Hey, boss, get me a word with the warden, first chance, huh?" No, Buster didn't talk about it, but he started to look around.

First he picked out Sonny Starr. He knew about Sonny, had a pal up in Dallas who'd done a little bank with Son. When the heat came down, Sonny hadn't talked about this guy; guy said that Sonny was stand-up. Still, Buster didn't tell Sonny what was up right away, he just got the name of a safecracker who would know how to get in touch with Sonny on the street.

John-boy Driggers was already out and on the ground when Boss Whitten first came to Buster, but Buster knew where he was, and thought about him right off. There'd been a ruckus about a year earlier over four cases of Spam that came up missing from Buster's locker. Buster knew who got them all right, a snotnose hot check boy from San Antone. All he'd had to do was mention it to John-boy, and John-boy got the Spam back in a hurry, breaking the hot check boy's shoulder. John-boy wasn't much between the ears, but he'd do a job right enough, if you just pointed him in the right direction.

During the second week in August, Buster paid a carton of smokes for some pressed duds from the laundry, got slicked up, and went to the board. He sat across a long table from two men in business suits, one young with black hair and the other in his fifties and bald, and a fat woman in a gray dress with a costume jewelry pin on the breast. The woman cleared her throat.

"Mr. Longley, the board first wants to assure you that your case will be given every consideration, from both the standpoint of your personal benefit, and the best interest of society in general. Now, I am briefly going over your file with you so that you may add anything you wish to add and we may correct any discrepancies in the record. Are we clear on that?"

Buster, clean shaven, was looking at the young guy, thinking, he looks like a wop. Probably him, yeah, this one, he's the contact.

The woman said, "Mr. Longley?"

Buster's gaze shifted to her. "Huh? I mean, excuse me?"

The woman wore round, black-framed glasses, which hung on a chain around her neck. She put them on. They sat perched on a little hump in the middle of her pointed nose. "I said, 'Is that clear?' Mr. Longley."

"Oh, yes, ma'am. It's clear enough."

She took the glasses off again and let them dangle, reading silently for a moment from Buster's file. Then she went on, saying, "Now, according to our records, you are serving a ten-year sentence for burglary of a building, and will first become eligible for parole on September 1. Your prior record includes . . ."

She droned on about the beef up in Danbury, the

one in Duluth, the state raps in Tennessee and Kentucky, and the prior Texas number, Buster watching the young guy. The dude wasn't looking up, just taking notes, acting like he couldn't care less, didn't know old Buster from Tubby's cow. Yep. It was him, all right. The older guy, light reflecting off of his bald head, was staring at Buster like a visitor in the zoo.

The woman was saying, " . . . and that seems to be the record. A rather lengthy one. Do you have any questions, or anything to add?" The pin on her breast had dull brown glass stones in it. She rubbed them with her hand.

Buster hadn't been paying much attention, but he thought she'd missed the South Carolina time. He said, "No, ma'am. I guess that covers it, right enough. I've made a right smart number of mistakes in my time. The good Lord must wonder about me, if I'm ever going to straighten out. But I want you folks to know, I've thought it over hard this time. I'll not be no more trouble to anybody."

The young guy, the contact, kept writing, while the fat woman turned her round head and exchanged glances with the bald man. The old guy had a hearing aid on. They looked in unison back at Buster.

In a high, cracked voice, the old man said, "Your record don't look like you've been trying too hard to change, Mr. Longley. Tell the board, what you going to do with yourself if you get paroled?"

Buster folded his chubby, freckled hands on the table in front of him, his eyes down. He tried to sound real, real solemn as he said, "Well, I don't want to go anywhere I've been in trouble, you know, take up old habits and haunts? So I've written to a man I know's got a construction company, and he says he'll put me on. He's—he's up in Dallas, is where he is."

Fat cheeks puffing, the woman bent down and started

to write. The old man fingered his hearing aid with one hand, writing with the other. The young guy barely glanced at Buster, keeping his cover, going on with his note taking.

The woman darted her glance both ways, making sure that the men's heads were down, then she looked up. She squinched her right eye, giving Buster a big, fat, knowing wink.

Buster thought, Jesus H. Christ on a crutch! Her?

Buster padded barefoot away from the window, across the carpet, and into the hall, crumpling his beer can and tossing it in the wastebasket on his way. The broad wasn't making a whole lot of racket, just some soft moans and sobs, but John-boy's bedsprings were creaking like a sonofabitch, so Buster quietly shut the bedroom door before he used the phone. He called the man. The secretary gave him a little shit about interrupting a conference, but Buster said that he was H. Brown Trucking Company, the code name, and she finally punched him through.

Yes, more money was available. Swell, said Buster. How much? Another hundred, if the job gets done. What job? Very simple. Find out if the lawyer, Phillips, knows about Buster and John-boy and the killing. Do it without any more violence, if possible. Buster snorted. What the fuck you think this is? You're paying a hundred grand to have a guy knocked off, another hundred to keep your ass from getting caught, and you're wanting no violence? Buster'd show him some fucking violence, he didn't come up with the hundred grand.

Buster put on shoes and shirt, and got ready to leave. He thought about telling John-boy. But just as he was about to open the door to the bedroom the broad squealed, "Ohhhh-wee!" and Buster changed his mind. He went out through the front and downstairs into the parking lot, thinking, Maybe John-boy will catch a dose, get scared, and leave without his share of the hundred grand. Serve him right.

There'd been this one time that Buster'd had to get a square job, so his parole officer would quit bugging him. He tried faking it a time or two, telling her he was working when he wasn't, but she kept checking up on him. So finally, Buster went to work. The job looked on the square, but it really wasn't.

Buster'd met this private eye, Jerry Peters, when Buster was making money being a puller. He'd get a call from a chop shop that was looking for a special part, like a chassis from a 1978 Olds or a fender from a 1980 Plymouth, and Buster would pull it. He'd swipe the Olds, Plymouth, or whatever, leave it parked in a certain spot, and call the chop shop to pick it up.

Anyway, Jerry Peters got himself hired by insurance companies to find all of these cars that were getting stolen—the companies thought that all the cops were on the chop shops' payrolls, which they were, and that they needed a cop of their own. So this Jerry Peters got a tip from somewhere, put the arm on Buster one day just as Buster was swiping a Ford, and made a deal with him. They started getting it both ways. When the chop shop got through taking whatever part they wanted, they'd have the car towed to another spot. Then Buster'd call Peters. Peters would find the car, collect the salvage from the insurance company, and split it with Buster. Sweet deal. So the time that Buster needed a square job, he went straight to Peters.

Peters put Buster on the payroll, taught him how to shadow guys. It gave Buster a paycheck every week to show to the parole officer and at the same time gave Peters a brand-new scam to make some money with.

This is the way it worked. Buster'd hang around all these singles bars in Manhattan, which is where Buster was living at the time. He'd play it real quiet, just sit there at the bar and nurse a beer, looking for a mark. The mark was usually a fat, balding guy in his forties or fifties, wearing a suit, with some jewelry on. Buster waited for the mark to score with a chick, then shadowed him. He'd find out where the chick lived, who the mark was, and how he made his living. If the mark was a phony, some guy playing high roller when he wasn't, Buster would cross him off. But if the mark was for real, had bread, and was married, Buster'd get ahold of Peters.

Then, one night while the mark was over at the chick's getting laid, *Boom!* Buster'd break the lock, slam open the door, and in would bust Jerry Peters—*Trick or Treat!*—snapping pictures. The mark would sweat it out for a couple of days, waiting for the blackmail call that never came. Peters wasn't no dumbo, not dumb enough to get nailed on a blackmail charge.

No, no blackmail, but here's what they'd do. When the pictures came out, usually with the mark in bed shaking his fist at the camera and the broad trying to cover her titties up, Buster would call up the mark's old lady. He'd sell the pictures to the old lady. Smooth as silk, no blackmail. Worked like a charm.

Where they finally fucked up was picking a mark whose old lady was screwing around, too—with the local U. S. attorney. That brought the F.B.I. into the caper, got them charged with mail fraud—Buster with two counts, Peters with four. Buster never did completely understand the rap, but it had something to do with mailing the pictures in to get developed. Understand it or not, it bought Buster a nickel up at Danbury, later reduced to a trey with a letter to the clerk.

The point is, working with Jerry Peters had taught Buster how to shadow guys. So, around one in the afternoon, when he stood across the street from the Davis Building, Buster knew what he was doing. He had the lawyer's car spotted where it sat in the parking lot up the street; its license number checked with the one that the man had given him on the phone. From where he stood, Buster could watch the drippy old building *and* the lot at the same time. The lawyer couldn't get around him. Wasn't no way.

Dante Tirelli looked through the picture window at the redwood deck and watched the water froth and bubble in the map-of-Texas-shaped portable spa that would seat twelve. Annabelle looked tiny on the recliner. She noticed him, flashed a picture-book smile, raised a slim arm, and beckoned. He pointed at his gold watch, raised both hands in a double five, closed his fingers, and flashed the double five again. Twenty minutes.

Without turning around, Tirelli said, "You know what really gets to me about all of this, Winnie?"

To Winnie Anspacher, seated at one end of the green, rose-patterned fifteen-foot sofa, Tirelli's outline looked hazy against the backdrop of the dim sunlight in the yard. Winnie's starched white collar felt a little snug as he said, "What's that, Dan?"

"It's that I could have handled it with one fucking phone call, and I didn't." He turned and faced Winnie, then took a couple of steps away from the window, hands in the pockets of his tailored navy slacks. "I didn't because I'm greedy. One phone call—Do me a favor—and it gets done. Then the next thing, a guy comes in town, says, 'Look, Dante, old pal, maybe we need to talk over a little vig.' Like, not much at first, just the poker games. Next the titty bars, little cut, I'd never miss it. A guy here, a guy there, pretty soon I got more partners than J. C. Penney. Look, Winnie, you want a grapefruit juice?" He moved behind the hand-carved wet bar and set a can of Texsun out, filling a tumbler with cracked ice from a silver bowl.

Winnie held up a stubby hand, palm out. "None for me, thanks. I see your point, Dan. Independence means a lot."

The church key made a crunching sound. The liquid glugged. "Yeah. That's what I thought." Tirelli squinted at Winnie through his glasses. "Twenty years ago, I come to Texas to get away from all that *Godfather* shit. Dallas was a burg, what, half a mil? Not even barroom licenses, brown-bagging it. It's changed a lot since then, and I got in on the ground floor. No partners, used my own dough."

"Self-made man," said Winnie. "My hat's off to you, right enough."

Tirelli sat at the opposite end of the couch from Winnie, crossed his legs, and propped the glass of juice against his knee, a diamond glinting on his little finger. "Even stuck to doing things they wouldn't want to do. Poker games, little cut, some stand-up craps. New York, they forgot about me. Once a guy came to me, wanted to set up Zigonnet. It's a game you never heard of, Winnie, fast action. It's dealt out of a box that's made in Italy, and there's only five of 'em in New York. Five families, five boxes. You want to play Zigonnet, you pay the families. You don't pay the families, you get dead. So you know what I tell this guy?"

Winnie put an elbow on the back of the couch and shifted, hands clasped, facing Tirelli. "Excuse me, Dan. What guy?"

"You don't listen good, Winnie. This fucking guy

that wanted to play Zigonnet in Dallas. I told him flat no, Zigonnet starts, he disappears. Zigonnet would bring the families. Partners, which is what I don't want. But this deal here, I'd of been better off making the call." Tirelli wiped his free hand across the front of his peach-colored knit shirt. His jaw bulged slightly, and his skin was smooth.

Winnie put a hand nervously on top of his bald head. "No, Dan, I think you did the right thing. We're getting things handled. The poll folks say that Art Stammer's a shoo-in. Even that little fiasco last night, why, we can work it to our advantage. Make Phillips look like a typical wild-eyed liberal, going around punching people in the mouth." He smiled. "Yessir, I think we can get some mileage out of that."

"Horseshit. Yeah, Winnie, we'll get some miles. The miles we'll get are the ones we'll have to put between us and this town, Feds on our ass, those two *Halloween, the Night He Came Home* motherfuckers of yours going up and down the street shanking people." Tirelli got up and paced back and forth in front of Winnie, taking little sips of the grapefruit juice. "All this time I could have run numbers, Winnie. You got any idea how much money you could make around here with the numbers? Shit, they print racetrack handles in the paper here, same as New York. Four, maybe five stations, ten runners going around town from each, dollar minimum play. I knew this guy in the City, Sammy Taglia. Died in the joint. The income tax guys, lousy bastards, went out to Sammy's house, boarded it up. You know what they find in Sammy's cars? Four million fucking dollars, that's what they find. Four million! And Sammy Taglia wasn't no biggie, just a South Manhattan office man, paid the vig to the Family. But me, no. I don't fuck with no numbers, keep the Family away from Dallas. You fucking look at me, Winnie, I'm talking to you."

Winnie's gaze had drifted to the redwood deck outside, where Annabelie was lifting one shapely leg out of the water, holding it straight up in the air. He snapped his head around and looked at Tirelli like a man watching green puke cascade onto the priest in *The Exorcist.* Tirelli went on.

"Now this malted-milk ball, this Bigelow guy, for some reason he gets his dick hard for me. Congressional subpoenas they're talking. Right there, Winnie, I should have made me one call. One guy, maybe two, comes down here. Slides up behind this Bigelow, slaps him on the back. One little pinhole, that's all. Guy's back in the City before they know Bigelow didn't have no heart attack. But I didn't, Winnie, 'cause I don't want to wind up paying no vig to no Family. Now, everybody thinks Dante Tirelli's a big muscle guy, but I ain't. Bunch of pansies around me I got. Like you, Winnie, a lot of phony dipshits. You, you tell me you're going to fix it, and it's three *Day of the Jackal* types we're getting. Hundred grand it costs me, not to mention the hick guard and the parole bitch—what's her name? *Day of the Jackal,* shit. Day of the Jack-off! Three punks, one of them busted for selling fucking weed, the other two which can't even search a fucking office without butchering a poor little girl what runs an elevator. What about those assholes? You got them the fuck out of town, didn't you?"

Winnie was silent, lowering his eyes, rubbing his hands together.

Tirelli said, "Didn't you, Winnie?"

Winnie kept his head down. "Well, Dan—you know, they're worried about what Phillips knows, just as we are, and they need money to—"

Tirelli took a long stride over in front of Winnie. He put a thumb on one of Winnie's cheeks, a forefinger on the other, and squeezed, making Winnie's lips form a compressed *O.* He held Winnie's cheeks that way, forcing Winnie's head up so that Tirelli was looking him in the eye.

"Winnie, I know you are not going to tell me that you told these two yo-yos they are getting more money. I'm sure of that, Winnie, just like I am sure we are sitting here in my den having this little chat. Do you know why I am sure of that? I am sure of that because if you tell me that, I am going to make this phone call. And then these two punks, they are going to get dead, number one. And number two, one big-shot lawyer in this town is going to get dead. And number three, I am going to have partners, which is what I don't want. So that will be bad for us all, Winnie—you, me, the punks." He released his hold on Winnie's face, now patting Winnie solidly on the cheek, palm slap-slapping. "Now, Winnie, I am going to ask you. Did you tell these two punks that they are getting more money?"

Suddenly, Winnie began to sob. He pushed Tirelli's hand away, put his own hands over his face, and blubbered into them, his small, rounded shoulders heaving. Tirelli stepped back, sipping the grapefruit juice, and watched him.

Gasping for breath, tears rolling down his cheeks, Winnie said, "Look what you've done to me, Dan. Look what you've done. I've got a family history here. A name. Sure, I made a few mistakes—but this! I just—well, what matters to me anymore? You've taken away my self-respect, is what you've done. It's—It's—" He cried again, unable to stop.

Tirelli watched, stone faced. Then he went back to the bar and poured three fingers of Jack Daniel's, no ice, walked over to Winnie, and handed him the drink. Winnie hesitated at first, then took a gulp. He choked and coughed, the liquor coming out of his lips in a fine spray.

Tirelli said, "Look at you, Winnie." He shook his head slowly from side to side. "Shit, ain't nobody done nothing to you. Anything done, you done it to yourself. Did I tell you to start hanging in the titty bars? Did I tell you to bang that young stripper, that—what's her name, Jolene? You come to me, Winnie. Shit, you come into my office, I don't know you from Adam. Oldest game there is, Winnie. Every broad in them joints is a doper, every one of 'em runs with dopers. What you expect? Slam-bam, thank you, ma'am, maybe a little blow job? Guys like you, they're easy. Them broads find out you got a little bread, they hook you but good. How much cocaine was it you bought her? Don't matter, you don't play ball, she goes to your old lady. You asked me for a little favor, Winnie, and I done it for you. You know, broad don't work in this town no more. I just want my favors back, Winnie. No different than you. You campaign, get a judge elected, he pays you back while he's on the bench. Federal judge, he's appointed, but it's the same deal all over. You maybe get that federal judge a little country club membership, maybe a charge account he don't have to pay the bill on, he pays you back. It's all the same ball game, Winnie, I'm no different from you. Now, Winnie, you quit that fucking crying and you listen to me. Ain't nobody going to hurt you, Winnie. You listen."

Winnie looked up slowly. He took a little sip of the bourbon, then, hand trembling, set it down on the floor by his foot. He got a spotless handkerchief out of his back pocket and blew his nose. His eyes were red and puffy, and his glasses had tearstains on the insides of the lenses.

"Now," said Tirelli, picking up Winnie's drink and carrying it to the bar. "Now here is what is going to happen. You're going to call off these two dogs, zappo. Me, I don't think this Phillips guy knows Jack Shit. I think the one punk was lying to the two punks. He knew anything, he'd of already been to the law. But

I'm gonna make sure." He grinned, bending over and closing the doors underneath the bar, filling the two now-empty glasses with faucet water. "We got a break, Annabelle being the lawyer's ex. Annabelle, she'll bring him to me. I'll find out, Winnie, what there is to know."

Winnie's eyes widened, and he shifted his gaze back to the redwood patio. Past about thirty feet of wood deck, past the huge, Texas-shaped spa where Annabelle now lay on her side, one round, bikini-clad hip sticking out of the water, the fall had stripped the backyard oaks of their leaves.

Winnie said, "Annabelle? Does Annabelie know about all of this? She knows a lot of folks that I know, too, Dan. People that grew up with us in this town."

Behind the bar, Tirelli walked to one end and leaned his elbow on it. "Only in America, Winnie. Only in America do guys do stupid things like letting wives in on business. You, I'll bet Sarah knows all of your clients' names, you sitting around the house drinking those fucking martinis and telling her what's what. That's what the fucking restaurant is for, Winnie. All that spaghetti, clam sauce, crab claws, pizza, and shit—far as Annabelle knows, that's what pays for all of this." He gestured around the house and out the window. "Ain't a piece of paper anywhere to connect me with a titty bar or a poker game. That's something I learned, real young. You let me handle my wife, Winnie; you try and handle yours. Mine will bring me this lawyer, won't know nothing."

Annabelle Bradley Phillips Tirelli thought, Maybe I will, then used a small hand as an anchor and floated to a position where the water jet cascaded a soothing, powerful flow on the back of her left shoulder. She drifted slowly, purposefully, the jet pin-pointing different parts of her neck and shoulders, thinking, but probably I shouldn't.

Bino was on her mind. And a lot of corny old phrases and scenes. We can never go home again. Though nothing can bring back the hour of splendor in the grass, of glory in the flower . . . Natalie Wood. Deanie: Are you happy, Bud? Warren Beatty: I don't think about that anymore, Deanie. *Jesus Christ, Annabelle!* She rolled in the water and directed the current onto her chest.

The window screen blocked most of what went on inside the house from her view. When Dante stood right in front of the window, the image was clear, but Winnie Anspacher on the couch was like a photo taken in deep shadows.

Winnie Anspacher, another face out of the dim, long-ago past that had turned up lately. Funny. Dante wasn't Annabelle's idea of one of Winnie's clients. Winnie's clients were from places like Yale and Harvard, wore Brooks Brothers, lunched at the Lancers, and played their golf at Preston Trails—all of the things that Annabelle had been getting away from when she married Dante.

Like marrying Bino Phillips. Different. Annabelle half-smiled, remembering all the different come-ons it had taken to get Bino, the big galoot, to ask her out in the first place.

Titters and questions at the Pi-Fi House. He's *such* a cornstalk that he's cute, Annabelle. *Mesquite?* My God, it's such a hole. We had a flat out there on the way to the lake. Had to interrupt a *checker game,* for goodness' sake, in the filling station just to get it fixed.

Highland Park Methodist Church, jammed to the rafters. Hart Schaffner & Marx and furs from Neiman's on one side, Penney's wash 'n' wear and sprayed beehive hairdos on the other. Pop Harrison, proud but cranky in a tuxedo, fumbling in his pockets for the ring, muttering, "Shit-fuzzy!" The minister, shocked, eyes widening. Annabelle raised a hand from the hot spa water and covered her mouth, giggling. Yes, maybe she'd dig up an excuse to call Bino now. But probably she shouldn't.

Dante? This life? Well, that was something else again. Her attraction to Dante really wasn't a whole lot different from what had first drawn her to Bino, years ago. She had wanted a change, a big one.

Yes, she'd heard. A gangster, that's what they said. The L.T.V. vice-prez who had first taken her to dinner at Tirelli's Italian—what was his name? Bert. Yes, Bert Johnson, as in, what's the forecast for Middle East prices, Bert? Let's work up a report for the board, Bert, for everybody to sit, smoke, drink ice water over, and kick around. Bert, only his eyes and businesslike nose visible over the dark red leather-bound menu, saying, "Boy, Annabelle, that's one thing about the Mafia. Really know how to throw the old meatballs and lasagna together. Remember what Sonny Corleone and the brothers were eating, right when they were plotting for Al Pacino to go out and plug the guy?" Sure do, Bert. Yawn. Annabelle remembered thinking, Bert is going to say that he brings some out-of-towners here sometimes, to give them a look at the seamy side. Then Bert had said it.

Suddenly, Dante Tirelli was next to their table in a blue silk suit. Jet black hair turning to iron gray, big, rough hands, man hands for a change, not soft, pink, boardroom hands. Dark eyes behind the glasses, alive eyes, moving from Annabelle to Bert as Dante talked, twinkling eyes, something hidden in their expression. Dante pulled up a chair, bought them a drink. Bert talked about steel prices and the big board, and rumors of mergers. Dante talked instead about shows in Vegas, and seeing Maris and the Mick go back to back, twice in one night. Annabelle listened, fascinated, felt her eyebrow arch at some things he said, watched him gesturing with his hands to drive his points home. She noticed the way his broad shoulders filled his suit coat, and she felt a little tingling sensation on the insides of her thighs.

Leaving her slim evening purse in the booth when she and Bert had left had been no trick at all. Getting rid of stodgy Bert at her condo door had been. She'd finally been downright rude, saying, "Sorry, Bert, no, and you can like it or lump it." She'd waited for Bert's taillights to disappear around the corner before going into the garage, keys jingling in her hands, and taking the green Corvette out of its space next to the yellow Mark. Her purse was in Dante's office, on the corner of his desk, and Dante was in his chair with his arms folded, a knowing grin on his face, waiting for her. Annabelle had three delirious, shuddering orgasms that night, remembering that it had been years since the last time that had happened to her. Since she'd left Bino.

No, she shouldn't see Bino again, not even after all this time. But she might.

The back door opened. Dante came out in silver Izod swim trunks and matching fishnet top, a yellow beach towel around his shoulders. The breeze generated by the swinging door sent some dried leaves skittering over the redwood. At the bottom of the steps that led up to the hot tub, he hopped on one foot, then the other, peeling off white socks and sneakers. The fishnet top rumpled his thick hair as he pulled it over his head, tossing it on the steps next to the towel. His chest hair was thick, a few gray strands in it.

Grinning, he said, "Make room, doll. Jeez, it's getting nippy out here." He went up the steps, towering over her as she lay in the hot tub, then put a foot in the frothing water, said, "Ow! Jesus!" and yanked it quickly out. The bubbling caldron gave out a heavy chlorine smell as he descended into it, checking the water thermometer reading as he inched downward, bitching about the too-hot water, then laughing at himself. Finally he sat on a bench next to her, his legs moving under the surface like strands of white seaweed.

She cupped a hand and scooped some water onto the spa's bank, watching it trickle back in. "Did you have a nice visit with Winnie?"

"Yeah—sure," he said. "Winnie, he's a barrel of laughs. Great guy. Glad I got to know him."

"Dante," she said, "you sure have been spending a lot of time with Winnie lately. You don't have any legal problems, do you? That I don't know about? I mean, Winnie Anspacher *is* a lawyer, a high-priced one at that."

"Naw, doll, nothing like that. Winnie and me, we've gotten to be pals, is all." He looked thoughtful. "But say, babe, it's real good that you asked. A little beef I'm getting, one with the state alcohol people. Something about the tax on the bar drinks we're selling down at the Italian. It ain't no big deal—little shitstorm is all, and I damn sure don't wanta cough up the kinda dough that Winnie's gonna charge to handle it. Not on a little deal like this here. So I was thinking. Listen, dollface, this Bino guy you used to be married to. Think you could call him up, go to see him? Maybe put me in touch?"

Annabelle rolled onto her side and put a hand on Dante's arm the spa glugging and bubbling. "Well, I don't know, honey," she said. "I guess I could get in touch with him. If it's for you."

"That's my girl," he said.

Later, on the sixty-eighth floor of InterFirst Tower, seated behind his massive desk, Winnie Anspacher counted the fifteenth ring. He hung up.

He swiveled his chair to the left. Winnie I glared at him from the wall in that direction, so he turned around the other way and looked out the window. It was dusk, getting dark. Winnie drummed his fingers on the desktop.

He picked up the receiver and punched the number for Buster and John-boy again. There was still no answer.

IX

Bino entered the ground floor of the Dallas County Courthouse at a half-walk, half-jog, thinking, I am one snakebit son of a bitch. Jesus! His dark brown attaché case was loaded down with papers, and its swinging weight thudded against his leg. As he stood and waited for an elevator, Bino checked his watch. Five after one. Maybe the hearing would start late. Maybe the judge had taken a long lunch. Maybe the roof would fall in. He shared the three-floor ride with two middle-aged women and an old man who leaned on a cane.

He stopped in his tracks just inside the 357th Court, in the aisle between rows of long wood pews. Beyond the railing, past the prosecution and defense tables, Assistant County D.A. McIver Strange was in front of the bench, saying, " . . .and three times there was no answer, Judge. We finally got his investigator on the phone just minutes ago. Mr. Phillips is allegedly on his way, but we haven't—"

From his position at the rear of the courtroom, Bino said, loudly, "Counsel for the defense is here, Your Honor."

Round shouldered, hair thinning, and with a pot on

him, Mac Strange turned slowly around. Criminal District Judge Ben Stevenson—youngish, full head of curly brown hair, clear eyes, nearly colorless plastic-framed glasses—gazed at Bino from his seat behind the high bench. The court reporter, a slim brunette in her forties, quit running the shorthand machine and looked up. County Detective Hardy Cole, angular and dark, looked over his shoulder at Bino from his seat at the prosecution table, a sarcastic grin on his face.

In an even tenor voice, the judge said, " 'Here' means here, Mr. Phillips. Here, in front of the bench, standing next to the prosecutor."

Bino mumbled, "Yes, sir," and approached the bench in the pin-drop silence. The rail gate creaked like *Inner Sanctum.* As he went by the defense table, Bino set his attaché case up on the polished surface. Top-heavy, the case fell over with a loud bang. The judge started. Finally, Bino stood at attention next to Strange. A giant Stars 'n' Stripes hung on a gilded pole to the judge's right; a flag of Texas was next to it, same colors, two huge stripes, one red, one white, mammoth white single star on a field of blue.

Judge Stevenson leaned forward, elbows on the bench top, and put his fingertips together. Surrounded by the billowing sleeves of his robe, Stevenson's forearms looked like thin sticks. Bino'd heard that Winnie Anspacher's firm had put up the money for Stevenson's campaign fund.

Stevenson said, "I thought I heard someone announce that counsel for the defense was here." He raised his thick eyebrows.

After about fifteen seconds of stony silence, Bino said, "Huh? I mean, excuse me, Your Honor? It's me. I'm—counsel for the defense." Strange snickered on Bino's right, his head on a level with Bino's shoulder.

Stevenson looked down at a file folder before him, then back up, saying, "How can that be, Mr. Phillips?

Counsels for the state and defense appear in this courtroom in a suit and tie."

Bino put a hand to his chest, feeling the soft knit fabric of his rugby shirt. He thought, Holy shit, then said, "Your Honor, there've been a lot of things happening lately, and, well, I've got to confess that this hearing had completely slipped my mind until right after lunch. My secretary, well, she took some dope—" He cleared his throat, thinking, Dumbass. "Prescription drugs, Your Honor, given her by the county coroner, and she had to go home. But she's been called, and she's on her way down here with some proper clothes, if the court will bear with me."

Stevenson regarded Bino for a moment, then bent over the bench, half-standing, and looked down and to his left at the court reporter. "Mrs. Bailey, I want to go off the record here." She sat back and folded her arms. Then the judge cocked his head sideways, looking at Bino and tapping a pink rubber eraser on the wood before him as he said, "Look, Bino, I don't know what kind of a shitstorm you've gotten into down at the federal courthouse, with Judge Sanderson. I don't know why a grown, adult man, and a member of the bar to boot, goes out at night and attacks a candidate for the United States Congress like a common brawler. And I don't know why your secretary is running around town with your clothes. But I do know that I am not going to put up with any bullshit in this courtroom. Now, I am about to call a half-hour recess, and then we're going to get on with the pretrial motion hearing. Your client is getting a sore butt from sitting on that iron bench back in the holding cell."

Bino swallowed hard. "Well, Judge, I'm afraid we're going to have to ask for a continuance in this matter."

Judge Stevenson opened the folder in front of him with an annoyed pop. "You're going to ask for what?"

"A continuance. Sixty days, to prepare for trial."

The judge glared at Bino. "I think we'd better get this on the record, Mr. Phillips." To the court reporter: "Back on the record, Mrs. Bailey." The shorthand machine began its barely audible clickety-clack. Judge Stevenson folded his hands and droned, "In Criminal Case Number Four-Eight-Seven-Oh-Three, the State of Texas versus Theodore Oliver Madrick, also known as Wimpy Madrick, charges of Burglary of a Habitation, the matter at hand is a hearing on pretrial motions. Now, are there any motions to be presented to the Court prior to this hearing?"

Bino coughed into his cupped hand, then said, "Your Honor, the defense wishes to make a verbal motion for a sixty-day continuance. We need more time to prepare for trial."

Stevenson now directed his gaze toward Strange. "Any objections?"

Strange moved a half-pace forward, his file open in his hands. The prosecutor had a file. The judge had a file. Bino was the only one without a file. Strange said, "If it pleases the Court, Your Honor, the State does object. This case has been pending for a year. Our records show a number of continuances—so many, in fact, that there isn't any room on the file jacket to mark down another continuance. We'll have to turn the jacket over and start making pencil notations on the back. We object, Your Honor." He stepped back, wearing black suit and polished black shoes, a white shirt with a high starched collar. Strange's round profile made him look like a formal penguin.

"Mrs. Bailey," said the judge, "I am going off the record again." There was an abrupt cease of clatter. Mrs. Bailey gave a little sneeze. Stevenson said, "Bino, are we going to waste a lot of time trying this case? I mean, your boy's been in jail for nearly a year. Why doesn't he cop out?"

Bino exchanged glances with Strange, who shrugged.

Bino said, "Wimpy says he didn't do it, Judge. Besides, as long as he's in the county he gets regular visits. If he cops out, goes down to the state pen, he won't get so many."

The judge chuckled, his head moving derisively up and down. "Visits, he wants, eh? Resume the record, Mrs. Bailey. Motion denied, Mr. Phillips. Now, I am declaring a half-hour recess so that you may confer with your client—and perhaps discuss a plea bargain arrangement with Mr. Strange. And, gentlemen, when we return we are going to carry this matter to a conclusion. Pretrial motions. Jury selection. Trial. Get dressed, Mr. Phillips." His banging gavel echoed. He left the bench and bustled to his chambers, the black robe swirling around his knees.

At the defense table, Strange said, "I can't believe that you're going to fart around with this, Bino. I mean, the cop caught the guy climbing in through the window, for Christ's sake. Tell you what. Five years. Five to ninety-nine, that's the beef. Five is the bottom; I'll give it to him to get rid of the damned thing."

Bino deadpanned it. "Wimpy drinks a lot, Mac. He thought it was his house."

Bino went out through the gate, Strange telling him to go fuck himself.

Dodie had crept in while the doings at the bench were in progress. She sat erect on the back pew, Bino's navy suit, tie, and white shirt in her lap with her hands clasped under them. There were little strain lines around her lovely eyes.

"Did you have any trouble finding them?" said Bino.

She smiled, almost a Dodie smile, but not quite. "Cecil helped me." Then, more serious, "Wow, that Mr. Strange sure has it in for poor old Wimpy." She blinked.

Bino took the clothes from her, draping the tie around his neck. "Your eyes look like forty miles of bad pavement, Dode. Go home."

She put her knees together and smoothed her dress. She'd changed to hugging red. "I'm staying. I'm not being a martyr, Bino, nothing like that. I couldn't sleep at home, even with that monster pill that Dr. Traynor gave me. Every time there's any kind of creaky noise around the apartment, I just come unglued. Like—well, like . . ." Her shoulders quivered and she folded her arms around her middle. "Well, I just want to stay, is all. Where there's people."

He felt a little twitch at the corner of his eye and said, "Okay, Dodie. Up to you. I'll buy your supper." Then, quickly, "And you can sleep out at Half's farm."

She let it pass. "Okay. Wow, you're gonna be here awhile. That Judge Stevenson, he really wants to put Wimpy to trial, doesn't he?"

"I've just got too much else to do the next few days to be down here trying a case. We haven't gone to trial, not yet, Dodie." He winked at her. "You hide and watch."

He changed in the men's room, fooling with the Windsor knot two or three times before saying to hell with it and settling for a poorly constructed slipknot. As he stood in front of the lavatory mirror in Jockey briefs and white dress shirt, the water closet door opened behind him and a young guy with shoulder-length black hair came out. He was in slim jeans and sleeveless blue T-shirt. The guy moved to the sink next to Bino and turned on the water, his glance in the mirror darting briefly at Bino's image.

As the slim long-hair dried his hands with a paper towel, he turned slowly and faced Bino's profile. In an effeminate tenor, he said, "Hi, there." He looked down, then slowly back up.

Bino's hands froze on the slipknot. His eyes widened. He thought, Jesus Christ, nodded curtly, dodged around the guy, and hustled into the navy suit pants.

As he finished dialing the hall pay phone, Bino

checked his watch. Still a little over twenty minutes. The other line rang twice before it was answered.

Half said, "Half here."

Bino couldn't say anything for a minute; finally he said, "Well, get *all* here. Jesus, is that the way you're answering the phone?"

"Bino. Sometimes the office phone rings, sometimes the black phone rings. I get mixed up, okay?"

Bino said, "Uh, listen, Half. Dodie's down here. She's got the heebie-jeebies about staying home alone after, you know, what went down. How about hanging around the office until we get there? Let Dodie spend the night at the farm."

"Sure. No sweat. How long's it gonna be?"

"Well, it—sort of depends on Wimpy Madrick, Half."

"Bino, you ain't going to be down there as long as Wimpy. I ain't got *that* long."

The clock hands had moved another two minutes. Bino said, "Nothing like that. It's a plan I've got. Look, Half, I'll call you back if we're gonna be too long. Got to get going. Oh, and Half—switch the office phone over to the answering service, will ya? I'll call through on the black phone." He hung up.

He deposited his casual garb in the courtroom with Dodie. She looked a little better. Then Bino took off to find Wimpy.

He went down a long, white-tiled corridor, his footsteps clicking with a slight echo. Wooden benches paralleled each other on both sides of him. Two Bandido cyclers were on one of the benches, in leather vests with hissing snakes and club emblems tattooed on their burly arms. One of them, fat cheeked and pit faced, had his head shaved. The other had a nasty scar running from his hairline to his cheek, bisecting one puffy, half-closed eye. On another bench, a chubby-kneed, stringy-haired pregnant girl was holding a crying baby. The federal courthouse was silent carpet and tall wood pillars. The county was a loud, bawling ghetto.

The holding cell was behind a door marked BAILIFF'S ROOM. Harry Bostick was obese. His metallic gray deputy's uniform was under stress; he sat behind a small table in the foyer with his enormous belly pressed against the table's edge. Harry'd been a county courthouse bailiff since before Bino'd started practicing law. A huge metal ring was on the table in front of him, four brass keys on it that looked like they fit the harem locks in a giant's castle. Behind Harry, the holding cell's steel door had a six-inch-square, eye-level porthole in it. Its swiveling metal shutter was closed.

Bino said, "You got Wimpy in there?" He gestured with his head toward the holding tank.

Harry's bulbous nose wrinkled. There were flaming booze veins around its edges. Harry said, "Can't you smell him? Jesus Christ, Bino, can't you get that sonofabitch to bathe? Six-man cell, I got fourteen prisoners jammed in it. Jesus."

"Uh, look, Harry, I have to confer with Wimpy. In the empty office next door, huh? We've got a hearing in about fifteen minutes."

Harry said he guessed so. He shrugged, struggled to his feet in unwieldy slow motion, picked up the jangling keys, and turned to the holding tank. He opened the porthole. A jet black face was pressed against the small double bars, large white teeth shining against pink gums.

The face said, "Man, you get this smelly-fish muthafuckah outta here. We'se suffocatin'!"

Harry said, "I'm gonna, I'm gonna. Front and center, now, Wimp."

In a moment, a white face with a buzzard nose appeared. There was a stubble on the full upper lip.

Bino waggled his fingers at the nose and said, "Hi, Wimp. They say they're gonna put us to trial."

Wimpy Madrick said, his shrill voice muffled by the cell door, "Fuck them."

Bino nodded to Harry. Harry put a big key in the lock and turned it. The door swung open on oiled hinges, making a hollow metal thud against the plaster foyer wall.

Wimpy stepped out. Bino caught a whiff and breathed through his mouth.

Wimpy said, "Anybody got a smoke?"

Bino kept his nasal passages blocked and breathed through his mouth. He sat in a cushioned leather armchair at a long conference table in the office next to the bailiff's room and watched Harry, fat-breathing loudly, handcuff Wimpy to the arm of another leather chair that was directly across the table from where Bino sat.

The office doubled as a witness-rehearsal room for the prosecution and a spot for lawyers to meet with their locked-down clients, trying to get the clients to cop a plea; in between it served as a retreat for the bailiffs and deputies to sit around in and shoot the shit. There was a small table with a coffee maker on it against one wall, this morning's black dregs thickening and caking in the bottom of the clear round pot. Next to the coffee maker sat a flat metal hot plate. Bino noticed an empty soup can in the wastebasket. Along the far wall, a low bookcase held a complete set of the Texas Criminal Code and the Rules of Criminal Procedure. The books were dusty, from lack of use.

Harry closed the bracelet around the chair arm with a metallic zip, stepped back, and regarded Wimpy like a man about to lance a boil. Then he turned to Bino and said, "I'll talk to the judge, Bino, get you a full quarter hour. He'll bitch about it, but it'll give him time to call his old lady."

Bino thanked him, and Harry left.

Wimpy Madrick had big, sad blue eyes on both sides of the widest, longest nose that Bino had ever seen. He looked like a Great Dane that had gotten lost. His forehead sloped into a high hairline. His neck was scrawny, and he kept moving his head back and forth like a stalking rooster. He wore a filthy tan jumpsuit with COUNTY JAIL stenciled across the back in large black letters. Wimpy rubbed his skinny wrist where the cuff held it.

Before Bino could speak, Wimpy said, "I got something for you. About Sonny Starr."

Bino sat back, remembering that it was Sonny who'd first referred Wimpy as a client. Like Ford referring Chrysler to Winnie Anspacher. Bino thought, at least Sonny *bathed*, and said, "What about him?"

"A guy knew Sonny just did thirty days, hit the street last week. We talked. A broad named Hilda, works the day bar at the Longhorn. She—well, best I can figure, she was doing old Sonny while the guy was doing thirty days. The guy's her boyfriend. She visited regular."

Bino made the mistake of drawing a breath through his nose. Whew! He said, "True blue, huh?"

"You got it. Anyway, seems a coupla days before Sonny bought the farm, two guys were by to see Hilda. They roughed her up some, which she mightta liked, and found out where Sonny lived. You know the F.B.I. broad, the one that's a looker, plays a hooker, then nails your ass to the wall?"

Bino said that he did, thinking, Wimpy's a poet and don't know it.

"Well, she come down to the jail to see the guy, the one doing the thirty days. Wanted to know about Sonny. Guy says he didn't tell her shit, but I don't know. He might've. Anyway, she came down."

Bino thought, If she knows, why is she asking *me*? He said, "Who were the two guys, Wimpy?"

Wimpy held a matchbook awkwardly in his cuffed hand and lit the lone Salem he'd bummed from the bailiff. With the cigarette dangling from one corner of his mouth, he said, "Don't know 'em. Real badasses, though. Redheaded dude name of Buster. Other one, Hilda says, is an iron pumper, a real stony cat, acts crazy. I know they scared the shit out of Hilda, okay. She says they probably did time with Sonny. Hilda ought to know, she's seen enough cons. Anyway, thought you ought to know, since you're Sonny's lawyer. I don't like guys which go around bumping my friends off."

Bino thought, Why don't you? He said, "What about this case of yours, Wimpy? You want to cop out for a nickel? You don't, they say they're gonna try you."

"Shit, no. Huntsville I don't like. Get the case passed, Bino. They'll come down off the five later on."

Bino took a ballpoint and a blank envelope from his breast pocket. "There's one way, Wimp. I'm going to write down some stuff, tell you what to do. Any heat comes down, you thought of it yourself. Got it?"

Wimpy said that he had it.

For five minutes, Bino talked and scribbled on the envelope. Wimpy listened and nodded.

As he got up to go find Harry Bostick, Bino got another dead-fish whiff. He said, "Uh, Wimpy. When we go in the courtroom, stand as close as you can to the judge. Okay?"

Wimpy looked thoughtful. "Why's that? He hard of hearing or something?"

Openmouthed, Judge Ben Stevenson took his glasses off, folded the earpieces down, and carefully placed them on top of the file folder before him. He put a thumb and forefinger on either side of his nose and rubbed. Then he looked into Wimpy Madrick's sad eyes, just a foot or so in front of him.

"It's 'Farr-*eh*-tah,' Mr. Madrick," said the judge. "Not 'Farta.' Faretta versus California. I'm familiar with the case."

Mac Strange's neck was reddening at the collar. "Your Honor! What kind of a grandstand—we object, Judge Stevenson. The State objects! Why, if—"

"You're sure right, Judge," said Wimpy. He was holding the envelope that Bino'd given him close to the end of his nose and squinting at it. "There's an *e* between the *r* and the *t*. See."

He turned the envelope around and stepped closer, holding it so that the judge could read it. He was practically in Stevenson's face now. From where Bino stood, behind and away from the action with his hands folded behind him, the judge's expression looked strained. Bino would bet that Judge Stevenson was breathing through his mouth. Directly behind Wimpy, Harry Bostick looked ready to bust out laughing.

Stevenson said, sounding as though he had a cold, "Are you sure that you want to do this, Mr. Madrick? There are a lot of pitfalls in the courtroom at trial, even for a trained lawyer. A man representing himself is at a real disadvantage."

Wimpy's birdlike shoulders squared, and he stood at attention, the COUNTY JAIL across his back parallel with the floor. "I got witnesses, Judge, that'll say I wasn't nowhere near the place. I'm fightin' 'em"—he jerked his head toward Mac Strange—"tooth and nail. I'm standing on my rights, Judge, that the Supreme Court gimme in this case here—old Faretta. From now on, I'm callin' my own shots."

From far in the rear, a soft feminine voice said, Attaboy, Wimpy." Judge Stevenson glared out into the courtroom, past lawyers, Wimpy, and bailiff. Bino turned. On the back pew, Dodie had her hand over her mouth. She was blushing. Her eyes were wide. Mac Strange stared daggers at Bino, who shrugged. Wimpy beamed at Dodie. Bino thought, Jesus. Perry Mason with terminal *C*.

Judge Ben Stevenson sounded like a man who'd

swallowed a chicken bone as he said, "That's—you're right, Mr. Madrick. But, just so you don't rush into anything, I'm calling a sixty-day continuance." He banged his gavel. "Off the record, Mrs. Bailey." Mrs. Bailey sat back, this time picking up a paperback novel. Judge Stevenson must go off the record a lot, thought Bino.

Now the judge looked at Strange. "Mr. Strange, I do not like trials. Particularly, I do not like trials where the defendant is trying to represent himself—they just drag on and on. The Court will not be pleased if this matter goes to trial, Mr. Strange. Good day, Mr. Madrick." He nodded curtly. "Bino." With that, Judge Ben Stevenson made his second grand exit of the day.

To Bino, Strange said, "Back time, you bastard. We'll reduce it to a misdemeanor, he cops out. He can be on the street today." He glanced at Wimpy, who had broken into a slightly buck-toothed smile. Strange said, "Jesus Christ, why don't he bathe?"

Bino's eyes twinkled. "Why, Wimpy's representing himself, Mac. You'll have to talk to him."

Wimpy said, "How'd I do, Bino?"

Dodie stood by with one tiny, spike-heeled foot in front of the other and leaned a shoulder against the corridor wall outside the courtroom while Bino jingled a quarter into the pay phone slot. She looked past Bino down the hall to where one of the Bandidos was ogling her with his good eye; then she did an exasperated head-and-eye roll. The Bandido grinned and kept staring.

In a metallic voice with static in the background, Karen Allen told Bino, "I'm away from the phone. If you will leave your name and number at the tone, I'll get in touch with you." Click. Just like that.

Bino had just thought of a pretty cute message to

leave, when the businesslike, high-pitched tone beeped, making his throat constrict and causing him to forget what he was going to say. Instead, he mumbled sheepishly at the fucking machine, "It's Bino Phillips. I've got some information for you." Then he stood there waiting for the machine to answer him. It didn't. The longer tone sounded, ending the message. He thought, real chatterbox, Bino, and hung up.

On the elevator ride to street level, Bino watched Dodie. Framed by soft blond curls, the strain lines around her eyes seemed to be lessening, and her pouty lower lip was in a thoughtful half bow. She opened her mouth as if to speak a couple of times, then changed her mind and didn't say anything.

As he held the swinging door for her and they left the white, rock-walled courthouse and entered the street noise, Bino said, "What is it, Dode? Something on your mind?"

She was a couple of steps in front of him, his slacks and rugby shirt draped over her folded arms. She smiled wistfully over her shoulder. "Oh—well, it's nothing." Meaning, yes, well, there *is* something.

Bino took the cue. "No, really, Dode. What is it?"

She stopped and faced him. "It's just—well, Bino, could you carry your own clothes? I mean, it looks like I'm your cleaning lady or something."

She held them out. He said, "Oh," and took them from her.

It was six long blocks to the Davis Building, and they dawdled a lot making the walk. Dodie window-shopped and Bino girl-shopped. Once she stopped playfully in front of him as he craned his neck at a redhead across the street. He bumped into her, stumbled, and held her arm to right himself, saying, "Whoops." She grinned. "You should watch where you're going, sir," she said, and batted her eyes.

Hot Dogs, Inc., had a gaudy red front and did a

pretty good job on a Coney Island. He'd promised her supper. As Bino steered Dodie to the stand-up counter inside, she said, "Wow. Thanks, Rockefeller," giggled, and ordered two regulars with the works. Bino shook his head and smiled to himself. She did things to him, Like-me things. Dodie'd do them to anybody.

Between bites, she said, "Hooray for poor old Wimpy."

Bino shrugged. "It's about dogs and days, Dode. They all got 'em."

It was nearly three when he followed her through the swinging door into the building lobby. She paused in the entrance for a second, the strain lines returning, then set her jaw and moved on to the elevators, heels clicking.

Across the street, Buster thought, About time, asshole. Where the fuck you been? Jeez, who's the long-legged bimbo?

It had been forty-five minutes since he'd called John-boy—Hey, get rid of the broad and get your sweet ass on down here. Now he was getting pissed, picturing John-boy screwing the broad and doing bench-presses at the same time.

As Buster hunched against the building wall and watched the lawyer and the luscious puss disappear into the drippy old building, hands deep in his pockets, the supercab pulled to the curb in front of him. John-boy grinned and gave Buster the thumbs-up sign.

Buster thought, What's so fucking funny, you dumb shit?

Bino worked late. It took a couple of hours in the front office—Dodie behind her desk putting them in alphabetical order with her brow crinkling, and Bino doing the legwork back and forth—to get the files back where they belonged. In between calls on the black phone, Half-a-Point wandered in and out, sitting down to chew the fat and get in the way.

Once Half said, "Look, Bino, the Dupard kid playing Saturday? The point spread's jumping around like some kind of Mexican bean. Tuesday, S.M.U.'s giving three, yesterday it's pick 'em already. Now the line's swung all the way to *Texas* as the favorite by one. The game ends in a tie, everybody that took Texas on Tuesday's gonna win, everybody that took S.M.U. today with the point's gonna win, too. The only one getting screwed will be me. Dupard plays, I like S.M.U. If he don't, I gotta lay off the Texas money. What about it, he gonna play?"

Bino was kneeling by the open bottom file drawer, his coat and tie off and sweat around his collar. He was poking files to the rear of the half-full drawer. He said, "Hamstrings are funny. Straight on, he can go, usually runs that way in the I. Wide stuff, he has to cut, it might give on him. Texas giving a point, huh?"

Half said, "You ain't answering me. Barney still play golf on Friday with that backfield coach—what's his name?"

Bino was on his way to Dodie, who waited with another stack of files. He took them from her and lugged them back to the cabinet. "What do you want, Half? Jesus, they're on probation more than Petey Webb—you know, the shoplifter, skinny kid comes down here? I checked on it. Last fifteen years, Petey's done three probations. S.M.U.'s done four. You can't pick up a rock on campus without some guy from the N.C.A.A. under it, snapping pictures. Now you're wanting us to pump an assistant coach, get gambling information? You gotta be out of your mind, Half. It'd scare the guy to death." He bent over and rammed some more files into the drawer.

Half-a-Point put his chin in his cupped hand and thought a minute. He was sitting on the red fabric waiting couch, a small table with one of last year's *Sports Illustrateds* and a four-month-old *Newsweek* on top next to him. A tall floor lamp was lit behind the table. Finally, he said, "Maybe Barney could ask him like somebody besides us wanted to know—big booster, guy like that."

Bino was on his knees again by the open drawer. He shook his head. "No way, Half. No can do."

Half shrugged. He smoothed his mustache with a forefinger, got up, went to his office, and grabbed the doorknob. As he turned it, Bino looked up and said, "Uh, Half?" Half turned, hand on the knob.

Bino said, "Put me down for a nickel, Half. On S.M.U., plus the one, huh?"

Dodie laughed, a file in her hand, ready to slide it into the stack in front of her. "That's the old school spirit, boss!"

As one, they looked at her. Then back at each other.

Half said, "You talk to Barney?"

A white lock of hair was damp on Bino's forehead. He wiped it back. "Yeah, Half, I'll talk to him."

Half grinned. "You got a bet." He took out a notepad, writing down the bet and whistling the S.M.U. fight song as he went into his office.

The file cabinets were at last straight. As Bino clanged the final drawer shut, he hefted the lone folder that he'd kept aside in his free hand. It was Sonny Starr's. He had the folder open and was leafing through it as he strolled into his office and sank into his cushioned swivel chair. He swung his long legs up and rested his feet on the corner of the medium-size light oak desk, crossing his ankles. The papers rustled as he thumbed through the file.

It was after five. Bino's office had a western view, and the late-afternoon sun was casting a slanted ray of light across his desk, highlighting the dust particles. There were two straight-backed armchairs directly across from him and a brown imitation-leather three-seater divan against the wall. Above the couch, the Final Four bunch raised exuberant clenched fists in the air. Bino was on the top row, with the giant conference trophy held aloft; next to him, a grinning Barney Dalton was stretching upward to get his arm around Bino's shoulders. Bino glanced at the picture, then steadied his gaze on it for a moment. He remembered the feint to the left, the shoe squeak on the polished hardwood Pauley Pavilion floor, the breathless drive to the baseline. And the bony, jarring hip from Alcindor, light ebony, sinewed arms flailing in a powder blue uniform. And the sickening thud of the sprawling three-point landing, gritting his teeth against the sudden pain. On the desktop, Bino's ankle gave a little twinge.

His black-framed degrees were on the wall behind him, the "B.B.A." and the "Southern Methodist University" in the prominent spot. One of Bino's printer clients, a counterfeiter, had done a little doctoring on the law degree, Bino shaving his fee some in trade. "Bachelor of Laws" was in huge black script, but one had to squint, step a little closer, to read "South Texas College of Law." His state bar and federal licenses were on either side of the degrees.

Sonny Starr had been a bad boy, but Bino'd seen worse. Marvin Goldman had been a little shifty about turning Sonny's F.B.I. rap sheet over to Bino. At the time, Bino hadn't thought much about it—Goldman was a little shifty about everything, including exactly what the charges were against Bino's clients—but Goldman had been a tad extrashifty about a little coke-and-weed-in-a-bar case like Sonny's. Now Bino knew why.

Sonny's story was the usual: Truancy at eleven, shoplifting at thirteen. He'd held off longer than most, made it all the way to eighteen before the first stickup and trip to the joint. A break-in here, a liquor store holdup there, penny-ante stuff. But a political hit? Naw, didn't jibe. Unless somebody didn't want it to jibe. You could get about anything done by dangling a money-carrot in front of a punk like Sonny Starr, and get it done cheaper than normal. The Feds would be carting a list of pros around, looking up a bunch of guys with thin black gloves and silenced Berettas holstered under Hart Schaffner & Marx. They'd run right past a cat like Sonny.

And the rest of it was beginning to come together. Bino could spot a potential snitch a mile off, and under all of the arrogant bullshit, Sonny had a weak chin. Sonny's fall partners in the Bigelow hit would be a pair who could spot it, too. Bino would have dropped Sonny like a two-inch putt if Sonny'd come to him to make a tell-off deal, but the two goons wouldn't have known that. Bigelow murder plus federal dope beef equaled dead Sonny. And who would they look up next, the guy Sonny was most likely to have put in the know? His lawyer.

Thanks a lot, Sonny. Old buddy-buddy.

He called Karen Allen again. The answering machine still had him buffaloed; this time he was able to gag out his home phone number.

When he hung up Dodie was just inside the office, the light at her back making a filmy veil of her soft blond curls. Half-a-Point was behind her like Dorothy's scarecrow.

Half raised a hand to shoulder level. "We gone, Bino. My little girl's gonna spell Pop on the phones some tonight—she's the only one that don't ever write anything down wrong." Dodie nodded, her face lighting up with the old Tinker Bell grin.

Bino cocked his head. "Dodie, are you sure you want to—? Oh, the hell with it." He held out Sonny's rap sheet. "Look, Dode, shoot me a copy of this, willya?"

She turned her head sideways toward the supply room door, then looked back at Bino. There was a nearly unnoticeable quiver to her lower lip.

Bino tried to remember whether there were any blood spots on the carpet in there. He put Sonny's info back on his desk. "Never mind, Dode. I'll take care of it."

She approached his desk, her lashes downcast. "Thanks, Bino. I'll be all right. Couple of days, okay?" Then, brightening, she held out five little pink call slips. "These came from the answering service. Cheerio, boss." There was a slight head-and-shoulder droop about her as Half followed her out.

Bino thumbed through the messages, tossing aside a couple of them, both from clients whose cases didn't come to trial for quite some time. He read the next one over, twice. Skip Turner, *Dallas Morning News.*

The guy who'd written the article in this morning's paper. What'd they call him around the newsroom, Skip the Scoop?

Bino wadded Skip the Scoop into a tiny ball and dropped him into the wastebasket.

The next one was even worse, from Anthony Perrino. As in Harvard Law School. As in mergers. As in Anspacher, Anspacher, and Mortarhouse, about fourth partner down the line. Perrino'd told the answering service that he was representing Art Stammer.

Stammer. *S* as in *suit.*

Jesus.

He slid the message under the corner of his desk blotter, and looked at the next one.

This one got him. He put his feet on the floor, stood, and moved over to the window. The afternoon sun had disappeared, long shadows from the skyscrapers putting the old Davis Building in early twilight. Rush-hour traffic was bumper to bumper on Main Street like an attic full of toy cars. His eyes softened and his vision blurred a little as he read the message again.

Mrs. Dante Tirelli. Annabelle.

It was all the way dark when Bino drove himself to the first floor on the elevator, Sonny's file under his arm. He'd paused just before going in to make the copy of the rap sheet, thinking, might need all of the file, you never know. Or maybe he just didn't want to go in there. Like Dodie.

Annabelle's call slip was in his inside breast pocket. He hadn't called her back. Not yet. He wanted to think it over.

A uniformed guard was at the sign-in desk, young, thirty maybe, a bit too chubby, with chipmunk jaws and fat pouches sticking out over the rear of his belted slacks. His billed cap was about a half-size too big for him. New guy. Poof. Like Teresa Valdez had never been there at all. Bino signed the book. The guy let him out.

A few solitary cars were making the drag, one an ancient Ford with a headlamp out. As it bounced over the gentle speed bump at Main and Akard, the dead light winked on, then off again.

Football cold was setting in. It wouldn't freeze for another month, but the evening brought enough of a nip to make you think about it. Bino wondered if the overcoat should come out of the mothballs.

He walked the block and a half to the parking lot at a pretty good clip, not really with a reason to be in a hurry, just being that way. A young black girl with a little thigh showing, who would have been pretty with a little less makeup on, eyed him as she went by in the opposite direction. He met her gaze, then shook his head. She shrugged her shoulders and kept sauntering.

He passed two Mexican men, one old and wrinkled with a snow white beard, the other younger and with an unshaven grizzle, both of them staggering, the younger one carrying the half-empty wine bottle. Bino closed his nasal passages to the sick-sweet odor. It was night. Downtown was scumming over.

Bino paid for the Linc and got his keys. The parking boys had moved it nose-on to the exit, and Bino'd just inserted the key in the doorlock when he felt the tingle.

It was a prickling sensation, a jumpy little quiver that started where his spinal cord joined his neck and worked its way upward into his scalp. He looked behind him, to where the night attendant sat in a little wood building, a single bare light bulb glowing. The attendant, a scrawny old fellow, was stooped over the desk, reading. Nothing. The street was in the other direction; nothing there, either. Just sparse nighttime traffic, lights going by. The hooker he'd seen earlier was across Main, doing her stroll now in the other direction. There was a new supercab pickup across the street at a parking meter, white with stripes that were probably blue in the daytime. Someone might have been sitting in the cab. So what? He thought, Shaky bastard, and climbed into the Linc.

He hit the doorlock with one hand, plungers thumping down, and fished the Mauser out of the glove compartment with the other. He loaded the gun with the shells in his coat pocket. Redheaded guy named Buster and a muscleman, huh? Thanks, Wimpy. Anybody with red hair or anybody that looked like he might work out went by, Bino'd probably draw on him. He started the engine, put the car in drive, and moved on.

The Linc's radials click-thud, click-thudded over the northbound tollway expansion joints as Bino smoked his first filtered Camel of the day and felt the padded steering wheel vibrate under his fingertips in rhythm to the Eagles, taking it to the limit on the wraparound. Visible in the upper-right corner of the windshield, a lone blue-white star twinkled bravely at him through the light Dallas smog. He made the gentle climb over Lovers Lane and glanced both ways at the lights strung out along the Miracle Mile. Bino was in no hurry. He was still a little pissed at Cecil over the push-up incident, and Cecil could just get hungrier.

By the time he rolled under L.B.J. Freeway, traffic backed up over his head from the bottleneck entrance to Valley View Mall a mile or so to his right, the Eagles were through with "Tequila Sunrise" and "Take It Easy" and were twanging mellow into the opening of "Lyin' Eyes." The right-turn signal bonked monotonously as he eased to the right and made the smooth curve through the gated entrance to Vapors North. He and Cecil lived there. He wheeled into his numbered slot, parked, got out, and felt the tingle again.

It was stronger this time. He directed his gaze into the complex, in between the two-story units that were wood paneled and painted dark brown, with stark white trim like frosting on gingerbread houses. The lights on L.B.J. Freeway glowed soft on the horizon, and the tall courtyard oaks had their leafless branches silhouetted against the brightness like twisted fingers. Bino didn't see anybody. He patted the butt of the Mauser, feeling its hardness against his belly through the soft fabric of his coat, shifting Sonny Starr's file up under his armpit, and whistling "Lyin' Eyes" slightly off-key as he strolled in among the buildings. There was sudden movement in low, pruned bushes to his right, and he spun in that direction. A small brown cat, stretching languidly, came out and meowed at him as he reached for the Mauser, ready to plug the animal. Bino thought, Jesus Christ, and walked to his front door.

He laid the file on the rough-surfaced bar between the spacious living room and the tiny bachelor kitchen, the light slap of the manila folder on plastic, louder than it ought to have been. His scalp was still tingling as he switched on the soft fluorescent light over the fireplace mantel. The rough white brick cast little shadows on its own surface, and the deep red of the overlong couch and the easy chairs shimmered. The blank fifty-one-inch screen of the Mitsubishi stared at him like a giant unseeing eye. Bino went to the tuner of the component stereo, switched it on, and pushed a cassette into the player; Bette Midler warbled and belted the scare out of the room. He liked Bette Midler, and to hell with who didn't.

Cecil had his nose to the glass, fins on hips. Bino ladled a minnow, and it darted madly into the lion's den.

A few minutes later, Mauser in the nightstand, he sat on the king-size's quilted green bedspread and put on soft white socks and Nike sneakers to go with his jeans and gray cotton sweatshirt. His suit was piled in the corner of the walk-in closet. At the kitchen bar, he glugged a neat Scotch into a rock glass; then he flopped on the couch and picked up the telephone.

He told Karen Allen's answering machine that he was at home, then punched the number for Joe Miller's Bar.

The cocktail waitress said, "He says he isn't here."

Bino wet his lips. "Tell him I need him. For old times' sake."

Silence for a moment, muted conversations in the background, glasses clinking. Then, "He says that this is new times."

Bino couldn't argue.

He said, "Tell him that I've got a sure winner."

He pictured her, hand with the receiver down at her hip, as she yelled, "Barney, will you please *talk* to this yo-yo? I've got tables to wait on."

The receiver dangled. Finally, Barney said, "It better be good. I'm drinking with the redhead, Syl's friend."

"The nutty one, that likes writers?"

"So now I'm gonna write a book. Whatcha want?"

Bino swirled the liquor around. "Look, who you playing with tomorrow?"

"Not you. We got a foursome. Coach Smith, couple of other guys. Besides. We want a golf game, not a fucking Easter egg hunt."

"No, Barney," said Bino. "I wouldn't want to horn in. And I've been having trouble with the driver lately. It's leaking off a little to the right."

"I've noticed. About two fairways."

Bino thought, Stronger grip? Maybe—

He said, "It's about the coach, Barney. I need you to find out if Dupard's gonna play Saturday. It's for Half. He's gotta know. Sort of."

Barney yelled something to somebody that Bino

couldn't understand. Then, "Look, Bino, I've got a position to maintain. I'm the pro, they're the members. Everybody wants something. Inside stock tips. Now inside football dope. I'm playing golf with the guy, I can't just—"

"Yeah, Barney, you're right. I suppose—"

"Lemme finish. I can't just walk up and ask him in the middle of the course, two other players standing there. So I asked him today on the phone, when we were setting the golf game up. I took S.M.U. and the one point, too, Bino. Dupard's going, full gallop. That all you want to know?"

Bino thought it over, then said, "That'll get it, Barn. Redhead's waiting."

"I know. Oh, and Bino. It ain't the grip. You're getting your hands up too high, blocking the shot out." The clinking and chatter of Joe Miller's ended with an abrupt click.

Bino stood. He set the drink on the glasstop coffee table and assumed his tee-off stance. He dropped his hands lower, nearer his crotch. Then he got the phone again and was about to call Half when the doorbell chimed.

Twice. Bong-bong, bong-bong, like someone was in a hurry. Bino's hackles rose; the pinpricks started again. As he went to the front door and opened the peephole, he wondered how long it would take him to get to the bedroom, get his hands on the Mauser.

Bino's clients were right. In tight, low-slung jeans, Karen Allen was a number. Add spike-heeled pumps, and make that a double number.

He opened the door.

Her elbows were bent, her hands jammed into the pockets of a light-colored, waist-length jacket with fur around the collar and cuffs. She was clutching a small evening purse, its rectangular end poking out of her right jacket pocket. The soft front bangs of her dark hair were slightly wild. Her right leg was in front of her left, its thigh having a confrontation with the molded blue fabric of her jeans. The fabric was hanging in there. Just barely. The pressure of her hands in the pockets drew the jacket's front taut against her body and pulled the fur collar snug around her neck like a soft, downy brace. Her lips were parted in a half question.

She said, "I don't have a warrant, Bino. Can I come in anyway?"

He closed his mouth, then said, a little embarrassedly, "Why, sure, Karen."

Her soft brown eyes did an it's-about-time roll, and she went past him as he closed the door. Different again. Same girl, third version. This walk had an earthy come-on about it, straight from hip discos, swinging singles bars. Below the waist-length coat, her buttocks struggled like two bear cubs under a thin blue sheet. Two very lean, very in-shape cubs. Her short hair bounced Dorothy Hamill–style around the back of her head.

Bino took her coat. She shrugged out of it, showing a clinging navy sleeveless sweater underneath that rose in front to twin medium peaks, then tobogganed sharply to a waist that Bino'd make to be about twenty-two inches around. Make the wager over or under twenty-three, Bino'd bet heavy on the under. Her soft brown hair tickled his chin. Tall.

He carried her jacket to the bedroom, folded it, and placed it carefully on the king-size. The purse fell out and landed heavy. He didn't need to look inside; the pistol barrel was sharply outlined. When he got back to the living room, she was on the couch, one arm over the back and one leg drawn up under her. The other foot was on the floor.

He said, "I was just having a drink, Karen. What would you like?" Real hip, Bino. Cool. Just like with the answering machine.

She arched an eyebrow. "Is that why you called?"

He froze, bent over with his hand on his own drink. "Why, uh—no, I've got very important information—you'll see." He grinned sheepishly, straightened, and went to the bar. Sonny's folder was still there. "It's about Sonny. Sonny Starr, you know. Here—his file." He dropped it in front of her on the coffee table.

She said, a half smile forming, "Well, then, I'll have a drink. White wine." She didn't say please. It irked him some.

The cool, tall bottle was in the refrigerator. As he filled a stemmed glass, he watched the back of her graceful neck while she leafed through Sonny's papers. Bette Midler was still warbling, muted.

As he placed the wine in front of her and sat down maybe three feet away from her on the couch, she said, without looking up, "This is real old stuff, Bino. Our own rap sheet. I've already got that. And a questionnaire that wants to know what kind of property he's got in case he can't pay your fee." She turned, soft light on her olive cheeks. "I mean, this isn't what I call real sleuthy material."

He took the questionnaire out of her hand, leaning over close to her and pointing out filled-in blanks as he said, "Aha, Karen. That's what the client thinks, too. Only a form. It's designed that way. See. Here I find out where he lives, where he used to live, who his relatives and friends are. And look. A space for his own version of the crime—see, these blank lines at the bottom. I can learn a lot about the client here—whether he has remorse, if there were extenuating circumstances, even how literate the client is. Things like that are important if you're going to put on a proper defense."

She was bent forward at her narrow waist, back straight as a ramrod. She retrieved the form and sank back against the cushions, holding the paper in one hand and the wineglass in the other. She raised the glass to her lips, her eyes moving left and right as she read. Her tongue licked the lower rim of the glass. Almost absently.

She lowered the glass to rest on her thigh as she said, "Well, whatever did you find out about old Sonny? He wrote, 'Sold coke and weed to narc.' He spelled the words right. Enter him in the next bee."

She had him. Bino remembered Wimpy's buddy, the one in jail. He chose his words carefully as he said, "Well, that's not really what I called about, the form. Or the file. It's something I heard—by accident, from one of Sonny's friends. Guy was in jail, down at the county. I talked to him."

He paused. She wasn't showing full house or busted flush, just sitting there holding the glass, fingertips light on it, base making a round damp spot right where her solid thigh muscle flowed. He went on.

"The guy was talking about a pair that roughed up a barmaid, wanted to know where Sonny lived. Description was a tall, black-headed skinny dude and a fat midget."

Still nothing.

"So anyway," he said, "that's what I've got. Not much to go on, but maybe you could check, who he did time with, that kind of stuff. Maybe the description—you think?"

She stood, looking thoughtful as she walked to the stereo. The Bette Midler tape was in its second round. Karen looked through Bino's other cassettes; he watched her from the couch.

She said, "Is it because I'm a woman?"

He glanced at her behind, thinking, You sure are, and said, "Huh? Is what because you're a woman?"

Karen turned. "That you're bullshitting me. I went through the school, Quantico, did everything. Guy comes to work and they say, come on, let's investigate, I'll show you the ropes. I was in the office two weeks before I did anything but get coffee. And then they put me out as a dope front, getting my butt pinched by every greasy fuck in town. I've earned my wings, or whatever you want to call it. So why are you bullshitting me? I talked to the guy in jail, too, Bino. Sonny's landlord put me on him." She was holding a cassette, gesturing with it. Elvis wore white and a sneer on the cassette's jacket.

He looked down, hangdog, then back up. "Hell, I'm sorry, Karen. I didn't know you were so touchy. You don't come on touchy. So okay, already, it's a redhead and a muselehead. Redhead named Buster."

Now she grinned. Triumphant. "I thought you were bullshitting me, Bino. The guy in jail wouldn't talk, clammed up. The girl act gets them, every time." He looked pissed. She said, "Don't be mad. I had to know."

Glum, he said, "I was going to tell you. I just wanted to see if you already knew, before you even asked me to check up on it."

"Sure you were." She came to him, picked up her empty glass, and held it out. "More." No please, again. This time she followed him to the kitchen, stood with her elbow on the bar, and watched him pour. The sweater was a mock turtle. There were smooth veins on both sides of her soft throat.

She looked at the tape in her hand. "Jeez, you actually play this stuff?"

He set her fresh drink on the counter and held his own glass steady on the rough surface, bottle ready to pour another for himself. He cocked his head sideways at the picture. "Well, yeah, sometimes. He *is* the King."

"Spare me."

"No, really. Part of American history. Barney and me—Barney's a guy, friend of mine—went to Graceland. A happening. An event, that's what he was."

She sipped her new, cool wine. "He died on the crapper, Bino. That was an event."

"You sound like a blasphemer, Karen. The King was probably in the middle of composing a hit—got too much drugs."

She gazed off to the side, the sweater molding with her as she turned her shoulders.

Bino turned his back to her, putting the wine away. When he turned around, she'd disappeared. From off to his right, behind the pillar separating the kitchen from the living room, she said, "Who's he?"

Bino carried his drink out of the kitchen. She was standing, relaxed, elbow propped on her cupped palm, drink to one side, watching Cecil. Cecil was doing his floating turd imitation.

He said, "Well, his name isn't Oscar."

She snickered. "God, I hope not. Oscar is what he is. Oscar fish. Oscar the oscar fish, now, that'd really be drippy."

He said, "I wish I'd said that."

She paused a moment, lips half parted, then decided to let that one go. She made a graceful standing turn on the balls of her feet and faced the couch and stereo. The bear cubs started their roughhousing again, and Bino followed her back into the living room in no mood to break the fight up. She went to the tape player and put the King in his place with a push that was a little firmer than necessary, then began to take the different tapes out and put them back in turn, looking each one over. Bino sat down on the couch.

Without turning around, she held one tape above the level of her shoulder, title side where Bino could see it. "Do you mind?" she said.

He squinted, glass at his lips. The Scotch went down warm. The tape was Bread. Bino liked Bread, and this time she'd asked nicely.

He said, "Sure, help yourself."

There was a vibrating pop from the speakers as Karen ejected Bette Midler, then another pop, followed by the silent noise of running tape. Then the familiar, smooth guitar introduction, Bino anticipating the words and melody even before the singer began. "Baby, I'm-a Want You."

As she walked to the couch, she said, "Is that it?" She glided around the coffee table, holding the wineglass carefully as she sat down and crossed her legs. Her firm roundness was less than six inches from Bino's thigh. Her scent was musk.

Bino said, "I beg your pardon?"

"Is that it? Redheaded guy and a muscleman, redhead named Buster. Nothing else? Like where they live, or might live?" She turned her head to look at him, her lips in close range.

He crossed his ankles on the coffee table, leaned over, and set his drink next to them. Then he sat back, arms folded. "That's it. It's something to go on, Karen. Like the Darrington Farm roster; I'd probably start checking on it for a pair fits the description."

She lifted, then dropped her shoulders. "Yes. It's a start. If that's it, then that's it."

Karen bent forward purposefully, with finality, her drink joining Bino's with a soft, glassy clink. Then she shifted her position, her knee nearly touching his, bending her arm and resting it on the back of the couch so that her elbow was just to the right of and behind his ear. Her left breast was a hair from his triceps. He sat still, watching her. She was half turned, facing him, her deep brown eyes softer yet, and having that look about them, like a novice swimmer taking her first highboard plunge. Her slim nose cast a shadow on one olive cheek. Her lips parted.

"So what do I do?" she said. "Take off my pants and flash you, something like that?"

* * *

The music from the bedroom speaker was muted by the drapes. From far away and down the long hall, the living room's mantel fluorescents put out a faint glow, soft footlights on a shadowy stage for Karen Allen. Bino was stretched out on the king-size, his Scotch resting on the bedspread by his hip, his hand lightly on it. There was a slight rustle as the hem of Karen's sweater moved up, upward still, slowly, gradually revealing smooth skin, a navel with sharply defined edges on a flat, hard belly. The pulling of the garment over her head left her soft hair wantonly tousled. Her eyes were half lidded, almost a smile on her face, changing at times to a lustful challenge. She wore a black lace half-bra, the tops of her breasts quivering against it.

Her slender arms bent, hands going behind her, the front of the bra tightening, then relaxing, the wispy thing dropping on the floor next to the sweater. Her nipples were large and dark, jutting slightly upward.

She did a long, gradual come-around with her hands, fingers brushing lightly down her back, tracing feathery paths on both sides of her rounded hips, slowly, slowly, hands moving toward one another across her belly. Her gaze stayed on Bino, moving from his eyes methodically downward to somewhere in the vicinity of his abdomen, her lips parting slightly as she looked there, then slowly back to meet his eyes once again. Her thumbs hooked under both sides of the button on her jeans, muscles in her forearms dancing as she undid it. There was a nearly inaudible, clothy pop as the front of her jeans came open. Then the tantalizing, metal slide of the zipper, the opening widening, nylon line across her lower belly, through the mesh of the panty hose another line visible, this one black.

She turned her side to Bino, still looking at him, used her toes as braces to take shapely feet out of one high-heeled pump, then the other. She bent from the waist, the points of her breasts falling slightly away from her body, and stepped out of the jeans, a sharp indentation where her ribs slanted to her tiny waist. The jeans fell next to the sweater and bra.

Bino raised his glass and took a long, warm swallow.

Karen sat down on the bed to discard the panty hose, lithe and slow, Bino moving some to give her room. Her graceful legs and hips were the same olive color as her cheeks and neck. She left the bikini panties on and moved beside him on hands and knees, hesitating, reaching and taking the glass from his hand. She set it on the nightstand.

She tugged at his waist, and he raised his hips, helping her. She stood by the bed, urgent now, yanking feverishly as she tugged his jeans down past his knees and ankles, finally dropping them out of sight behind the foot of the bed. Bino sat up to take his shirt off, the cool air in the room flowing on his chest. Once again, she knelt beside him, her soft, dark nipples just inches from him as she bent over. He reached for her breasts. She stopped him.

"Lie still. Let me." It was a hiss, a command. He lay back. She reached down to his erection. He closed his eyes.

He felt her tugging his shorts off, then gentle nails raking his chest, and down past his hips, then a firm pressure, the palm of her hand smooth on his member. He kept his eyes closed, waiting for the warmness of her mouth, then feeling it, the sliding in and out.

He opened his eyes and looked down. The back of her thigh and her rounded buttock were near his arm, her head going down, slowly back up, moving from side to side as he felt the caress of her lips and tongue. He slid his hand up the inside of her leg, stretching the crotch of her panties aside and probing her with his fingers. A vibrating rumble started deep in her throat.

The thrusting of her head increased its tempo; Bino

continued to work his fingers, massaging. Then he sat up quickly, stopping her, directing her with the pressure of his arms on her waist and at her shoulder. As she slid her body over his, finally on her back next to him, he worked his hands under the tops of her panties and took them off. Then he mounted her.

Her head was propped on the bolster pillow against the carved headboard, neck bent. She was eye to eye with him. Bino felt her hand between his legs, grabbing firmly, helping him enter as she moved her pelvis tight against him. She watched his eyes.

Her face began to change expression, her jaw thrusting forward, her upper lip curling with earthy lust, her bare even teeth shining in the semilight. Her breath came in short, harsh gasps; between them she whispered fiercely to him.

"Give it—God—give it—give it—" And he did, for a long time.

When he felt the explosion coming in his thighs and midsection, he tried to hold back, couldn't. As he pounded inside of her, her tawny legs encircled him, locking ankles at his back, squeezing, her lusty breathing continuing.

Spent, they stayed entwined for moments. Then he stretched out next to her. There was a sticky wetness at his groin.

Bino looked at the ceiling, relaxed, his hands folded on his chest, his legs crossed at the ankles. Next to him, her breathing slowed. Her smooth upper arm was against his. He rubbed the back of his hand across his upper lip, the short hairs tickling. Her musk smell was there.

He had to go to the bathroom. He lay there for a time, his bladder swelling, grasping for the right words. Excuse me? Going to the little boys' room? Say nothing, just get up and go?

To hell with it, he had to piss.

He rolled to the side and stood up, the padded carpet springy under his bare feet. "Nature calls, Karen." His voice a little deeper than normal. Not bad. Her chuckle was throaty. His neck grew warm, flushing in the darkness.

The bathroom was through a big, carpeted dressing area to the rear of the bedroom. He had to go around the foot of the bed to get there, noticing her long, tawny suppleness out of the corner of his eye. He was nearly to the dressing area.

She said, "Bino . . ."

He started to turn around.

She said, "Remember the King, Bino."

He looked. She was laughing silently, propped up on her elbows, her head thrown back, shoulders heaving. He went through the dressing area into the john.

When he returned, she was sitting up, back against the headboard. Bread was still playing. He went around the bed and sat next to her.

"You know that you're probably a target, don't you?" she said. "Might very well get killed if these two guys aren't stopped."

He took his drink from the nightstand, swallowed, set it back down. "Yeah, it's not the most pleasant thought in the world. They think I know they killed Richard Bigelow, know their names, the works. Funny thing is, if they hadn't come down to the office and—well—done what they did, I never would have known. I swear, Karen, I had no idea. About Sonny, any of it. If I had, I never would have represented the little bastard."

"Well, it's working out good, Bino. Not the little girl, the elevator operator, that's horrible. But if they hadn't made a move, we might never have I.D.'d them. It's just a matter of time, now, with the description. Who knows if we ever would have, with Sonny dead." She drew a bare knee up under her chin and hugged it with her arms.

Bino ran his fingers through his hair. "Well, if I'm going to be—"

Karen put a hand firmly over his mouth, stopping him. She was suddenly tense, rigid, her head cocked, listening. She looked at Bino and put a silencing finger to her lips, taking her other hand away from his mouth.

Without another sound, she rolled away from him, moving quickly, gracefully, like a cat. When she reached the far edge of the bed, she stretched her arm toward the floor, out of his sight. Then she was up on silent bare feet, moving fast into the dressing area, and through it into the john, her small purse dangling from one slender hand.

Bino watched her cute bare fanny disappear, thinking, What the fuck? Hide-and-seek? I'm it or something?

He was going to scramble across the bed and go after her. But as he moved in that direction, something nudged his bare shoulder from the rear. Something metal. Something round. Something hard.

As Bino started to turn around, a mellow, twangy voice said, "You make that turn slow, asshole, if you want to make it with your head still on your shoulders."

Bino made the slowest head turn of his life.

Twin barrels of a sawed-off shotgun, about six inches away, were pointed directly at his face. Behind the shouldered stock, a beefy man in a white T-shirt was outlined against the light from the hallway door. The man had a beard. His hair was bushy and kinky, and the soft light shining through it held a red tint.

The guy next to the shotgun was taller, with massive shoulders and arms protruding from a sleeveless vest. He was grinning from under thick, dark brows and a receding hairline, black hair above and behind the smooth half scalp. The muscles at his neck bulged like ropes under tight burlap.

Muscleman and a redhead.

The fear was in Bino's stomach like a hard knot of

cancer. The shotgun prodded him again, motioning. At its direction, Bino sat back against the headboard.

The beefy redhead's voice was slurred, like that of a man chewing tobacco and needing to spit. "Hell, John-boy, this here feller was screwin' so hard he didn't even hear us come in. Wasn't no need to be quiet about it."

John-boy was holding a large, wicked-looking buck knife loosely in his fingers. He wore cotton gloves. He hefted the knife from one hand to the other. "Yeah, Bus, bangin' away." He chuckled low. "Lady went to relieve herself, I reckon."

Buster held the shotgun steady and looked for a place to spit. There wasn't any. He cut loose a stream on the carpet. "Go fetch her, John. Me and Mr. Phillips here, we'll wait on you."

A massive biceps expanded as John-boy scratched an elbow. "Party time, huh, Bus?" As he moved to the foot of the bed and started to go around it, he said to Bino, "You go for parties, don't you? Big lawyer, sure you do." He wore high black motorcycle boots. They squeaked.

John-boy's shoulders rotated in a swaggering strut as he walked. He'd reached the corner of the bed nearest the dressing area, a confident grin of anticipation on his face, when Bino caught the flashing movement in the shadowed dressing area out of the corner of his eye.

It was with a graceful, flowing stride that Karen entered the bedroom. She stopped dead. Her tawny, olive legs were spread apart, feet at shoulder width, fine hipbones jutting forward, upper torso slightly back, arms in front of her, bare breasts pressed together. Her slender right arm was straight, her left arm slightly bent, hand clutching her right wrist, steadying it. The compact Walther PPK 380 loomed big in her tiny right hand. No one-eye-closed peep for Karen Allen; both eyes were open, the pistol lined up with the bridge of her nose. Her tousled dark hair bobbed on her forehead.

John-boy stopped, puzzled, started to say something.

The Walther made a noise like a mallet on a solid block. Brief flame spurted from its barrel. Karen's hand recoiled upward and slightly to her left.

The entry of the bullet was somewhere in the vicinity of John-boy's nose. His body jerked, started to fall back. As Bino watched, the back of John-boy's head exploded.

It was like a sprinkler turned on in the heat of a summer afternoon, when the first droplets from the sun-baked hose are the temperature of bathwater. A hot mist filled the air, drifting. Something wet clung to Bino's arm. He looked. The wet thing had strands of hair on it. John-boy went down out of sight below the surface of the bed, the thud of his fall vibrating the room.

Buster grunted. The shotgun's aim shifted away from Bino's chest to point at Karen. She looked toward Buster even as she steadied the kicking Walther and started to move its short barrel in his direction, her feet still planted firm. She was never going to make it.

Bino lunged. Both hands came up hard. The metal on the underside of the shotgun's barrels stung his hands. He was on one knee, shoving upward, when both barrels exploded. They were pointed at the ceiling.

The blast was a physical force, stinging his eardrums, deafening him. The buckshot ripped into the ceiling, dust and shards of plaster raining down, clinging to the patches of John-boy's red wetness on Bino's chest and shoulders.

Buster staggered backward, his jaw slack, disbelief in his eyes. He faced Bino that way for a split second, then shifted his stunned gaze past Bino to where Karen stood. Suddenly Buster turned and made tracks. As he lumbered out of the bedroom and down the hall, another slug from the Walther splintered the door frame.

Buster fled down the hallway into the living room, his breath short, his body jarring with each heavy footfall, thinking, Who'd believe the fucking *broad* with a gun? He went by a tank with some kind of fat, round, black fish gaping at him.

John-boy's a pure goner. Goddamn, she took the back of his head off. Broad knew what she was doing with that Walther, shit, did she ever! Some kind of fucking cop this lawyer is screwing.

He charged outside and made for the parking lot, the empty shotgun banging against his leg. Get to the supercab, get the hell gone. Forty-five auto in the cab.

What about the keys? Jesus, the fucking keys.

Did John-boy leave them in the truck? Asshole was supposed to. He damn sure better have, or old Buster'd had it.

The pickup loomed closer.

Bino was conscious of the chalky odor of plaster dust and a burning sensation in his hands from the shotgun's blistering metal as the Walther's bullet whined close to his ear and thunked into the wood of the door frame. He froze in his tracks, hearing the heavy feet of the redhead thudding down the hall. Then he yanked open the nightstand's drawer, junk inside sliding and rattling, and took out the Mauser.

As he released the Mauser's safety and took a long, running stride in the direction of the bedroom door, Karen said, from behind him, "I'd use this, Bino. You never know—"

He turned. She was standing with the Walther down at her side, relaxed. In her other hand she had the fluffy beach towel that was normally hanging on a rack just inside the dressing area. She tossed it to him.

Bino snatched the towel out of the air and drew it clumsily around his waist, the Mauser getting in his way. As he raced down the hallway and into the living room, holding the ends of the towel together with his left hand and waving the pistol in front of him in his right, he thought, What the hell are you looking at, Cecil? Go fuck a fish.

Outside, the sidewalk concrete slapped hard on the soles of his bare feet, and the soft terry cloth of the towel clung to his pumping legs. He was aware of sudden lights in windows, patio doors sliding open, people on balconies. Somewhere, a guy yelled, "Pipe down, dammit!"

He was gasping for breath by the time he reached the asphalt of the parking lot. The chill of the night air on his bare shoulders and chest was beginning to register, raising goose bumps. Matter from John-boy's head was beginning to dry and cake.

Off to his left, a supercab pickup's door was swinging. It slammed. Bino'd seen the truck before. Downtown, near the office. Tonight.

There was movement in the pickup's cab, visible through its rear window.

Its starter chugged once, then its engine roared and raced. The truck jumped as it went in gear, then lurched forward, gathering speed.

Bino pointed the Mauser, arm extended, the pistol trained on the rear driver's-side window. As the truck reached the turn that led to the street and started to go that way, Bino's trigger finger was beginning to squeeze.

Just beyond the truck, a patio light came on. A young blond woman, curlers in hair, was silhouetted in the door. She was directly in the line of fire.

Bino relaxed his hand and pointed the Mauser straight up in the air.

As he shrugged, arms now limp at his sides, and

turned to go back the way he'd come, a nearby auto horn gave a short, high-pitched beep. Bino looked over his shoulder.

Fifty feet from where he stood, both front doors of a Dodge Caravan station wagon opened at once. Two men alighted.

The driver was a smiling, pleasant-enough young guy wearing wire-frame glasses and a yellow windbreaker. He was a little under six feet, with sandy hair neatly combed. He carried a spiral notebook in one hand, a pen in the other.

The other guy was shorter, stockier, older, part bald, and wearing a plaid sport jacket. A camera was suspended by a strap from one shoulder.

They approached Bino. Bino stood puzzled, clutching the towel in one hand and the Mauser in the other.

The young guy said, "Mr. Phillips? Bino Phillips? I recognize you from your hair—and from last night." He chuckled dryly. "Mr. Phillips, I'm Skip Turner, *Dallas Morning News*. And this is—"

Jesus Christ. Skip the Scoop.

"—Stan Jones, one of our cameramen. We were in the neighborhood, and I wondered if maybe I might get your side of—"

The sound of Skip the Scoop's voice faded as Bino made a mad dash for the sanctuary of his apartment. Behind him, the camera flashed.

Marvin Goldman didn't look as though he liked being in Bino's apartment. He was in one of the easy chairs, with his shoulders hunched forward and his elbows on the armrests, hands clasped in front of his belly, and his feet on the floor, crossed at the ankles. Occasionally he'd glance to the right at Bino or straight ahead at Karen. But mostly he kept his eyes directed to a spot in front of him on the carpet and looked pissed.

He said, "I don't guess there's any way to make it look as though he got shot in here, stumbled off into the bedroom." It sounded like a question. Goldman stroked his goatee.

Bino was on the couch, his head resting atop the corner where the endpiece joined the back. His face was pointed toward Goldman, but he kept his gaze on the ceiling over Goldman's head. His arms were folded, and he didn't say anything.

Seated in the easy chair to Bino's right, her legs drawn up under her, Karen continued to massage her shower-damp hair, looking smaller in Bino's pale blue, too-big-for-her robe. She said, "The back of his head is gone, Marvin. How's he going to stumble off into the bedroom?" She rolled her eyes.

The front door cracked open. The stocky, dark-suited F.B.I. agent on the porch stuck the upper half of his body into the room and motioned. The skinny, dark-suited F.B.I. agent who was seated on the couch next to Bino got up and went to the door. The medium-sized, dark-suited F.B.I. agent who was still on the couch watched them intently.

Bino heard the guy who'd just gone to the door say, "Tell them fifteen minutes." Bino looked through the open entryway. There was quite a crowd out there, necks craning. In the front row were two uniformed Dallas cops. As the F.B.I. inside closed the door, the one on the porch faced the mob and folded his arms. The skinny agent sat back down next to Bino. Bino looked back at the ceiling, over Goldman.

The skinny guy, hair combed straight back from a receding line, took three or four pages from his inside breast pocket. They were folded over twice, like business letters. He spread them open. In the corner of his eye, Bino saw the wording, "U.S. Government Memorandum."

The skinny guy said, "We've got a bigger problem than that, an internal one. It—has to do with the Walther PPK."

Karen stopped drying her hair, letting her hands fall into her lap, clutching an end of the towel in each one. Her lips parted. The skinny guy went on, talking to the agent on his left more than anyone else.

"The problem is that Agent Allen here doesn't have any Walther PPK registered with the bureau. A Beretta. A Browning twenty-two. No Walther PPK three-eighty." He looked at Karen. She looked at her lap.

The medium Fed on the skinny one's left was a blond, with short-cut sidewalls. He arched an eyebrow at Karen. "That can't be, Agent," he said. "Everybody's handguns are registered with the bureau. Every single one. The Walther's an expensive piece, practically a collector's item. There must be some mistake."

Goldman spoke up. "What about a Llama? It's a three-eighty. If the gun were lost, the ballistics guy wouldn't have anything to compare it with. She got a Llama registered? Maybe we could—oh, the hell with it." He looked at Bino's knee.

The skinny agent took a ballpoint from his pocket and clicked the button down with his thumb. He held the end of the pen in the corner of his mouth, clenched lightly between his teeth as he said, "That's a good point, Mr. Goldman. If she had a Llama registered, we could probably get by with saying she used that. But she doesn't." He took the ballpoint out of his mouth and scribbled something on one of the pages, using his knee as a desk. Then he said, "It's hell. We can't even get out a memo, make it retroactive. Not on a Walther PPK, gun like that. Where'd you buy the gun, Agent Allen?"

Bino sat up a little straighter and pulled down the leg of his jogging shorts. He was getting interested.

Karen moved the tip of her little finger along her lower lip. "It isn't mine," she said. The two agents glanced at each other, then back at Karen, not saying anything. She kept her gaze on her lap as she said, "It belongs to Bill Featherston."

The blond agent's jaw slacked. "You call him 'Bill'?"

"Now wait a minute," said Goldman, talking partly to the male agents and partly to Karen, ignoring Bino. "Are we talking about the same guy here? The guy in Washington, Featherston?"

Bino was grinning, ear to ear.

Karen's voice sounded like a little girl's as she said, "The one and only."

"And I suppose," said Skinny, "that you've got a

good explanation of what you were doing with that gun, Agent."

Karen shrugged. "There's really nothing to explain. I carried it for him in my purse, when we went out to dinner. When he went to his plane, he forgot it, that's all. We—I was going to get it back to him, first chance."

Skinny got up and paced, hands behind his back. The blond guy watched him. Karen wrung her hands in her lap. Goldman watched the floor. Bino set his right ankle on his left knee, scratching the inside of his bare thigh, still grinning.

Skinny said, "So. We're going to report that while Agent Allen was shacked up with the dead suspect's lawyer, she blew one of the other suspects away with W. E. Featherston's gun. Is that it?"

"Like hell we are," said the blond guy. "We're going to shoot this one straight up the ladder. It's Featherston's problem, let him figure it out. Let the locals in long enough to do their job, get rid of the body. Keep everybody else out, especially that frigging reporter—what's his name?"

"Skip," said Bino.

Buster cussed John-boy's dumb ass the whole time that he was looking for a good spot to dump the supercab. Hot son of a bitch, he had to get rid of it. He'd eyeballed the lawyer in the rearview, the big s.o.b. standing there aiming that monster pistol, Buster flinching every second of the time and waiting for the rear window to shatter. But it never did. Guy like that lawyer, though, he'd have the supercab's tag number nailed for sure.

Buster cruised East Dallas back streets, old houses on the narrow bastards with most of the paint flaked off and gray wood showing through, thinking, John-boy, he screwed it up but good. The truck was registered in John-boy's real name, and at the North Dallas apartment address. Buster couldn't go there, couldn't even go downtown and pick up his own Chevy, 'cause with Buster's name on the apartment lease it wouldn't take no time for the cops to put two and two together. And Buster with a lousy eighty bucks in his pocket, the rest of the bread at the apartment, stashed in Buster's footlocker.

It was the shits, is what it was.

The .45 had eight rounds in the clip and one in the chamber. Big deal. May as well use it to come up with some kind of a bankroll. But where? Not in this old beat-up end of town, with a bunch of assholes sitting on the wooden porches, rocking and shooting the shit. He held his breath as a black-and-white squad car passed him, pictured a squealing one-eighty, rooflights flashing and siren screaming. But it didn't happen. The cop kept cruising, made a right, and disappeared.

Buster thought, Fuck it. If he was going to get some money, he'd have to have some wheels. Hot or no, he'd need the supercab, for a little while anyway. He found Washington Street, wound the supercab through some more old neighborhoods to the Central Expressway, and went north. Green-reflecting freeway signs whipped by on both sides. Traffic was light, and Buster kept the needle on fifty-five, cracking the window and feeling the cool air rush in with a roaring sound. He needed a chaw, but the Days Work package was empty.

He found what he was looking for on Mockingbird Lane, close to Abrams Road, pulled the supercab in, parked, and cut the engine. His knee felt stiff, so he rubbed it while he sat for a time and listened to the motor tick and cool, measuring with his eye the distance from the truck's nose to the hissing electronic doors that were the entryway to the all-night Skaggs-Albertson's. The parking lot was around a quarter full, fifty cars maybe. Buster watched people moving up and down the aisles inside, taking their time and fucking with the merchandise. Bright fluorescents glowed; over one counter the huge letters PHARM— —were visible, the outside brick wall blocking the rest of the word from Buster's view. Lotta dough in there, stuck in them registers.

Getting inside without somebody noticing that big-ass .45 was going to be a problem. Buster thought that one over. He didn't have a jacket, nothing on but a flimsy T-shirt and jeans.

Goddamn, the whiskey. John-boy'd bought a pint just before they'd gone to that lawyer's place. Buster fished under the seat and came up with it, brown bag rustling as he took the bottle out and dropped the gun inside. Buster took a warm slug of the bourbon and shuddered. Made him feel okay, his nerves pretty steady. People kept filing in and out of the store, nobody noticing him.

Buster climbed down out of the cab, the door squeaking some and closing with a hollow thud. The chilly wind that had kicked up, nipped at him. He plodded across the asphalt and toward the entrance, the sack with the gun inside swinging loosely in his hand. An old woman, wrinkled and gray, head down, passed him in the opposite direction, determinedly shoving a half-full shopping cart into the parking lot. Buster heard her breath whistle through false teeth as she went by.

Just outside the entry, Buster paused and gave the place a once-over. Six of the twelve registers were in action. All the other aisles had chains draped across them, and there was a chromed iron railing with a one-way turnstile entrance to the shopping area, all to make sure that everybody who came in had to go out past the checkout stands. Buster thought, Jesus, they don't trust nobody these days, then giggled to himself as he stepped on the mat in front of him. There was a sharp hiss, and the door popped open. Buster went in.

The calm of the store's interior felt a little strange after the gusting wind in the parking lot, and Buster paused for an instant to get his bearings. The registers were too far away for him to make his play here, across wide counters and behind plastic shields that were probably bulletproof. Man'd have to go through the checkout from the inside shopping area, throw down on the clerk, take the money, and keep on going into the parking lot. No other way made sense.

Buster moved to the iron railing, the .45's swinging weight tugging on the sack in his hand. He was just about to go through the turnstile when he noticed the T.V. cameras.

You couldn't see them from the parking lot. They were mounted on top of a ledge in the high wall, over the electronic entries. There were twelve of them, one trained on each register, each with a red light glowing, indicating that they were on. Pull a stickup and be a star. Buster rolled the turnstile, went through it, and then screwed around with the interlocking shopping carts while he thought about the cameras. He rattled one of the carts loose and steered it up an outside aisle marked HOUSEHOLD GOODS AND APPLIANCES.

On purpose, Buster stayed behind a skinny girl in black corduroy pants who stopped every few feet and took a knife, can opener, or bowl from the shelf, looked it over, and put it back. Every time she stopped, Buster'd stop behind her, fooling with merchandise and looking both ways. So far so good. No gun-toting security guards, not yet. But those damn T.V. cameras had him bugged.

He wandered over to the fruit-and-vegetable counter and dropped four or five apples in the basket. Still no guards. He held one of the clear plastic bags for a time before he tore it off the roll and really looked it over. No way. Most he'd do with that over his head was suffocate, and the damn thing wasn't tight enough to disort his features any. Something like John-boy would think up.

Come to think about it, did the cameras make any difference? Buster'd made up his mind to put a whole passel of miles between him and Dallas before tomorrow. They sure as hell were going to have a make on him anyway, once they got John-boy and the truck I.D.'d, so what did a grocery store holdup matter? Didn't amount to a hill of beans. 'Course it didn't. Buster herded the shopping basket toward the checkout stands, feeling pretty dumb for having farted around so long.

On the way, he made a couple of stops. He dropped a carton of cocoa in the basket at one counter, a sack of candy bars at another. Had to look like he was going to buy something. There were short lines at every counter, but Buster got behind a silver-haired guy in the express lane. That was where the cash would be; most of the folks in the other lanes were writing checks and flashing credit cards.

The old dude in front of him had on green coveralls and was carrying two boxes of saltines. A dark-haired woman of about thirty with a kid riding in her cart, facing her, fell in behind Buster. The boy was around six or seven with front teeth missing, too big to be riding in the cart. He grinned sort of goofy; Buster thought, Kid must be half off or something.

The kid said, "I want a Three Musketeers, Mom."

"No sweets, Jimmy," said the woman. "I've told you that. Ask one more time, and you'll find yourself marching out to the car alone, young man."

Buster glanced. The woman had on makeup, her hair was fixed nice, and she wasn't bad looking. There wasn't anything wrong with the kid, either, just spoiled as hell and too lazy to walk. Buster felt down inside the paper bag and touched the pistol's handle as he turned back around and faced the register. There were four people in front of him.

It probably wasn't over five minutes, but it seemed like hours to Buster, until it was his turn. The old guy in front of him argued about his change, jawing with the clerk, and didn't know how close he came to getting robbed himself, just for good measure. He finally left. Buster stood relaxed and watched the cashier, smiley little thing with short dark hair and braces on her teeth, ring up the crap in the basket. Buster was leaning back with both elbows on a low counter behind him, sack with the gun in it dangling loose. Next in line, the pretty woman slapped the kid's hand and snatched a Three Musketeers away from him.

The clerk paused and grinned, silver metal reflecting over her teeth. "Will that be all, please?" There were dark freckles across her nose.

Saliva came up in Buster's mouth. As he straightened and loosened the sack's neck, he said, "You got a Days Work?"

She nodded, bent, and fished under the counter, still smiling. A green bag of Days Work in her hand, she raised up. Buster had the ugly, blue-black .45 pointed straight at her. Her eyes widened, her smile froze. To Buster's left, the woman with the kid drew a sharp, hissing breath.

Buster said, "Just go ahead and drop the tobacco in with the other stuff." She did so mechanically, eyes riveted on the gun, while Buster said to the woman behind him, "Don't say a word, lady, and act normal."

Surprisingly calm, the woman said, "Be still, Jimmy."

Buster handed the now-open whiskey sack to the stunned cashier. "Cash, little lady. Quick about it."

Her hands trembled; her glance flicked beyond him, past his shoulder. Buster looked that way, keeping the .45's barrel trained on a point between the cashier and the lady with the kid in the cart, ready to swivel its aim in either direction. Clerks' heads were down; they were busy sacking purchases. Customers looked unconcerned; nobody was paying any attention. For now, Buster had himself a three-way party, four if you counted the kid. On the high exterior wall, the T.V. cameras glowed like a row of traffic lights.

Buster pointed the gun once again at the cashier, saying, "You ain't moving fast enough, hon. I said quick, now."

She hit the NO-SALE button, the register's computer tick-ticked, and the drawer slid open. She held the sack in one hand and poked the ones, tens, and twenties into it with the other. She held the bag out to Buster.

He said, "All of it. The big ones, too, under the drawer."

She nodded vacantly, her lower jaw moving slightly from side to side. Her face had paled, and her freckles stood out. She lifted the cash drawer, found a few fifties and hundreds underneath, and added them to the bag's contents. The kid in the basket began to snivel. Buster jerked his head in that direction. "Shut him up, lady."

The woman stood firm. "He's just a little boy, for goodness' sake."

Buster nodded to her and turned his attention back to the cashier. He took the bag from her. "Now don't either of you make a move till I'm outside. I hear a peep, I'll turn around and shoot you both."

The cashier put shaking, petite hands on the countertop, looking down at them. "Yes, sir," she said, her voice barely above a whisper.

Buster said, "Oh, yeah. Gimme the Days Work."

She looked up. "I beg your pardon?"

He gestured with the gun. "The tobacco, girlie. I want it."

She nodded and handed the pouch to him. The tobacco made a swelling bulge in the hip pocket of his jeans as he stuffed it in. He half grinned, saying, "Thank you kindly," as he moved out the aisle and into the open space, shoving the .45 into the bag with the money. He was about halfway to the exit when the electronic door hissed open. A uniformed cop came through it, dropped to one knee, and leveled a .38 snub-nosed revolver at Buster. The bluesuit said, "Hold it, right there. Police. You're under arrest." He was a fuzzy-cheeked youngster, with some baby fat still on him. His voice quavered.

Buster's glance flicked up toward the ledge on the high wall. His heartbeat thudding, he thought, Christ! Live cameras, some asshole somewhere on a monitor phoning the law. He stopped for an instant, acted like he was going to raise his hands. Then, without warning, he dropped suddenly to the tiled floor, rolling to his right, digging in the bag as he did.

The cop didn't move fast enough; he was probably spooky about shooting his gun in here with all these customers. His split-second hesitation gave Buster just the time he needed. Buster rolled over twice, rib cage thudding on the floor, the .45 pointed at the cop after the second revolution of Buster's body. The horse-kick of the .45 jerked Buster's hand up in the air as he pulled the trigger. The boom echoed loudly in the store. Somewhere, a woman screamed.

Buster had to admit, it was a lucky shot, after rolling and shooting wild like that. Could have hit most anything, including the ceiling.

The slug ripped into the cop's left shoulder just above the heart, sending the bluesuit sprawling backward, blood spurting like a geyser, .38 clattering useless on the floor. As the cop grunted in pain, the plate glass in the window behind him shattered. He hit the floor on his bloody, numbed shoulder, rolled over once, and lay still.

Buster was up, ducking, the money bag still in his

hand, moving back toward the aisle and the register from which he'd come. Visible through the smashed glass, backup cops on the sidewalk scattered for cover. Buster thought, Officer down, huh? *Fuckin'-A,* you assholes.

The woman with the kid and the cashier were still there, frozen. Throughout the store, people ducked behind counters, yelled nothings, ran pell-mell to the rear of the shopping area.

Buster shoved the rolling cart aside, the kid whimpering, and grabbed the dark-haired mother by the arm. Slender muscle moved on slender bone in his grasp. She wore a black wool sweater-jacket and green slacks. Buster jerked his head toward the front of the store and the street beyond. "Come on, lady."

She shrank back in his grip, shaking her head, terror in her eyes. Buster pointed the .45 at the kid's midsection, saying, "It's you or him. Come on."

Her eyes widened. She gasped and nodded.

Buster shoved her along in front of him; she stumbled slightly, then he gripped her shoulder with one hand and yanked her close. As they approached the front door, he placed the barrel of the .45 against her temple. Her back was still to him.

He said into her ear, "What's your name, lady?"

"Sally." She was rigid with fear but spoke calmly.

"Sally, huh? Well, Miss Sally, we're going for a little stroll. Cops stay clear, you got no sweat. You better hope they do. That's a nice little boy you got."

Strangely, she said, "Thank you."

They stepped carefully around the fallen officer. He moved and let out a bubbly groan. Buster thought about going ahead and finishing the cop, then changed his mind. Might need the fucking bullet.

The exit door made a soft gust of air as it swished open. Buster now encircled Sally's shoulders and upper chest with his free arm, keeping the pistol muzzle braced against the side of her head. They went outside.

The wind had quit. With it the chilly nip had gone from the air; only a cool stillness remained. Buster quickly counted six sets of flashing rooflights, the black-and-whites in front of the store's entrance in a wagon-train half-circle. Billed hats were visible behind the hoods and trunks of all the cars, faces underneath the caps. A few pistol muzzles. At least one rifle barrel. Behind the cops, the lot had been cleared of people; only the parked cars remained. The supercab was straight ahead, fifty yards or so behind the squad cars.

A guy in a soft-brimmed hat and a suit stepped from behind a car. A bullhorn was raised to his lips.

The bullhorn said, "Throw your gun down. Release the woman and raise your hands in the air."

Buster thought, You're shitting me.

He squeezed Sally a little harder, yelling, "You got one minute to get all those cops over to my right, out of the way. One minute, or this lady dies. You hear me?"

Bullhorn leaned over and said something to somebody who was out of sight behind a car. Bullhorn was portly. There was a small feather in his hatband. Buster thought that the suit was brown, but in the artificial light he wasn't sure.

Bullhorn straightened, his loud mechanical voice saying, "Don't be foolish. You can't get away. Let the woman go."

Buster shouted, "Thirty seconds." Sally gasped.

Another whispered conference behind the cars. Finally, amplified by the bullhorn, "Stay calm. Don't do anything rash. We're moving. To your right, you say?"

Buster nodded, gesturing with his pistol, thinking, You better get a move on, asshole. Red from the rooflights flashed on him and Sally like a disco strobe.

Slowly, carefully, a dozen or so bluesuits rose from

behind cars, moving warily until they had formed a group far to Buster's right in the parking lot. Pistols and rifles were lowered. Only the man with the bullhorn remained in the center.

To the plainclothesman, Buster yelled, "You, too, man. I mean it. You get over there with the others, or she's dead."

Bullhorn obeyed, moving sideways around the cars and facing Buster all the way.

Keeping Sally between him and the circle of cops, Buster edged through the small clearing that was formed by the half-circle of cars. When he reached the hood of the middle vehicle, he stopped, .45 cocked against Sally's head.

"Listen, you pigs," he snarled at them, "I'm gonna count to five. Now, if there's still any cops behind these cars here, they better move on over with the rest. They might get me, but you'll be washing this lady's brains off the sidewalk if they do."

Nobody answered him.

"One . . ." counted Buster. "Two . . ." He felt the woman tense up, heard her constricted breathing.

"Three."

Still silence.

"Four."

Footsteps sounded. A cop rose from behind the trunklid of the car nearest Buster and jogged to the others. Buster chuckled, his laughter echoing in the dead stillness.

"Okay, Sally," he whispered.

The soles of Buster's shoes made little rustling noises as he and Sally went between the cop cars. When they were in the open parking lot, he backed slowly toward the supercab, using Sally as a front between him and the officers all the way. They remained in a knot, Bullhorn at the front of the pack.

Finally, Buster was close enough to touch the pickup's door handle. He stopped dead and yelled at the cops; the woman flinched at the sound of his voice.

"Stay right where you're at, pigs. We're gonna get in the truck, now."

Buster was a little bit worried about how he was going to maneuver himself and the woman both up the high step into the cab and still keep her in front of him. He thought it over as he used his gun hand to grope for the doorlatch. The .45 clunked and scraped against the truck's metal shell. Just as Buster's fingers closed on the handle, Sally thrust an arm forward, then reversed its direction and drove her elbow into Buster's midsection. Hard.

Buster never would have believed that the fucking little woman could hit that hard. The breath whooshed out of his lungs in a startled grunt. At the same time, Sally ducked her head and sank her teeth into Buster's forearm where it was draped across her chest. Buster screamed once, loud. Then the woman twisted away from him and ran for the store, footsteps clicking. Buster made a grab for her, but she was gone.

He thought, Fucking bitch, goddamn you, and leveled the .45 at her narrow, fleeing back. As he did, a loud *boom* sounded from within the circle of officers, about fifty yards away. Buster caught a flash of light in the corner of his eye. Something rocketed underneath his arm, missing it by scant inches, and whanged into the metal side of the truck. The supercab rocked hard on its springs.

Buster forgot about the woman and scrambled for safety. Two more bullets sizzled and clanged against the truck as he opened the door and climbed aboard, breathing in short, heavy gasps. He dropped the .45 next to him on the seat and started the engine, flooring it, pistons churning. He popped the lever into drive. The rear tires squealed and burned rubber as

Buster started to turn right and go parallel to the store's front. More flashes. More bullets thunking.

From close on his left there was a louder explosion, a bigger burst of flame. The cop's dark silhouette flashed by, and a ray of artificial light glinted from the riot gun's shiny barrel. The front left side of the truck bucked high, raising Buster off the seat. Then it hit the pavement with a stunning jar, sparks flying as the churning rim tore the blown-out front tire into shreds.

The truck lurched, straightened out, nose lifting as it rolled onto the sidewalk, crushing two shopping carts that had been left there. Buster let go of the wheel, screamed, and covered his eyes with his forearms as the glass front of the store loomed close.

The truck rammed the storefront. Glass tinkled and flew in jagged shards. The truck's bumper collided with the storefront's lower brick facing, the bumper twisting and crumpling. Buster's chest banged against the steering wheel. His chin thudded on the dash. The supercab jarred to a halt, the rattling of the broken glass still vibrating the air.

Dazed, Buster shook his head and blinked.

The door handle rattled, and the pickup's door banged open. Buster looked to his left as a .38 snubnose poked its way into the cab and pointed its barrel at his head.

"Please, motherfuck," said the cop. "Please try something."

Buster raised his hands. He grinned, friendly. "Ain't doing nothing, boss. Bus don't want no trouble."

The cop grabbed Buster's shirt and yanked. Buster came down on the sidewalk, stumbling, grabbing the truck's door for support.

The cop said, "On the pavement, asshole. Facedown." Buster hit the deck.

More bluesuits surrounded him. As rough hands

patted him down, a voice over him said, "What's your name, you fuck?"

Buster twisted his head to one side. Out of the side of his mouth, he bawled, "Ain't saying nothing. Not till I see a lawyer I ain't."

One cop said, "He ain't gonna talk, Henry."

There was a heartbeat of quiet. Then a second, deeper voice said, "He ain't, huh? Good."

A hard-toed shoe kicked Buster in the ribs. He grunted in pain.

From farther away, a woman said, "Kick the dirty bastard again."

Buster wasn't sure, but he thought it was Sally's voice.

Bino spent the night on the couch, what was left of it. By the time the Feds had monitored the Dallas cops' comings and goings, the County Medical team, minus Shoesole Traynor for once, had carted John-boy off to keep Sonny Starr company, and all the tents were folded up, it was after three. Pumped up like a gallon of pure caffeine, Bino spent most of the night rolling, tossing, sitting up, then rolling and tossing some more. It was dawn when he finally slept. When he awoke to the steady drumbeat of rain in the outside metal gutters, the glowing digital clock next to the tape player read 8:09 and his eyeballs stung like he'd put in new contact lenses. Bread was still plugged into the tape player. Bino popped the control over to F.M. and listened to the KVIL-icopter report that Royal Oaks Country Club was turning into Lake Mead as he went to the front window, drew the curtain aside, and peeked out.

Rain. Rivers and lakes of the stuff. Two gutters were joined at a top corner of the building across the way, and the water was brimming out and falling in a thick waterfall line to splat in the graveled plant bed underneath. The little cat that Bino had nearly shot last night was huddled under a cedar bush. He'd gingerly stick a paw out from beneath the branches, then yank it back quickly when he felt the rain, showing pointed teeth in a helpless mew. Bino knew just how he felt.

The bedroom looked like the aftermath of a blitzkrieg. The dust from the blasted ceiling had coated the furniture, floor, and bedspread like chalkdust on a blackboard. There were large gouges in the Sheetrock wall where the skinny F.B.I. agent had dug out fragments of Karen's (or Featherston's, whoever the hell *he* was) bullet before the locals could get their hands on it. John-boy had ruined the carpet with a huge crimson stain that still looked damp. Bino didn't touch it to see. He showered fast, put on jeans, Nikes, and a sweatshirt, threw a hooded slicker over himself, and dodged puddles to the manager's office—or almost dodged, he landed a size twelve in the middle of one of them so that his pants were soaked to the knee when he ducked inside.

A few minutes later, Tilly Madden's padded shoulders lifted as she put her elbows on her desk. She held a plastic cigarette holder between her thumb and middle digit and tapped on it with her forefinger. A long row of ash fell from the end of her filtered Virginia Slim and went to pieces in a round glass tray.

Tilly said, "Do you have any idea what those are?" She gestured to what looked like between twenty and thirty square pieces of pink paper that were impaled on a brass spike in front of her.

"Well, they look like call slips to me," said Bino. "We use the same kind down at my office."

Tilly had deep red hair, center parted and hanging straight to her shoulders on both sides. Her long nails were painted to match her hair. She said, "That's what they are, all right. All from residents." Her fall suit was red also. There was a gold ring on each finger of both her hands.

She puffed on the holder, inhaled, and blew out a long plume of smoke before saying, "I'll bet we can guess what those calls are all about now, can't we?"

Bino sat in a straight-backed chair across from her and didn't say anything. His damp jeans were beginning to feel chill, and a sneeze was coming.

"Bino, dear," said Tilly. "Have you heard about Trails North? Just opening up, now leasing? Pool and spa. Maid service. Hot and cold running secretaries. It's really in, Bino."

Bino cleared his throat, then sneezed into his palms. He quickly got a handkerchief from his back pocket and cleaned his hands and nose. "Well, Til," he said, "after five years, I'm really attached to Vapors North. I call it home. A lot of new places opening up, but I've got my roots right here."

Tilly's mascaraed lashes rose as she glanced at the ceiling. She lifted her upper lip and scratched a spot of crimson lipstick off of a front tooth. "That's what I was afraid of," she said. "So, Bino. What can I do for you this rainy day?"

Bino hesitated, decided he wasn't going to sneeze again right away, and stuffed the hankie in his rear pocket. He leaned forward with elbows on knees, saying, "Tilly, my place is a real disaster area. There's a shotgun hole in the bedroom ceiling. And the carpet is ruined—you don't want a blow-by-blow of what caused that, believe me. Sheetrock dust all over. I need it fixed, right away. I mean, I can't even sleep in my bed until it's—you see?" His eyes were pleading.

As Bino talked, Tilly got a spiral Daily Planner and inserted a red thumbnail under a tab in its edge. She opened the book and flipped pages, looking each one over briefly. Then, she said, "How about the twenty-seventh?"

"The twenty-seventh? That's over two weeks from now."

"It's hard to get good help these days, Bino. You know, they come and go. We've got move-ins, and the crew is really tied up. Then there's Thanksgiving, and you can forget about having anything done around then." She really looked sympathetic. "Gosh, I know it's going to be a problem to you, but I just don't see how our boys could—"

Bino said, "How about if I pay for it myself?"

Tilly brightened. "Now that's a horse of a different color. There's a small remodeling company, new around here. They came by, left some flyers. I think they'd get right on it. Today, if you'd like."

Bino stood. Outside, the torrent had slacked to a drizzle but looked as though it might pick up again. Bino said, "Hey that's great, Tilly. Tell you what. I'll drop a signed check off with you on my way out." He fished, came up with a pen and a business card of his, and turned the card blank side up, ready to write on it. "What's the name of the company? So I can make the check out."

She didn't bat an eye. "Madden and Madden."

Bino glanced up, pen in hand. "Oh? Who is it, your husband and you?"

She grinned. "Not me, Bino. Jimmy. He's my boy. They do good work, dear."

He gave up, thinking, Tilly should be doing holdups with the two goons from last night. He wrote the name down. As he turned to go, Tilly said, "Oh, Bino."

Bino looked. She was holding a morning paper out, folded.

"You'll probably want to look this over," she said. "You're featured. Along with your towel." Tilly looked ready to break into giggles as he took the newspaper from her.

He read Skip the Scoop's story over quickly, then again with care. There was mention of possible court action by Art Stammer over the slugging incident, followed by a lot of innuendos, ending with "Phillips declined comment." Usual stuff. And a caption underneath a hazy photo of a guy running away with a towel around his middle, a guy who could have been anybody. But not a word about the gun in Bino's hand or about John-boy's shooting. Nowhere else in the paper, either. He checked thoroughly, page by page. The Feds had really done a job on somebody. Bino was looking the picture over as he called the office. Dodie answered.

Bino said, "How'd it go?"

The typewriter was clickety-clacking in the background as she said, "Baylor down to seven. Tennessee up to eight-and-a-half." She was forcing it some. But not too much.

"No, I mean you, Dode," he said. "Feeling any better?"

"Great, boss." The typewriter hesitated while Dodie swallowed something. There wasn't any static, so she didn't have the speaker phone turned on. Bino pictured the receiver cradled between her shoulder and soft neck. The typewriter started back up. She said, "Listen, Bino. That Mrs. Tirelli's called three times. Says she needs to talk to you, right away."

Images of Annabelle hurrying to class with a stack of books hugged to her bosom. And a sequel picture, of a sapphire ring on her finger, of her standing there with Dante Tirelli's arm about her slim waist.

"Yeah, Dode," he said. "I'll call her."

"Do you need the number?"

"No—I've got it. Listen, Dodie, have you seen this morning's paper?"

"Yes," she said. "But Half made me promise not to mention it. So I won't. Bye." She hung up.

Bino spent the next half hour figuring out reasons why he shouldn't call Annabelle. The first solution was easy—the folded call slip with her number on it just wouldn't be where he could find it. But it was the first thing his fingers came in contact with when he reached in the coat pocket of the suit he'd worn yesterday. First solution down the tube.

Then he made two columns on a ruled pad, nos on the left, yeses on the right. When he was through, the left side listed six completely logical reasons, five of which involved Dante Tirelli, and the sixth a drivel: "For Annabelle's own good." Then he moved to the right-hand column. He sat for a full ten minutes, pen frozen in his hand, but couldn't come up with a single reason why he should. Just as he thought. He shouldn't.

He picked up the phone and punched in the number.

A male voice, British accent, said, "Mr. and Mrs. Tirelli's residence. How may I help you?"

Bino thought, Jesus, an English butler? At Tirelli's house? Come on.

He said, "This is Bino Phillips, attorney. I'm returning a call from Mrs. Tirelli."

"Oh, yes, sir. I've been expecting your call. The madam is indisposed at the moment, but says you're to drop by around one. If it's convenient."

Bino hesitated, then said that it was. He copied the directions down as the limey gave them. Las Colinas. Spendthrift heir to old-money Highland Park.

When he was sure that he knew the way, Bino said, "Thanks, Jeeves. I'll be there."

"It's Radcliffe, sir. The madam will be expecting you."

Las Colinas was like a strip of Southern California, say Newport Beach, cut out by a giant, transported half a continent west, and jigsawed in between Dallas and Forth Worth. The spires of its glittering office complexes, complete with moats and floating barges covered in plant life, were visible from westbound Highway 114 like the Emerald City. But the homes were hidden from the freeway by low wooded hills, and you couldn't see them until you'd jogged a mile or so to the south on a street that started out like a winding country lane, then gently widened into a four-lane boulevard. When you finally did get a look at the houses, they'd knock your eyes out of their sockets.

Bino didn't like it. The homes just didn't fit in together, like a very gaudy, very expensive piece of jewelry that had diamonds, rubies, and emeralds clustered in rows. Big bucks, bad taste. A mammoth Rolex looking like a Mickey Mouse watch on a very skinny man's wrist. Or a neighborhood where a Dante Tirelli would live. As he made winding turns and checked his written directions, Bino wondered how Annabelle fit in around here.

He found the address. It was a rambling one-story Spanish, red-tiled roof and all, that was set between a two-story colonial, with white pillars yet, and a huge Gothic mansion spotted with too many arches in the front. Best of three worlds, thought Bino as he pulled the Linc to the curb in front. Spanish house, English butler. Probably a French cook. Perfect. Look, Mom, see how much money I got?

Bino walked up on the porch and rang the bell. The morning thunderstorm had vanished, and a heatless November sun was beginning to peek through the cloud cover, making flashes in sidewalk puddles and shadows in the wet, browning grass. The scent of moisture hung in the air.

Bino had Radcliffe pictured as late fifties, tall and thin with wavy silver hair, and wearing a vest and black bow tie. In a few minutes the door's peephole opened and closed. Radcliffe then pulled the door wide, and Bino saw that he'd been wrong. The bow tie was navy with white polka dots. The rest of Radcliffe was just like Bino had pictured.

Radcliffe said, "Mr. Phillips, I presume." Bino nodded, and the butler said, "Please, sir, right this way." He held the door for Bino, closed it with a solid thud, and led the way into the interior of the house. Radcliffe walked with his back straight as a ramrod. His vest and slacks were coal black, making his starched white shirt look even whiter. The collar looked like molded cardboard. Bino was wearing a charcoal suit and maroon tie that he had thought were pretty spiffy when he'd put them on. Radcliffe made him feel as though he was wearing his grodies.

The entry hall was wide, with a rich-looking, deep red throw rug over gray stone tiles. A grandfather clock was on the right, its three-foot gold-plated pendulum ticking and tocking. A clustered group of pictures was on the wall next to the clock. Annabelle on horseback. Annabelle and Tirelli on a sailboat. A small photo of Annabelle's dad in a western suit and a ten-gallon, the same picture that once had hung in Annabelle's and Bino's place. Bino looked away from it.

They went into the arena-sized den with its wet bar on one side, a long divan, and floor of stone tile like the entry hall.

An enormous, high-ceilinged kitchen was off to the rear of the den, an island stove and grill in its center. There was an exit from the den next to the bar, rich-carpeted stairs leading to what Bino supposed was the master bedroom. A couple of oil paintings hung on the wall, western scenes. One a pack of rustlers making a score, the other cowpokes around a campfire. The pictures didn't quite go. Neither did the couch. The bar was okay. Bino leaned an elbow on it.

Radcliffe said, "Would you care for refreshment, sir?" He made a sweeping gesture toward the bar.

Bino thought it over, then said he'd have a Coke. Radcliffe produced a two-liter plastic bottle, a big tumbler, and an ice bucket. As the butler plunked solid cubes into the glass, Bino said, "Say, Radcliffe. You don't feel a little out of place here, do you?"

Radcliffe gave a thin-lipped smile as he poured. "I'm learning Spanish, sir," he said. He gave Bino the fizzing Coke and disappeared up the carpeted stairs.

The windows gave a view of the redwood deck and shaded yard. Bino sipped the Coke and looked out at the giant hot tub that was shaped like Texas itself. More of the same. Bino was beginning to wish he hadn't come.

Behind him, Annabelle said, "It was Dante's idea. I wanted a smaller one, with a recliner and one bench. Might seat four. Perfect for two."

She was still reading his mind. He turned around.

Annabelle was standing with one foot on the floor and the other still on the bottom step, her lips parted in a half statement, half question. The mirth that Bino remembered in her hazel eyes had faded some. One dainty foot came off the stair in graceful slow motion and went down next to the other one.

"There's just too much room for other people," she said. "You know?" Bino supposed that she meant the spa. He wasn't sure. If she was pitching, he wasn't catching. Not yet.

He said, "Your man Radcliffe gives good directions. I couldn't have missed it if I'd wanted to."

"Good directions and good service. I'll have one, too. Whatever you're drinking is fine." She went to the couch to sit. Annabelle was wearing white denims and a black shirt, the sleeves rolled to the elbows and the tail out, artist fashion. The top two buttons were open at her throat. The shirt's hem caressed her hips. She flowed into a corner of the divan and propped one elbow up on the back.

Bino went to the bar, found the necessities, and poured her a Coke. "I'm at your service, ma'am," he said. "What's up?"

"It's Dante. He wants to hire you, Bino. Something about taxes at the restaurant—liquor taxes, I think."

He gave her the drink. She held it in both hands and made circles in the frost with her thumbs. There were two straight-backed chairs with cushioned seats against the wall underneath the painting of the rustlers. Bino got one of them and sat down across from her. Her slightly arched eyebrows said she didn't like that.

He said, "That's a little out of my line, Annabelle. Why me? Why not Winnie Anspacher, or some tax lawyer that Winnie knows?"

She took a dainty sip. "Beats me. It really does. It was his idea; he says Winnie's firm charges too much. He—he was supposed to be here now, to talk to you. But he called not fifteen minutes ago. He's tied up." She'd seemed ageless the other night at Winnie's. Daylight added some years. Tiny crow's-feet around the eyes.

Bino said, "I don't get it."

"Get what? What is there to get, Bino?"

"The whole thing. All your—your husband knows about me is that you married me once, I'm a lawyer, and I throw punches at Republicans. And if he's read this morning's paper, he knows I run around in the parking lot of my apartment with a towel around my middle." There was a small end table by the couch with a cork-centered coaster on it. Bino set his drink down. "And you call like this was an emergency or something, which it isn't. And then I show up, but Tirelli doesn't. So like I said, Annabelle"—he crossed his legs—"what's up?"

It flustered her, as Bino had intended, and she lowered her eyes. Richard Bigelow's assassination, followed by Sonny Starr's killing. Then the thing at Bino's office while Bino was conveniently out of the way at a political rally. Winnie's story about Art Stammer's wanting Bino to come, then Stammer's reaction to seeing him there—a total blank. Stammer hadn't been faking it, either; Bino'd seen enough phonies like Art

Stammer to know when it was an act and when it was for real. Somehow, Tirelli was behind it all. And now Tirelli was using his own woman as bait for—what? Bino didn't know, but whatever hots he'd been working up for Annabelle were cooling off, but fast.

Annabelle said, "I don't really know. It was a bolt out of the blue to me. Yesterday, Dante told me to get in touch with you. I didn't try to analyze why"—she set her drink next to Bino's, interlocked her fingers in her lap, and looked up—"and frankly I didn't care. It gave me something to do, and it gave me a chance to see you. Is that awful?"

She sucked her lower lip between her teeth. It was another thing about her that hadn't changed, a mannerism that Bino remembered from the days when he used to memorize everything about her and carry the image with him wherever he went. Now she was just a beautiful, lonely woman, living in a house that was too big and too gaudy and chewing on her lower lip. A cheerleader sitting on a bench in a vast empty stadium long after everybody'd gone home, wishing they'd come back so she could get up and strut her stuff once more.

Bino picked up his drink and went to the bar. He put his elbows on it and held the glass in both hands, his back to her. There was a breakfront cabinet behind the bar with weblike latticework between polished glass, like crystal. He turned to face her.

"No, babe, it isn't awful. It just isn't the right beat, is all. Wrong time, wrong place. Too many hard miles down the road, or whatever it is that they say. I can't slam-dunk it anymore, Annabelle, or carry your books to class. You make me feel like Rip Van Winkle. One day, poof, she's gone. Then I sleep for a decade or so and poof, she reappears, lovely as ever. Only I haven't been asleep all that time. Too much has happened. And I don't think you're in on it, babe, but I think that Tirelli is using you as bait. Exactly why I'm not sure. But I'm not taking the bait."

Annabelle was gazing out the window, still twisting her hands in her lap and biting her lip. Her profile was to him. It was gorgeous.

He walked to the hallway that led to the front door. "I'm going now, Annabelle. You can tell Tirelli that I'm in the book, if he wants me." She didn't turn her head. She was still looking at the blue water in the shape of Texas as he left.

He paused outside and glanced back, his thumb on the door handle of the Linc. The English butler was visible in the front picture window, brushing something with a feather duster. The butler didn't look at him.

Bino got in and woke the Linc up. It whinnied, purred, and pointed its nose in the direction of the real world. It was moving at a near-full gallop before it had gone a block.

Dodie said, "You need to call Mac Strange at the county D.A.'s. It's urgent. Have you been listening to the radio?"

Bino leaned against the phone booth's glass wall. Beyond the sleek body of the Linc, the front door of Joe Miller's Bar invited him into the dark quiet of the interior.

He said, "No, I haven't, Dode. Why?"

"Wow, it's all over the news. They've arrested a guy in a supermarket robbery. The radio says he's one of the guys that—that were in here the other night. And that he's a suspect in the Richard Bigelow shooting. Along with Sonny Starr and another guy. Did Sonny say anything to you, Bino? About Richard Bigelow?"

"No, Dodie, he didn't. I'll give Mac a call."

He did.

"Where the hell have you been, Bino?" Strange's office was in a high rise on Stemmons Freeway, along with the rest of the county D.A.s'. He'd be gazing out his window at the massive bulk of the World Trade Center.

Bino said, "Oh, around. I had a couple of fires to put out."

"Well, you've got another one. What have you done, joined the Feds? How's come we didn't know that the bozo we've picked up is the same one that shot your pad up last night? You know who told us? Not you. Not the fucking Feds. The creep himself, that's who. He says he wants to see you."

Bino thought, Jesus, what's he want to see *me* for? I might shoot the bastard.

He said, "When can I see him, Mac?"

"I think you'd better come on down here, Bino. First we want you to look at a lineup. Christ, the witness is gonna identify the guy, then the guy wants to spill his guts to the witness. Beats anything I ever saw. Anyway, Goldman is on his way over. He's bringing a lady F.B.I. agent with him. Let's see, her name is—"

"I think I know her, Mac. They'll be wanting to tie your boy into the Richard Bigelow killing. Listen, Mac. Look out your window in about fifteen minutes. You'll see me coming."

Bino gave Joe Miller's Bar one last wistful glance as he herded the Linc out of the parking lot.

Bino said, in a side-of-the-mouth whisper, "What do you think, Karen?"

On his right, Karen Allen shifted in the darkness and dug a sharp elbow into Bino's ribs. Marvin Goldman coughed into a cupped palm on Karen's other side.

Arnette Geron (Buster) Longley was two places from right of center under glaring lights, his red beard shining and the puffy white flesh of his belly showing under the hem of a too-small T-shirt. The guy next to

Buster on his right was skinny, a foot taller, and black-haired. A dumpy balding cop who Bino'd seen before was on Buster's left. Buster was the only redhead in the group.

Bino looked to his left at the dim outline of Mac Strange's chubby profile. Bino said, "Why don't you draw a black cross on the front of his shirt, Mac?"

Strange was chewing on an unlit cigar. He bit the end off and spat it out. "Vaudeville's dead, Bino. Just I.D. the fucking guy, huh?"

Bino needed some time. This was all lopsided and wasn't getting any rounder. Besides, if worse came to worse, Karen could give them a make. And if they hung the Bigelow hit on the redhead, it was all they needed. The paid-for murder carried life in the Fed if the indictment had the right wording, and it was a capital crime if they wanted to let Texas prosecute him. So what if he'd killed Teresa Valdez and gone after Bino to boot? What were they going to give him, two lifes? Or two deaths?

Bino said, "I don't know, Mac. It was awfully dark in that apartment."

Strange's chin raised suddenly, a full two inches. "You—? Jesus Christ, Bino—"

"Now, I'm not saying it wasn't him, Mac. Don't get me wrong. But—well, as a citizen I want to be real, real sure before I go around fingering someone for something as serious as this. That's what you want, isn't it? Witnesses who are careful about making positive I.D.'s?" Bino was grinning and wasn't sure if Strange could tell or not in the dark.

Strange moved his chair back a little and looked over his shoulder to the rear. "Get the lights, Hardy. And clear 'em out, you know where to take the suspect. I knew it wasn't our day. First the Feds, covering up. Now for a star witness we got to have Funny Guy Phillips." He made a snorting sound. "Come on, Hardy. Now."

The lights came on and Karen's round thigh appeared taut against a navy business skirt. She was back into her "Effa Bee Eye" character. Sophisticated and cool.

County Investigator Hardy Cole made his way down to the front of the room, thin but angular and tough. He smirked at Bino as he went by. A door opened at the rear of the lineup stage, and the chorus line moved out. Cole put a hand on Buster's shoulder, held him up until the others were gone, and then personally escorted Buster outside. Cole looked over his shoulder and sneered one more time at Bino as the entryway closed behind him.

Goldman asked Strange, "That's the only way he'll have it? Won't talk to us, only to Bino?"

"That's what he says," replied Strange.

Goldman stood and faced Bino. "Karen's filled you in on what we want him for, Bino. It's big. Political assassinations are top priority. In fact, there's nothing bigger. Not drugs. Not espionage. Nothing."

Bino glared at Karen, then back at Goldman. "What about Featherston's gun?" he said. "You know—the guy in Washington? That's bigger, isn't it?"

The room was square, about ten by ten. Its walls were blank. They'd once been white, but now there were yellow streaks and gray splotches, the result of too many cigarettes being smoked by too many cops grilling too many guys, the guys allowed to smoke only after they'd told the cops what they knew. Or had what the cops wanted them to say committed to memory, down pat. There was a door off the lineup room and another closed door that led to a hallway that led to buses and vans parked at the curb outside. County jail shuttle. Cole shut Bino inside the room with a soft click, then waited outside.

Buster was seated in a hard plastic chair on one side

of a long narrow table. He was studying his freckled hands as if they held the answer. The hands were folded on the table. Bino sat down across from Buster.

Without looking up, Buster said, "Something told me we shouldn't have fucked with you, man." There was a purple welt above his eye that looked fresh.

There wasn't anything for Bino to say yet, so he put his elbows on the table and hunched closer to Buster.

Buster said, "I wanta make a deal. I got something to trade."

Bino got nail clippers from his pants pocket. He opened the blade and cleaned his already spotless nails while he let that one sink in. Then he said, "You're talking to the wrong guy, pal. First of all I don't represent snitches. Killers. Baby rapers. Guys that sell secrets to Russia. But no snitches. Besides, and this is the main thing, they got me down here as a witness. And I'm not exactly in love with you, if you know what I mean. You've been doing your damndest to fuck with me, man. Naw—you want to make a deal, you need somebody that can be your lawyer. Not me."

Bino thought, And I know just the guy, guy I went to law school with. Frank Bleeder. Old Bleed 'Em and Plead 'Em.

Buster looked up. Under his thick red mustache, his upper lip curled. "I ain't no snitch; you can shove that. But there's some you can snitch on without getting the jacket for it. Like baby rapers, you can snitch on them all day long and nobody gives a shit. Now I know a little bit about law and lawyers. You can't be my lawyer on anything that's gone down about you, 'course you can't. Not the stuff that happened at your office or the stuff that happened at your pad. Not even what happened to Sonny Starr, 'cause he was your client, too. But what I got has to do with the Bigelow hit. You know, Bigelow, the congressman? You got no conflict of interest there, man. And I want you.

Without you as a go-between, nobody gets Jack Shit from me. They can give me the needle, all I care.

He meant it. One look at the way he was saying what he was saying, showed it—he meant it, but good.

Bino put the clippers up and scratched above his right eye. "How much schooling you got, Arnette?"

"It's Buster. Arnette's a fag name, don't nobody call me that. My old man moved around a lot. Guess you could say fourth grade, only I was in it three different times, three different years. Why?"

"Fourth grade." Bino shook his head. "Fourth grade, and you know more about attorney-client rules than ninety-nine percent of the lawyers I've run across. That may tell me something about what law school's worth." He folded his arms and tilted his chair. "Buster, is it? Okay, Buster, I'm all ears. I'm not committing myself, but starting now anything you tell me is privileged. And that goes even if I don't represent you. Oh, and Buster. A lot of lawyers give you a lot of bullshit about privileged info, then run down the street and spill everything you tell them to the first somebody that'll buy them a beer. Not me. Whatever you tell me stays right here."

Buster grinned a mean-looking grin. "I got that figured out, man. That's why I want you."

For the next half hour, Buster talked and Bino listened, Buster studying his hands for part of the time, scratching his belly occasionally, smoothing his read beard and mustache every once in a while, his jaw working nonstop. Bino sat with his arms folded, not moving. Occasionally Bino would raise a white eyebrow.

Bino interrupted twice. Once when Buster told about the parole board woman, Bino asked her name. Buster didn't know. Bino let that pass; finding out who sat on Buster's panel would be a snap. There was only one woman, two men.

The other time Bino cut in was when Buster said he'd met with "Winston B. Anspacher" in a Houston office.

Bino said, "Winnie Anspacher?"

Buster said, "Winston. Winnie, shit, I guess it could be. Why? You know him?"

Bino didn't answer, told Buster to go ahead with his story.

Finally, Buster said, "So that's it. I got to tell you, man, there's another guy somewhere. Bigger guy. This Anspacher's a pansy. He didn't think all this shit up, not on his own. The big guy I can't give you, 'cause I don't know."

Bino shrugged. "I think I may know who it is. Like you say, Anspacher's a pansy. Put a little heat on, he'll give the other guy up."

"No question. So what do you think?"

Bino's right leg was going to sleep. He stood, bending and rubbing his knee, looking thoughtful. "Well, you ain't getting out of jail, Buster. You can forget that. You'll do life. But with what you've given me I think I might save your ass from the death penalty. You ain't going anywhere before Monday. Let me think this over."

He got up and went to the door, ready to knock for Cole to let him out. He had a thought and turned. "Look, Buster. You got any bread?"

Buster said, "Huh?"

"Bread, man. Green stuff. I get a fee for this kind of shit."

"Yeah, well I figured you would. I had a sackful of it when I got busted."

Bino shook his head. "No good. The law will have that. What about at the place you were living?"

Buster leaned back and scratched his head. "Potful. It's in a footlocker in my bedroom, if the Feds ain't been there."

"They haven't. It's going to cost you a grand up front. You got an apartment key in your jail property that you can sign over to me?"

Buster grinned. "Naw, man. It's unlocked, always has been. Wouldn't nobody rob me and John-boy."

Marvin Goldman probably stood in front of a mirror and practiced looking disgusted. At least every time Bino saw him, Goldman looked that way. Bino tried to remember seeing Goldman when the U.S. prosecutor had looked pleasant. He couldn't.

Mac Strange, on the other hand, was a pretty happy guy when he didn't have a problem. He'd even been known to join Bino and hoist a few cool ones at Joe Miller's from time to time. With a few beers in him, Strange was a pretty funny guy. But right now he had a problem. So instead of being happy or a funny guy, Strange looked disgusted, like Goldman.

Strange said, "Hell you are. Representing *who*?"

Bino was standing in front of Goldman and Strange, who along with Karen were seated in a semicircle. Bino thrust his hands in his pockets and said, "You heard me, Mac. Arnette Longley. Buster Longley. He's my client."

They were in the lineup room, the stage now dark and empty. A few minutes ago Cole had cuffed Buster and led him off to take a van ride to County Jail.

Strange hunched his round shoulders. He looked up at the suspended light fixture for a few seconds, then at Bino. "Jesus Christ," said Strange. "I've seen it all. Last year I had a guy that we wanted to cop to a burglary charge tell me he'd rather plead to armed robbery. But somebody who's going to be the lawyer for a guy who busted in and tried to kill him? Naw—this I ain't seen."

Bino'd seen Karen in a lot of different moods. She smiled sweetly under those soft brown eyes. "You're crazy," she said.

Goldman tugged on his goatee as if he was trying to pull it off his face. He looked like he was about to say something, then closed his mouth.

"Well, I might be crazy," said Bino. "My client might be crazy. But that's the way it is. My client wants to make a deal."

"So what's new?" said Goldman. "I want to make a deal. Everybody wants to make a deal. But Longley? We got a guy who a gun dealer is going to I.D. as one of the guys who bought the rifle that was used in the Bigelow hit. We got the same guy in your apartment trying to blow away a federal agent with a shotgun. So what kind of deal? Jaywalking, what?"

Bino thought about sitting on the corner of a long table that stood in the center of the room behind him. He brushed his hand across the table's surface and looked at it. It was gray and grimy. He dusted his palms lightly as he faced the group again.

"For the right plea bargain agreement," said Bino, "my client is willing to testify against the guy who paid him and the two others to shoot Richard Bigelow. And throw in a couple of state prison officials to boot. Without my client's cooperation, you're never going to make a case against anybody but him. And I'm not even sure you can do that. The case against Buster is pretty skimpy, the way I see it. At least on the Bigelow murder."

Goldman sat up a little straighter. Karen uncrossed her legs and put both feet on the floor, shapely nyloned calves side by side.

Strange rested his forearms on his thighs and put his fingertips together. He said, "The Bigelow assassination is one the Feds have got. They've told us to back off of it and so far we have. I'm talking a supermarket robbery and shooting a cop. Kidnapping maybe, on grabbing the woman in the store. And felony with a firearm. Adds up to a lot of time with this boy's record. If the Feds'll give us a go-ahead to prosecute on the Bigelow thing, we're talking murder for hire. Death penalty." He swiveled his head to look at Goldman. "What about it, Marv? We got anything to talk to Bino about, the two of us?"

"We might," said Goldman. His gaze flicked from Strange to Bino, his pupils hidden from Bino's view by knitted eyebrows. "Who paid your boy, Bino?"

Bino shook his head. "Not without a deal, Marv. No way. But I don't think you can pin a thing on Buster Longley without his help. The break-in at my office and killing the—the little elevator operator, I don't think the cops turned up any prints on that, not a shred."

Goldman said, "Let's think on it, Mac." Then, to Bino, "We'll let you know. Monday, huh?"

Bino stopped off on the way home. The money was in a footlocker in the bedroom, right where Buster had said it would be.

Bino woke up on Saturday morning, remembered where his money was riding, and decided to go to Texas Stadium. There he'd sit in an ocean of red and blue, sing alma maters and fight songs played by the best-dressed band in the land, and blow raspberries and give the finger to a sea of orange and white across the way. He was fired up and ready to go. He took Barney Dalton.

Barney said, "It still doesn't seem right, Bino. I mean, time passes and all. But the Cotton Bowl had real class. Ghosts of the Doaker and Dandy Don Meredith along the sideline. Ben A. Matthews on the P.A. system. Kern Tips in the radio booth. This Texas Stadium is too glitzy. A pile of glass, fancy skyboxes, and computerized scoreboards. Hell, the Cotton Bowl had class even when they had to keep time on the sideline when the clock broke down." He took an expansive drag from the fat cigar he was smoking. The Linc's passenger window was cracked open, and the smoke was whipped into rapid circles and yanked outside by the car-generated wind.

Bino had his right foot on the accelerator and his left on the brake, speeding up and stopping quick in the thickening traffic on westbound Highway 183. Texas Stadium's semidomed roof loomed over the Linc's nose, the mammoth structure growing steadily larger on the horizon. Elvis was playing low volume on the stereo. "Suspicious Minds."

Bino said, "You're living in the past, Barn. The Cotton Bowl had its day. So did the Stanley Steamer. You want to ride in one? I'll give you class. The last time I went to a game in the Cotton Bowl was at night. Lessee, the Rice game, I think, seventy-nine or eighty. I had a date with me, Bonnie Miles. You know, used to hostess at Cattlemen's Steak House. Now on the way to the car after the game I get hit on by three different hookers. Right in front of my date. And that's not all. Just as we're getting into the car a guy hollers at me. It's one of my *clients*, for Christ's sake. I'll tell you, Barney. When my clients start hanging out around a place, all of the class is long gone."

"You got a point," said Barney.

Yesterday's rain had gone, and the hood of the Linc shone stark white in the noonday glare. A Monte Carlo loaded down with coeds crept by, pennants waving and red and blue streamers trailing in the breeze. The girls made Bino feel good, and he tooted the horn at them. They smiled pretty smiles and waved.

They parked in the stadium lot, gravel crunching under the tires, got out, and joined the mobs streaming in through the gates. Guys in orange shirts and white string ties made the "Hook 'Em, Horns" sign at one another; a few of them were already loaded and a lot of them getting that way.

Just before they went through the wire-fenced gate into the stadium, Bino put a hand on Barney's shoulder and stopped him. Bino looked up and to his left, where lines of fancy ten-gallon hats and high-priced dresses were on display on people riding escalators to the Circle Suites.

"What is it?" Barney was in a red windbreaker and navy slacks, his thick sandy hair parted on the left and his mustache combed neat. He was three inches shorter than Bino.

Bino'd worn a powder blue western-style sport coat, designer jeans, and tan Dingo boots. The bootheels raised him a couple of inches more over Barney. He said, "Just eyeballing the rich, Barn. Doesn't Winnie Anspacher's law firm have one of those skyboxes?"

"Probably. Everybody else in town's got more money than sense has one. Why not Anspacher? Come to think of it, I'm pretty sure he does. I know somebody sat with him in it once, at a Cowboy game. Why?"

"Aw, nothing," said Bino. "Look, Barn, I may leave you at half time and go visiting. I just remembered I got to see Winnie for a minute."

They matched for hot links. Barney called even. Both coins came up heads, and Bino got in the concession line, bitching about it. He was behind a man with thinning hair who was wearing a tan sport coat and a chubby freckled kid of about ten. Bino bent his elbows, stuffed his hands in his jeans pockets, smelled the franks cooking, and watched the ladies go by.

When Bino was next in line, the freckled kid said in a penny-whistle voice, "Can I have an ice cream?"

The man had piled wrapped hot dogs on a cardboard tray and was putting paper cups full of Pepsi in round slots on the tray's corners. His sport coat had dark brown patches at the elbows. "Let me tell you, Danny. For what I just spent for three hot dogs and three Pepsis I can take your mother out to the Old Warsaw with chocolate mousse for dessert. No ice cream. It'll bankrupt us." He left carrying the tray, the kid following behind him and looking ready to bawl. Bino'd been holding a five-dollar bill. He fished in his pocket and added another five before stepping up to the counter.

Bino was munching on his first full bite, tasting the tartness of the mustard and the tangy sweetness of the pickle relish, and washing the link down with Pepsi, as he took long strides up a concrete ramp that led to the vast openness of the stadium and started down the aisle toward his seat, elbowing his way through congregations of people. Barney was hustling along behind him.

Far away and below on the green Astroturf floor, musicians in red blazers and navy slacks were in snappy formation, a monstrous block *S* with a smaller *U* and *A* before and after it. Light glinted from big gold tubas. A conductor on a stepladder waved a baton. Long-limbed majorettes struck a one-leg-straight, one-knee-bent pose, forearms straight across in front of their chests, each with a shiny baton in one hand pointing down toward the ground. In the stands, a packed crowd, close to sixty thousand strong, was on its feet. The band struck up the national anthem.

The opening bars filled the arena clear to the rectangular opening in the semidomed roof as Bino hustled down the aisle, Pepsi sloshing. A slickly groomed woman was standing in front of an aisle seat, her right hand lightly touching the red-and-blue streamered mum that was pinned to the left breast of her tailored navy suit. She turned her head and hissed at Bino as he went by. He halted in his tracks and stood at attention. Barney collided with him from the rear. Bino's Pepsi hit the cement steps, cup rattling and liquid splattering.

Their seats were low, seventeen rows from the bottom. By the time they'd reached them it was time to stand again. The band had broken formation and double-timed it to one end of the stadium, forming a double row that extended from both sides of an opening in the wall underneath the stands. Big athletes in red-and-blue uniforms with white numerals on the chest and back charged pell-mell between the lines of musicians, who were now playing a jazzed-up version of "She'll Be Comin' Round the Mountain." Cheerleaders in red-and-blue thigh-length skirts turned flying somersaults, showing navy panties. A black Shetland pony dragged two handlers, who were holding on to ropes for their lives, behind him on either flank as he charged across the striped green field with nostrils flaring.

On Bino's right, Barney yelled, "Go, Ponies. Attaway, bunch—go, you hosses!"

Across the way the orange-and-white team charged on to bump shoulders and high-five it around the opposing bench, a massive roar erupting from the visitors' section and an orange-and-white band blasting "Texas Fight."

Now Barney hollered, "Fuck 'em. Fuck them Steers! Go, Ponies!" He was jumping up and down and waving his arms.

Bino said, "Where's Dupard, Barn?"

"Fuck 'em! Fuck them—Huh? What's that?"

Bino pointed at the red-and-blue team as they huddled. "Dupard, Barney. He's number twenty-one. Ain't no number twenty-one down there."

Barney squinted and looked closer. "Naw. Gotta be. Coach Smith told me—Oh, my God. Jesus Christ, Bino, look down there. Jesus." He pointed toward the team's entry ramp with one hand and clamped the heel of the other on his forehead.

Dupard came onto the field, ebony features in a grimace. He was in a red pullover and jeans. He was hobbling on crutches, a cast on his right foot.

Bino said, "Is that a gallop? I mean, is that what you call a full fucking gallop? Jesus Christ, Barney."

Barney cupped his hands in front of his mouth in the direction of the S.M.U. bench. "Hey, Smith.

Asshole! Is that a gallop? I'm giving you two strokes a side and you gotta do this to me?"

In front of them, people turned in their seats and glared in Barney's direction.

One time Dante Tirelli knew this guy with the tall white-haired lawyer Bino Phillips. Knew him in the City, Eatin' Eaton, dealt a few craps and had the one Family's Zigonnet box for a game three times a year plus did a little running for a horse book out on the Island. What the fuck was Eatin' Eaton doing with Bino Phillips?

Jesus, can't be right. Eatin' Eaton, shit, he'd be near seventy by now. Must be these damn binoculars of Winnie's, outta focus. Keep looking. Round outlines merged together, Bino Phillips's white head a few inches above the other guy's, sometimes somebody or other going up and down the aisle and getting in the way, looking big as hell. Tirelli's index finger turned the knob on top of the binoculars, bringing things into sharp focus. Shit, that ain't no Eatin' Eaton. But Jesus, spitting image. Same hair, mustache—Eatin' Eaton was here, he'd think he was in a fucking time machine looking at himself.

At Tirelli's elbow, Morrissey Mortarhouse giggled like Petunia Pig. Up close she smelled like almond brandy. She said, "Come on now, Dante. Naughty, naughty, looking at all those young cheerleaders. My turn now, gimme peek."

Tirelli thought, The fuck, naughty, naughty. He turned to her, her monster boobs heaving against the front of a blue suit, hips bulging wide, belt cinched with rolls of fat spilling over. Jesus, Annabelle lets herself go like that I'll tie her to a stake in the yard, let her graze and think about it.

He smiled and held out the binoculars. "Yeah, those college girls're cute, okay. Want to have a look,

Morrissey?" She took them in chubby hands, burped, and trained them in the band's direction, the field spread out below the Anspacher, Anspacher, and Mortarhouse Circle Suite like a smooth green pool table for jolly giants.

Morrissey said, "Whee, what fun. Things sure have changed since mine and Annabelle's day. If Daddy had ever seen me in a skirt like that he'd have tanned my behind good and proper."

Tirelli glanced at her ample backside, thinking, Hell he'd ought to, ass like that.

He said, "Look all you want to, Morrissey. I've gotta go see Winnie about something. 'Scuse me."

Winnie was on the top level of the Circle Suite in a green Ultrasuede coat and pale green golf shirt, holding a beer and grinning behind his glasses, first at Annabelle on his left and then at Ted Mortarhouse on his right. Mortarhouse was a beanpole with sagging cords in his throat. Mortarhouse's old man was partners with Winnie's old man. Grandpas before that.

Tirelli edged around Sarah Anspacher, who was seated in a cushioned swivel chair and looking at the bands and cheerleaders on the giant-screen closed circuit. She twisted and tucked a swinging high-heeled foot to let him by, smiling in a bored way.

He climbed the three carpeted levels, past the stocked refrigerators and wet bar, thinking, What a waste of fucking money. This kinda dough, you get a bank of T.V.'s with four, five games at once and a hotline to every bookmaker in every town what's having a game. He passed a row of swivel chairs where Art Stammer was talking up votes to a couple of guys, his jaw still puffy. Jesus, Bino Phillips, he can hit. Maybe we shouldda backed him and not this Stammer bozo.

Winnie Anspacher is sure the wrong guy to get mixed up with. Nothing but a wimp. Standing up there looking back and forth and grinning like it was his birthday. Not a word from Winnie this morning about why after I told him to get rid of these two lunatics, get them the hell outta town, one of them is all over the radio and T.V. being in the county jail for trying to pull a stupid holdup. Jesus. And what about the other guy, the one Winnie said was one of these killing machines with ice water in his veins? Not a word about his ass. Probably to top everything else, now the other guy'd wind up busted for hanging around in front of the mayor's house with a Molotov cocktail. Something like that.

Winnie saw Tirelli coming and grinned, with his round eyes magnified by those thick glasses of his. Winnie's bald head showed a crease across the top of his skull. He was grinning and saying, "Your wife is quite a lady, Dan. She's got Ted and me hypnotized here." He shoved his beer in Annabelle's direction like a toast.

Mortarhouse's loose throat skin wiggled as he said, "Sure is, Dan. You really cornered yourself a jewel here." Annabelle looked pleased with herself.

Tirelli put an arm around Annabelle and squeezed her shoulder as he said, "Yeah. Well, you don't see me complaining, huh? Say listen, babe"—he smiled at Annabelle through his tinted wire-frames, his pink alpaca sweater billowing at the sleeves—"you mind keeping company with Ted? I need to see Winnie about the state thing. You know, the liquor taxes down at the restaurant."

Annabelle got the drift. She was wearing a gray wool suit and white blouse. Classy. Frosted curls springing. A shy smile. "Sure, dear. Ted, I hope you won't mind being stuck with me for a bit." She took Mortarhouse by his skinny arm and led him away.

Winnie sat down in a leather chair by a little mahogany gin table. His knees were bent, his toes barely on the floor. "You want to have a chat, Dan?" His eyes were wide and innocent.

Tirelli flopped down across from Winnie. He leaned forward and propped his chin on a cupped hand, elbow on his knee. He said, "Yeah, I want to have a chat, Winnie. A fucking chat about why one of your loonies is in jail for sticking up a grocery store. And what we're gonna do about it. I thought I told you to get rid of those two assholes, Winnie."

"I can explain that, Dan. Or rather I can't really explain it but I'm going to try." He set his beer on the table and looked like one of Tirelli's bartenders about to lie about why the cash register is short. "I told them, you see. Just like you said, Dan. They should have been gone. I'm as surprised as you are." He tried to look surprised, but didn't make it.

A monster roar came from outside the skybox. The announcer was saying that Rhoden had brought the kickoff back to the Mustang twenty-two. At the front of the box, Morrissey Mortarhouse was squealing and clapping her hands.

Tirelli said, "I've been thinking, Winnie. How long you think it'll be until this guy figures out he can give you up, Winnie? Save his ass. He probably figured it out on the ride downtown."

Winnie took his glasses off and rubbed his eyes. "Oh, Dan, I can't tell you how much I'd give not to be mixed up in this." He was about to cry.

"Too late for that shit, Winnie. You're mixed up in it plenty. Now we're going to make a plan, us two. I don't know what. But I'm telling you one fucking thing, Winnie, so you'll understand. I don't give a shit what this punk does, you ain't giving up no Dante Tirelli to no law. You better get that good and straight, Winnie. You want to keep walking around, you get that."

* * *

Barney said, "You can't ever tell, Bino. Remember one time the Colts had to do without Johnny U.? He got hurt. They had this garbage-can halfback name of Matte that they stuck in there at quarterback, damn near took 'em to the Super Bowl."

At that instant Dupard's replacement carried into left tackle. Five or six orange-shirts attacked him and nearly cut him in half. The ball squirted into the air and did a crazy end-over-end dance in the direction of the S.M.U. goal. A jubilant Texas player captured it just outside the ten-yard line and charged to his bench waving the ball over his head. His teammates tried to suffocate him, pounding and hugging. The crowd stood and yelled. Barney and Bino had to get up to see.

When the noise died down, Bino said, "The only place we're being taken is to the cleaners, Barney." He looked behind him, past rows of people standing up. Past a gentle elevation of faces, each row a little higher than the one in front of it. Mostly a sea, but some of the faces stood out. A woman in a flaming red pantsuit that she was too fat to wear, too much heavy makeup making a thick crimson slash of her mouth, and the puffiness under her eyes making them look nearly closed. A stocky man in a brown suit with a nasty scar on his neck. The man putting a voice box against his throat and saying something. Most of the faces watching the game. Past all the faces to the row of picture-window openings that were the Circle Suites. He wondered which one was Winnie Anspacher's. People in those suites looking down and seeming to be a lot more comfortable than the people in the grandstands. A woman with straight black hair to her shoulders leaning forward from the waist in a theater seat and raising a champagne glass to her lips. A man standing behind her with one hand gently on her throat and a champagne glass in his other hand. The man was visible only to his shoulders; the rest of him was hidden in the shadows. As Bino watched, the woman reached up and gave the man's hand on her throat a little squeeze.

Barney yelled, "Two minutes, gang. Two minutes till halftime. Hold 'em." His voice carried up to Bino from around Bino's knees. Bino realized that Barney and the rest of the crowd had sat down and Bino was standing alone. As he realized this, his gaze met the stare of a bearded guy two rows behind him. The guy frowned and said, "Down in front, huh?" Bino mumbled "Excuse me" and sat down.

To Barney he said, "Say, Barn, you ever been up to the fancy Circle Suites?"

"Huh? Have I—" Barney half-stood, grimaced, and sank back down into his chair. "Jesus Christ. Would you look at that? What can you say?" He was looking at the playing field like a man about to throw up.

Bino looked over the heads of red-and-blue players along the sidelines with hands on hips and coaches with earphones strapped on. One coach in a red sweater and navy slacks had his hand on a tiny mike that was suspended in front of his mouth, his jaw working. Past this row of players and coaches, a referee in white was grabbing a jersey here, an arm there, pulling orange men and red-and-blue men off of a pileup. The referee was sighting down the white line to the marker, turning to the goal line, waving first down. The official spotted the ball a foot or so from the S.M.U. goal. Players were on defense in three- and four-point stances digging in while the orange team huddled. Linebackers were jumping around, crouching, then moving again.

Bino said, "You think I can get in up there if I tell them I know Winnie?"

On the field S.M.U. called a time-out. Players sat down in the end zone and stared at each other.

Barney said, "No way. But wait a minute. Yeah, I know a guy. Forty-five seconds it'll be halftime, we'll both go. There's a guy used to work in the locker room at school. He remembered me from basketball the one time I was up there in the suites. Bound to know you. Yeah, we'll go see him."

Now this particular guy Bino remembered. The hair had thinned and grayed and the pants were a few sizes bigger around. But the shining eyes and the ear-to-ear grin were the same. Sure, Tony. Ptomaine Tony, used to guard the dressing-room door and keep out the gawkers and the reporters who weren't writing good things about the coach. Tony knew them all by sight.

"Bino, big man. Howsa boy? Come on, how's my all-time favorite?" Ptomaine Tony pumped Bino's hand like he was drawing water from a well. The words had a familiar ring. Bino remembered Tony outside the dressing room years ago, Tony shaking hands with an old grad who'd come by. Tony asking the guy, "How's my all-time favorite?" At the time Bino'd thought the old grad looked pretty washed up. Now Bino was the old grad.

Bino said, "Great, Tony. Barney told me he'd seen you working up here. Come to think about it, though, things could be a lot better, if the football team was doing a little more."

Tony waved his hand in the air. "Ten–zip? What's ten–zip? We'll get 'em back. Huh, Barney? Tell this character, Barn." Tony hadn't changed. His veins still had red-and-blue ink running in them.

Barney had both hands shoved deep in his windbreaker pockets. He shrugged. "We're pulling hard for 'em, Tony, Bino and me. Believe me. You don't know how hard we're pulling."

Bino and Barney had just come off the up-escalator and were at the turnstile entrance to the Circle Suites. Ptomaine Tony was in a gray Texas Stadium employee's uniform, watching the turnstile. As they talked, people would edge past Bino, show Tony a pass, and go on in. There was a long carpeted corridor behind Tony, acoustical tile on the ceiling and both walls. The corridor led to the suites.

Tony said, "You know, this is a small world, Bino. Who comes through the gates this morning but your old flame? Pretty as ever."

Bino's eyebrows raised. "Old flame? Tony, you mean Annabelle?"

Tony snapped chubby fingers. "Annabelle. Sure. I had to fake it, Bino. For the life of me I couldn't remember her name."

"Was she with a guy?" asked Bino. "About fifty, six feet or so, curly gray hair, glasses?"

"I'm paid to know 'em all, Bino. Sure, that's him, Dante Tirelli. And Mr. Anspacher. You know, Winston Anspacher? Lawyer. You might have gone to school with him, Bino. There was a big group of 'em, Mr. Stammer, the politi—" He stopped in midsentence, something dawning on him. Then he said, "Oh. I read it in the paper, Bino. Stammer is the guy you took a poke at the other night. Probably served him right. Between you and me, Bino, I don't like the guy."

Barney said, "Yeah. Anyway, Tony, what I was wondering was if maybe we might get in for a little bit to see—" Bino had nudged him. He stopped in midsentence and looked questioningly in Bino's direction.

Bino thought, No way. Not with Annabelle up there. And Stammer. And particularly not with Dante Tirelli around.

He said, "What Barney was going to say is that we need to see Winnie Anspacher. It's funny you should mention seeing Winnie, Tony. He's the very guy we came up here to find. I've got some business with him, and I wanted to get into his Circle Suite. But—well, you probably don't remember this, Tony, but that girl

Annabelle and I got married one time. And, well, it's sort of painful and—"

Tony's eyes softened, and he reached over the turnstile and gave Bino's elbow a little squeeze. "Hey, Bino, I got it. I got an ex-missus myself. Don't worry about it, huh?"

"Thanks, Tony," said Bino. "I still need to see him, but—gosh, I hate to ask this, is there maybe a little room around here, like for meetings?" Past Tony and down the long corridor there were a few closed doors in the walls. "And maybe without causing a bunch of commotion, could you maybe go and get Mr. Anspacher, tell him there's somebody out here needs to talk to him? Without saying who it is?"

Tony's round cheeks puckered in a frown. "Yeah, there's a room. Little office down there." He pointed behind him, down the corridor. "These big shots use it from time to time. And I could stretch a point, let you use the room as long as nobody gets wise to it." He stopped, nodded, and smiled to a well-dressed man and woman who nudged their way between Barney and Bino, showed Tony a pass, and went through the turnstile. Tony went on. "But I can't walk off from my post. I mean, it'd be my ass, Bino, if nobody's watching the turnstile."

Bino scratched his jaw as he thought that one over. Then, his eyes lighting up, he said, "Look, Tony, that jacket you're wearing. What size is it?" He looked Tony over, visually measuring his shoulder width, then did the same to Barney.

The office was postage-stamp size, maybe ten by ten. Bino sat down behind a half-moon–shaped desk of blond wood and wondered what kind of deals were made in here. "Yore driller's fulla shit, Bobby Joe. We can put the well in fer four hunnerd K, tops." Or maybe, "Yeah, we're gonna merge. Made the deal this month at the directors' meetin'. Buy all the Turd-O stock you can get. Oh, and while you're at it, slide me in a coupla thousand shares."

A small low cabinet with accordion doors in the front sat against the wall opposite the desk. Bino supposed that glasses were inside, along with bottles of Chivas and Jack Daniel's Black. On the other side of the corridor door from the cabinet was a small brown leather couch.

A table model color T.V. was on top of the cabinet, closed-circuit picture on, volume off. Bino lit a filtered Camel, leaned back, and watched S.M.U. take the second half kickoff and get going. A razor-sharp quarterback used stinging short passes to move to the Texas twenty-five. A longer toss found a receiver at the Texas ten, who took two steps toward the end zone before an orange-jerseyed player leveled him. The ball rolled free and Texas recovered. Bino's stomach churned.

The door opened. Winnie Anspacher took two steps inside the office and froze. Bino caught a glimpse of Ptomaine Tony's round outline as the door closed, leaving Bino and Winnie alone.

Winnie hadn't grown any. In his green Ultrasuede coat and pale green golf shirt he looked like a small parrot.

Winnie sputtered through pudgy lips. He said, "I've got nothing to say to you. I told you the other night you'd be hearing from our lawyer. Now if you'll excuse me I'll just—"

"I want to talk about Richard Bigelow. And Buster Longley," said Bino. He was snuffing out his cigarette in a black plastic ashtray.

It was as though someone had punched Winnie in the solar plexus. His features froze for an instant, then relaxed, air coming out of his lungs in a long sigh.

Without another word Winnie sank down on the leather couch.

He seemed to be deep in thought for a few seconds. When he finally opened his mouth to speak, Bino was pretty sure that Winnie was going to lie. He could tell from Winnie's expression.

Winnie said, "The Bigelow murder? My, yes, that was a terrible, terrible tragedy. One of the worst things that has happened in our lifetimes, Bino. And—I'm sorry, Bino, but the other name that you used escapes me. What was it? Buster who?" He blinked through thick lenses.

Bino thought, Not bad. Part of the education, growing up in Winnie Anspacher's circles. Standard curriculum. Ruthlessness 101. Lying 201.

Bino leaned back and folded his arms as he said, "I'm going to tell you a little story, Winnie. A lot of it you're not going to understand. I grew up simple, a lot like Richard Bigelow did. Folks out in Mesquite don't understand how you're supposed to do things. They think that when you tell somebody you're in favor of getting tough on criminals, that's what you're supposed to mean, not that you might go easier on criminals if going easier on them means getting more votes in the door. Now I defend a lot of bad guys, and I'm not very proud of my clients or the way I go about defending them sometimes. But one principle, if you want to call it a principle, that I've always had is that I don't represent snitches. Snitches are just as guilty as anybody, but they get off just because they go and be stool pigeons. Very despicable guys, Winnie. Not as despicable as the law enforcement agencies that operate through snitches, but still real dirty fellows."

Bino checked. Nothing yet. Winnie's jaw still had the droop it had had when he'd first sat down, but otherwise he was expressionless, just an occasional blink. Bino went on.

"And Buster Longley is a guy that I hate a lot more than I do the run-of-the-mill snitch. I mean, I'm human, Winnie. I got feelings. First Longley and a couple of other maggots killed a fine old man. And if it wasn't for this fine old man who's dead now, I'd have never gotten to practice law on my own. Then he tears up my office, him and another punk, not to mention raping and killing a sweet little eighteen-year-old girl in the process. Eighteen, Winnie, just starting to live. And then you know what? Buster Longley tries to kill me. Probably was going to torture me a little, maybe get some information. Which I didn't even have, Winnie. That surprise you? If I'd known Sonny Starr was in on the Bigelow thing, I'd never have been his lawyer. No, Winnie, Buster Longley is a guy I don't like very much."

Bino caught movement in the corner of his eye and paused. On the T.V. screen, a red-and-blue player stepped in front of a sideline pass, intercepted, and high-stepped into the end zone. Bino thought, Jesus, what's going on? He looked back at Winnie.

"But suddenly I am representing Buster Longley. He asked me to and I took the case. And you know why? Buster Longley is paying me a little fee, so it will be official. But that isn't the reason I'm representing him. I'm representing him because as low a sonofabitch as he is, he's still a cut above the guy that hired him. Which is you, Winnie, you dirty little shit."

It was beginning to take hold. Winnie bent over, elbows on knees, and stared at the floor. His lower lip was beginning to quiver. Bino wasn't about to let up on him.

"You will very likely get the death penalty when my client gets through snitching on you, Winnie. At the very least you will be in jail until you're too old to care. Now, you know why I'm telling you this? Because rotten little worm that you are, without testimony from you nobody is going to get Tirelli for all of this.

"I'm leaving in about two minutes, Winnie, walking out of this room. You can go with me. I'll take you somewhere safe, get you protection. I don't know what kind of deal the Feds will make with you. It's up to them. But I know the sorry rotten bastards, and believe me they'll make a deal. Monty Hall should have been a fucking Fed. Now you can go or stay. But if you don't go out of here with me, you'll be in jail before nightfall. I guarantee you that. I'm not bullshitting you one bit, Winnie, you'll be there."

Winnie looked up slowly, like a frightened child. Tears were streaming down his cheeks. All of the pomp was gone.

His voice quavered as he said, "My—my wife, Bino. Sarah. She's in the suite. And Tirelli's in there. My God, I can't go and leave Sarah behind."

Bino felt his own face soften. He'd known Winnie Anspacher, rich, spoiled Winnie Anspacher, for over twenty years. This was the first time that Bino had ever felt sorry for him.

Class is the word, the only one, thought Bino. Class showed through. People with class didn't have to have looks, didn't need money to look classy, they just looked that way. Acted that way. It was a bearing about them, a manner of speech, a way of getting along with people. And without it—well, all the furs, diamonds, and suits that Saks Fifth Avenue could sell in a season wouldn't cover up a lack of it. Sarah Anspacher had class in spades.

She followed Ptomaine Tony down the long corridor with style, no panic in her walk but not fooling around either, putting one high-heeled shoe in front of the other in smooth graceful rhythm, her narrow shoulders back. No stoops for this tall lady; she walked like a queen. The first time that Bino'd seen her at the door to her home, he'd thought her too thin, her nose too long, her features too bony. The way she smiled wiped out all of that. She looked lovely. She was in a slender purple dress with puffed sleeves and lace at the hem. She belonged in lace.

Her eyebrows were raised in a question. "Well my goodness, Winnie," she said. "You could have invited Bino in. Art Stammer would probably hide under a chair, but I think everyone else would be glad to see him."

Bino was leaning with one hand on the outgoing turnstile, the escalator behind him sending an endless line of grooved metal steps forty-five degrees to the ground level far below. Standing next to Bino, Winnie looked even shorter than he was. Winnie's hands were in his pockets, and his head was down. As Sarah approached, Barney took off Tony's gray uniform jacket and traded it for his Crooked River windbreaker.

Winnie kept on looking at his shoes as he said, "Something's come up, dear. We—you and I, we're going to have to be leaving."

The trouble hadn't dawned on her as yet, but it was beginning to. An uncertain look crossed her face, just a flash, then it was gone. She smiled, her eyes crinkling. "Why, whatever for, Winnie? Just like that? Leaving all those vultures with the food and booze?"

There was a silence that weighed a ton. Bino shuffled his feet nervously and looked away from them, down the escalator and past its foot to the concession booths, a few short lines of people in front of them. And on past the booths to the crowded parking lot. The fall sun was going down, and the mammoth bulk of the stadium had put all but the most distant rows of cars in deep shadow. Highway 183 beyond the lot had slight traffic whizzing east and west. After the game it would be a logjam.

Winnie said, "I'm afraid it won't be safe to go back in the suite, Sarah. It—" His voice broke, and for seconds Bino was sure that Winnie was going to cry. Then Winnie stood up a little straighter, looked directly at his wife, and went on. "I'll have to tell you while we drive, dear. We have to go now, is all."

Winnie took her arm, and she hesitated for a moment before going through the turnstile with him, her short dark hair swept forward and cut in a perfect curve at the back of her neck. When they were side by side on the escalator, Winnie's bald head was on a level with her earlobe.

Bino turned to Ptomaine Tony, who was back at his station, a slight frown on his chubby face. Bino said, "Thanks a million times, Tony. We'll be seeing you soon, huh?"

Tony glanced to where the top of Sarah's groomed head was sinking from view, then looked back at Bino. "Yeah—sure, big fella," said Tony. "Don't make it a decade next time. You're my all-time favorite." Tony looked worried. Bino winked at him, gave the thumbs-up sign, and followed Barney out through the turnstile.

On the ride to ground level Barney clutched the rail, saying, "Look, Bino. I'm not asking you to tell me what's going on. I'm not going to try to find out why I've got to put on an usher suit and stand around while Texas runs off with my dough, or why the hell Winnie Anspacher is leaving with his old lady. But I am going to tell you that the score is now ten-seven. And if you try to make me miss the end of this football game, then you and me might be in Knuckle City."

As they neared the bottom of the moving staircase, a giant roar filled the air from within the stadium, vibrating the metal steps. Bino said, "Sure, Barn. Wouldn't miss it. I got to go meet Winnie after the game, but it can wait. We'll see it, see the end." As he spoke Bino watched Winnie and Sarah, far away now as they hurried into the parking lot.

Bino watched the thick hair on Barney's head bob up and down as Barney jogged up the stadium entry ramp in front of him. Bino's chest was heaving, and his breath was coming in quick gasps. Just inside the vastness of the arena, Barney stopped. Bino's chest collided lightly with the back of Barney's head as Bino put on the brakes.

Everyone in the park was standing, silent. On the field a red-and-blue player was kneeling on the Texas thirty, arms outstretched in the direction of the center's rump. Behind the holder a soccer-style kicker was taking practice leg swings.

Bino looked quickly at the scoreboard. It was still ten-seven, Texas. The clock showed one second remaining.

Barney hissed, "Jesus Christ, we got a chance. Bino, he makes it we win. We got one point." He held his hands up, fingers crossed.

Bino took a deep breath and held it.

The ball spiraled to the holder, and a low rumble started in the crowd that grew quickly into a massive din. The opposing lines thrashed at each other. The kicker took one graceful, crosslegged stride and swung his leg into the ball with an echoing thump. The kick was high, end over end.

A guy yelled, "He made it!"

Another guy said, "Wide, wide."

Bino's heart thudded.

Just in front of the goalpost the ball hooked sharp left. It banged into the upright and dribbled harmlessly in the end zone, no good. Texas players hugged each other and jumped up and down.

Barney yelled, "Choker! Jesus, Bino, why don't they hire an American to kick the fucking ball?"

* * *

Barney's car was at the pro shop. By the time they'd bumper-to-bumpered their way out of the football traffic and wound through far North Dallas to Crooked River, it was dark. As Barney went through a ring of jangly keys one by one to unlock his office, Bino gazed out on the course. The night was moonless. He could see the roller-coaster swells of the eighteenth green and the white pin and dark flag. Beyond that the mowed wideness of the fairway was made into a corridor by lines of trees on either side. The columns of trees extended into the distance and faded in the dark into nothingness.

In the office Bino sat down beside a gleaming set of Haig Ultra irons and a polished Hogan 4-wood and used the phone. Barney sat across from him, set his cigar in a hole-in-one ashtray with a lacquered golf ball affixed to its edge, and picked up a copy of *Football News.* He went over tomorrow's pro line while Bino punched buttons on the phone.

For once, Karen Allen was there.

Bino said, "I've got news for you, Karen."

"Let me guess." Her voice was slightly nasal, like she had a cold. "You've been committed. You were hallucinating that your client didn't really try to blow you away. You just—"

"I've got the guy who hired Buster in cold storage. And I think he's going to testify against the real biggie in the Bigelow case."

Silence. Then, "Where is he?"

Bino glanced at his watch. "Just about now he'll be checking into the Holiday Inn—Central."

"God, that purple monstrosity? On Central Expressway, close to the Fitzhugh exit?"

"That's it, Karen. It's sort of off the beaten path, and the guy is somebody that would be looked for at a posher address."

"Who is he?"

The receiver was sticking to Bino's ear. He switched to the other ear. "Not just yet. I've—I've promised the guy protection, and I want to talk to him before your people do. He's registering under an alias, is going to need cover round the clock. Probably three shifts, two agents each. He's going to give you somebody big, Karen. I want an hour. Then you can have him."

"Bino, you're not working for the government. You can't commit the F.B.I. to—oh, the hell with it. You've got your hour. I'll bring some backup. What name is he registered under?"

He looked at the ceiling. He didn't want to tell her. It had seemed pretty cute at the time, but now—Finally he said, "He's under the name of Bill Featherston, Karen. From Washington."

"You're a real putz, Bino," she said. "You know that?"

The Holiday Inn was on the corner of an old street and an old freeway. All three of them were outdated. Bino took the Fitzhugh Avenue exit and wheeled under the garish purple awning that stretched over the lobby entrance remembering when they'd all been new. It didn't seem that long ago.

The desk clerk was a skinny kid with jerky movements and acne that he wasn't quite old enough to shake. Without checking the register he said, "Mr. Featherston is in two thirty-one, sir. It's right at the head of the stairs."

The staircase wound in an escalating half-circle out of a wide, deserted lobby. The carpet was worn thin; light-colored backing showed through the deep purple in spots. Bino went up to the second floor thinking about a Fiji party he d attended here back when the motel lobby thrived and the first-floor disco was wall to wall. Now they didn't even have to look in the register to give you somebody's room number. Two thirty-one was two doorways from the head of the steps. Bino knocked lightly.

Sarah came to the door in the same dress she'd worn at the stadium. The look was there. Bino wasn't sure how much Winnie had told her, but it was a lot.

She faked it, smiling and doing a damn good job. "Cloak and dagger, I'll say. Come on in, Double-oh-Seven."

The room had side-by-side king-size beds, a table with a lamp by the window, and two stuffed chairs, one on either side of the table. Winnie was in one of the chairs, with his feet barely touching the floor, like a little boy's. Bino sat down on the bed nearest Winnie. Sarah took the remaining easy chair and gracefully crossed her legs.

Bino said, "I'm glad you came, Winnie. I confess I thought you might take a powder." He looked around. "No luggage? You haven't been home, eh?"

Winnie rested a pale hand on the table's surface and looked at it intently like he was studying his knuckle. He didn't look up as he said, "Run? No, Bino, I wouldn't . . ." His voice trailed off and the sound died in his throat.

Sarah said, "No, whatever comes, Winnie is going to face up to it. And no, we didn't go home. I—we thought it would be better if we came straight here. Bino, I'm going to ask you to give me a lift to the house. I'll get Winnie a few things and bring them down. I—well, I won't be staying here." She turned a steady gaze on Winnie, then shifted it in Bino's direction.

And that was that. She had taken charge, and Winnie was going to do whatever she said to do. Bino didn't doubt it for a minute.

Bino now talked to Sarah as though Winnie wasn't

even in the room. "Sure, Sarah. I'll take you. There'll be some folks from the F.B.I. here soon. I suppose we should wait for them."

She glanced at Winnie's feet, then raised her eyes slowly until she was looking her husband directly in the face. He couldn't meet her gaze. "Yes, Bino," she said, still looking at Winnie. "I suppose we should."

Sarah didn't speak to Winnie again while they waited. Then Karen Allen didn't speak to Bino when she showed up with two agents in tow. One of the agents Bino'd seen before, and it took a few minutes for the memory to snap in. It was the curly-haired guy who had been with Karen at Winnie's fund-raiser.

As Bino and Sarah were leaving, Bino heard one of the agents say to Winnie, "Well, what's for dinner, Mr. Featherston? What's going on in D.C. these days?"

Bino heard the other male agent snicker and felt Karen's eyes on him as he quickly shut the door behind him.

Sarah didn't talk much on the way to her home, just murmured a quiet, "Thank you" when Bino held the Linc's passenger door for her and made a few murmured responses when Bino tried to pass the time of day. She sat erect beside him. He watched the road, feeling her presence more than seeing her in the shadows.

He walked up the front steps with her. Porch floodlights cast the cherub's shadow over the goldfish pond, turning the water black as the night. There were no stars. The entire city was under a thick black curtain that let no light in. Sarah faced Bino when she had the front door partway open.

She said, I have a twenty-two-caliber pistol. Winnie doesn't even know—my dad gave it to me years ago. Should I take it with me?"

It surprised him. She wasn't the type to have a gun.

Bino said, "No, Sarah. He'll have plenty of protection. And believe me, those Feds won't let him out of their sight."

She started to go in the house, then paused, her head down. "You don't have kids, Bino. Until you do you won't understand this. Winnie's torn us, he and I. It's over, never can be much again. Right now I can't stand the sight of him. But Tad's sixteen, Mary twelve. They're all I can think of now. There's nothing I wouldn't do to protect them. Nothing." For the first time he detected a quiver in her voice. Then she got her composure back, looked at him with that same steady gaze. "I'll be here, once I take Winnie a few things. If you need me." The style and grace were back in full flower as she left him.

On his way home Bino thought, Winnie's too much of a creep to have that lady. Go back a lot of years, he'd like to trade Annabelle for her. Would in a heartbeat, knowing what he knew now.

Dante Tirelli drew the sash on his purple robe tight around his middle. He was naked underneath, and the robe's satin was cool against his skin. He blinked, then squinted his eyes. The hall light was burning, and the door to the bedroom was open slightly, so there was a dull illumination. He bent over until his nearsighted eyes were inches from the nightstand's surface, finally recognizing the folded earpieces of his wire-frames in the dimness. He put the glasses on. As he did, Annabelle stirred.

She was lying on her belly, and the covers made a soft rustling noise and the box springs creaked some as she scooted onto her side and hugged a pillow to her chest. One smooth white leg bent and slid, finally relaxing its taut muscles when her knee was a foot or so from her chin. About half of a pink nipple was visible at the pillow's edge. Tirelli felt another stirring in his groin and shifted his gaze away from her. Her breathing was slow and even.

Tirelli went quietly out of the bedroom and down the thickcarpeted hall thinking, What the fuck happened to that punk? Him and his old lady both disappearing like that, saying nothing to nobody. And Stammer, the silly asshole politician saying, "Winnie must have important matters at the office. Maybe some mergers going on, who knows?" Stammer trying to take over like he owned the fucking Circle Suite or something.

Jesus, but that Morrissey Mortarhouse is strong for a fat broad. A fat drunk broad. Tirelli'd tried everything, hints, jokes, all he could do, but that damn Morrissey wasn't going to give him the binoculars. So he'd finally got pissed off and yanked them away from her, the silly bitch acting like she thought it was a game or something, hanging on like the fucking binoculars were glued to her hands. Then Ted Mortarhouse, the skinny creep, bitching about Tirelli grabbing the binoculars from Ted's old lady. Then Annabelle getting into it, raising hell with Tirelli, all pissed off at him until he just gave her a good hosing a few minutes ago. God, but Annabelle was one horny woman. Always. And even with all the shit going on in the suite, Tirelli'd seen what he wanted to see through the field glasses. That whiteheaded Bino Phillips, he was gone just like Winnie. Might not mean nothing. But might mean plenty, too.

The den was pitch dark. Tirelli peered inside, trying to make out the shapes of the couch, chairs, tables, and T.V. He thought that he was seeing them but maybe he wasn't. Maybe he'd just been in this room so often that he knew right where everything was and was imagining he saw them. He groped for the wall switch and flicked the hidden overheads on, making everything in the room suddenly visible. He sat on the couch, put a beefy hand on the white Princess phone, and thought about it.

Any other way, he wouldn't do it. For years he'd stayed away from it, just like he didn't know anybody outside of Texas. Dallas was Tirelli's own thing, and that was just the way he wanted it.

But there wasn't no other way. He shook his head as he picked up the receiver, hesitated, then hung up grinning, laughing at himself. He got the phone book and flipped through the beginning pages. Jesus, it had been so long he couldn't even remember the fucking area code. Finally he had it. 212. The City. He dropped the heavy book on the end table and made the call.

They brought Buster Longley an open-faced hot roast beef sandwich on Sunday night. That's what the guard called it when he set it on the ledge of the six-by-eight-inch pan hole in Buster's cell door. The meal was in a tinfoil tray. Buster tried attacking it with the plastic knife and fork they'd given him, but he couldn't cut a dent in it. The meat was just too damn tough. Then he put the roast beef between two soggy pieces of whole wheat bread, took a bite, and spit it out. Underneath the thick, lukewarm canned gravy the meat was blood raw.

Buster thought, six of one, half a dozen of the fucking other. The Feds are gonna feed you good, give you a soft bed, and make you stay down in the pen for so long that nobody'll know you time you get out. The state's gonna let you out pretty quick, if sleeping on a stone cot with cockroaches running over you and eating spoiled raw meat don't kill you first. Buster yelled, "Fuck this shit!" to nobody in particular and slung the tray of food out the pan hole. It made a tinny, sloppy noise on the stone corridor floor. Somewhere nearby a hoarse voice shouted, "Pipe down, asshole. This ain't no Hyatt House."

The white plastic thongs on Buster's feet slapped loudly as he plodded deep into the cell's interior and sat down on the hard bunk. Big-town county jails were all alike. This Dallas County joint was a new, fancy big building on the outside—electric doors, T.V. monitors. But it was the same old shit in a lockdown cell. High ceiling that you couldn't reach, recessed light up above you covered with two-inch-thick clear plastic. Light kept burning round the clock, a little dimmer maybe from ten at night until five in the morning, but on just the same. Stainless-steel privy in one corner of the six-by-eight cell. Iron bunk welded into the wall about two feet off the concrete floor. Filthy dirty floor, no way to clean it, wouldn't even slide you a mop inside for fear you'd whack them with it. Inch-thick green plastic mattress stuffed with rags. One blanket, no pillow, no sheets. The Shits, with a capital *S*.

Buster took his feet out of the sandals and rubbed their callused bottoms. One of the thongs was too short and was digging into his bare heel when he walked on it, making the bottom of his foot raw and sore. He was in a jumpsuit that was too small for him and restricted his movements when he bent over, so he stood, took the suit off, and flopped down on the cot in dirty T-shirt and boxer skivvies.

So the man, Winston B. Anspacher, was with the Feds, huh? Buster thought about Bino Phillips's visit earlier today, the cotton-topped lawyer looking at ease in the booth—he knew his way around. Pretty smart, Bus. Sure wasn't no fuckup getting Bino Phillips for a lawyer. One cool sumbitch.

Buster'd told him, "You just make the deal, let ole Bus worry about the parole." That lifetime sentence was a lot of shit. Right now Buster was all for copping to state charges, going ahead with the hard time. Knowing the state would parole him one of these days. Fucking Feds might not ever. Yeah, ole Bus would be back on the street one day. Bet on it.

Bino Phillips was an okay dude. Buster'd wanted him to know there wasn't nothing personal about what him and John-boy were going about doing, just something had to be done. Bino Phillips just looked at him in the booth with those steady blue eyes of his, not saying anything. He hoped Bino Phillips understood, wasn't too pissed off at him.

Buster's eyelids grew heavy as he lay there thinking. Pretty soon he was asleep. Best way there was to pass the time in lockdown. Dream your way outside. Buster'd learned the trick long ago.

He was little again, him and Jimmie Bratton fishing, their bare feet in cool mud on the river's edge, cane poles stuck out over the water. Two tiny corks bobbing side by side in the green murk, sun peeking between the high trees and making flashes on the water's surface. Shit, never has been another fun pal like Jimmie Bratton. Never would be again, neither.

The water rippled, became suddenly crystal clear. The riverbank changed its shape and molded around the water, becoming a white porcelain bathtub. Big man-knees rising out of the water with wet red hair clinging to white calves. Beyond the knees a red-haired chest, flabby male breasts. Above the chest a square, red-bearded face. Crazy eyes, wild-drunken eyes, a clear, half-full gin bottle raised to the lips. The man in the tub taking a long swig, then wiping his mouth with the back of a hairy hand.

Buster's father sneered, his lip curling. "Whatcha doin' in here, you little shit? Can'tcha see I'm bathin'?" His words slurred.

Buster stood at attention, with his chubby arms straight down at his sides. His heart was thudding. "I'm hungry, Pa. Near starvin'—really." He felt his nose about to run and sniffled.

The tub water rolled and splashed as the man scrambled to his feet, the eyes now wild with rage. Thick red hair at the crotch. The gin bottle clutched tightly at his side. "I'll give you hungry. I'll teach you to fuck with me, you little—"

Buster turned and tried to run. Warm water sprayed on the back of his neck as a big hand clamped on his shoulder like a vise. His ears rang with pain as something slammed hard into the side of his head. Tears welled in his eyes, and he began to struggle. The hand was too strong. Buster twisted in its grasp as his father raised the bottle to strike again.

Light glinted from an open straight-razor's blade on the sink. The tears blurring his vision, Buster reached for it, felt the hard plastic handle in his grasp. He struck out blindly, one wild and murderous swipe fueled by terror and rage. The big hand released his shoulder.

The gin bottle crashed to the floor, glass flying, the odor of the liquor filling the room. Buster's father stared at his open hand in numb disbelief, watched the red blood spurt.

"You—you've cut me, you little bastard! You've fucking cut me."

The words faded; the picture of his father disintegrated. Buster came to dull consciousness in his cell, aware of leather-soled footsteps retreating from him. He opened his eyes.

He could feel that his right hand was stretched out behind his head. He tried to move it, couldn't, felt the tug and heard the chain rattle. Buster's right wrist was handcuffed to the head of the bunk.

The man's receding form was thin; his body cast a moving shadow in the cell's overhead light. Buster could make out the gray jail guard's uniform as the man went to the half-open cell door.

Buster said, "Hey, man, what—"

The door wheeled shut behind the guard with a resounding clang, and Buster was left alone. At the same instant something wet and warm and sticky exploded against Buster's cheek in a gush, receded, then spurted again. His left wrist was slashed to the bone.

Panic welled in his throat like bile. The blood continued to spurt in pulsating rhythm as he reached for the bracelet on his right wrist and yanked. It wouldn't budge. Blood shot onto his fingertips. He stared dumbly for seconds until it finally dawned on him that his handcuffed wrist had been cut also.

He screamed.

It was a wordless, reverberating yell, a long sound from deep in his throat that echoed down the corridor. He lay back and listened while the noise faded, then died, felt his heart thudding as though it would pound its way through his rib cage. There was no answer.

Buster screamed again. The sound was weaker this time, and the effort made him dizzy.

From down the corridor the same hoarse voice that had yelled at him earlier came to him again. "I thought I told you to pipe the fuck down, asshole."

The blood was making a splatting noise as it pumped onto the plastic mattress. Buster tried to yell, "Jesus Christ, get somebody, I'm fucking dying in here!" But he couldn't talk. Only a strangling croak came out of his mouth.

Finally a red haze filtered over Buster's eyes. He lost consciousness and dreamed the final moments of his life away, fishing with Jimmie Bratton. Mercifully, the image of his father didn't reappear.

When Bino found out that Buster Longley was dead, he spilled his coffee. It wasn't shock or grief. It was just that Dodie had set the paper cup of steaming black liquid too close to Bino's arm, so that when he tried to reach for a notepad without taking his feet off the corner of his desk, he knocked the cup over with his elbow. The coffee gathered into a dark puddle on

Bino's ruled pad and began to spill over and soak into his desk blotter.

To Mac Strange, Bino said, "Wait a minute, willya?" Then he pressed the hold button, leaving the light on the phone blinking steadily as he got up and hotfooted it into the outer office. "Kleenex, Dode. Paper towels, anything."

Dodie was in a filmy, beige-tinted blouse and dark blue skirt, her hair tied at the crown with a matching blue bandanna. She said, "You need a heavy mug, Bino. One that's anchored. This is the third time this month and . . ." She kept a running stream of chatter going as she snatched a handful of paper towels and went to Bino's desk, soaking up what she could. Bino got back on the phone.

"Let me get this straight, Mac. You're telling me that while my client was in the custody of the Dallas County Sheriff's Department, somebody went into a locked-down cell, handcuffed him to a bunk, and slashed his wrists. And nobody knows anything about it?"

After a pause Strange said, "That's about the size of it. We're investigating."

"Does Goldman know?"

"Yup. I just hung up from talking to him."

Bino said, "Let me think for a minute, Mac," then put the prosecutor on hold, pushed back from his desk, and let Dodie finish cleaning it. Her bra line was visible through the thin blouse.

Bino thought, Could be any of 'em. Tirelli. Winnie Anspacher, though that's not likely. Maybe even somebody higher up, someone whose name hadn't surfaced. Somebody with the dollars and the connects to put together a hit in a lockdown cell.

Back on the phone, Bino said, "I can testify, Mac. To what Buster told me. And Winnie Anspacher." Thinking, Winnie didn't really *tell* me anything. Just didn't deny anything.

"Well—I'll have to think about that one, Bino. The kind of case we're talking about, you know as well as I do there's going to be some top-notch defense lawyers runing around. I don't know if we could get what Longley told you into evidence or not, him being dead and nobody to back you up." There was an odd, hesitant pause in Strange's voice.

Bino rubbed his hand on the desk blotter. It was damp. "Yeah—well, you think on it, Mac. After all, we wouldn't want to go to trial without a lock if there's a chance the D.A.'s office might *lose* now, would we?" He banged the receiver into its cradle, opened his tab directory under *H*, and called the Holiday Inn.

The voice on the line probably belonged to the pimply faced kid who had been working the front desk on Saturday night. It sounded like him. "No sir. Mr. Featherston checked out last night."

Bino threw his pen down. "Can't be. Would you check that out again, please?"

"I don't have to, sir. I was on duty. Featherston is a short, bald-headed guy with glasses. He left with a lady and two gentlemen." After a short pause, "Between you and me, they looked like cops."

Bino thought, Yeah, this kid would know. A desk clerk at a motel can spot a cop a mile away. Bino thanked the kid and hung up. He made another call.

An impersonal female voice said, "F.B.I."

"Agent Karen Allen, please."

"I'm sorry, sir, Agent Allen is no longer with this office. Her cases have been transferred to—"

Bino hung up. Jesus Christ.

At first Marvin Goldman didn't want to talk to Bino at all. Finally he said, "Look, Bino. Just do yourself a favor and butt out. The lady's been transferred. You're not going to find out where. *I* don't even know where, for sure. Go away, Bino. It isn't your concern."

Bino's neck was getting warm, and he was clutching the receiver in a death grip. "What about Winnie Anspacher, Marv?"

Goldman was choosing his words like a man checking for rotten fruit as he said, "Winnie Anspacher? Why, we don't know anything about Winnie Anspacher, Bino. You want to talk to him, try his office or his home."

Bino's voice was dead cold. It was dawning on him, what was going on. "You aren't getting away with this, Goldman. So help me you're not."

"Getting away with what, Bino?" said Goldman. "Look, buddy, I'd love to visit but there's another call holding. Keep in touch, huh?" The line went dead.

Bino's pulse was racing as he redialed the county number and asked for Mac Strange. He hesitated when the switchboard operator asked who was calling. Then he shrugged, saying, "This is Bino Phillips." Might as well find out if Strange was in on it, too.

In a few minutes there was a click followed by, "Bino?" It was a harsher voice, a deeper twang. It wasn't Mac Strange.

Bino said, "Yeah?"

"This is Hardy Cole," the voice said. "Listen, Mac's tied up right now, Bino. Something I can do for you?"

"You know fucking well what you bastards can do for me, Hardy. Let's cut through the bullshit. Are you gonna make a case against Winnie Anspacher and Tirelli, or aren't you?"

The investigator left the line for a moment, and Bino pictured whispered questions to Mac Strange, the chubby county prosecutor sitting within arm's reach of the phone. Then Cole said, "Bino, you know where the Hidden Door is? Bar right off of Lemmon Avenue, opens at eight in the morning?" He chuckled. "Some drunks don't know what time it is."

The place was only a few blocks from Joe Miller's. Bino said, "I know the spot, Hardy."

"Yeah. Well, look, Bino, meet me there in an hour. I got some things to go over with you."

There's nothing quite like the sound and smell of a bar that opens its doors at eight o'clock in the morning. In the Hidden Door the odor wasn't quite a stink. It was stale beer mixed with stale smoke in a solvent of stale air. The sound was a faint tingling buzz, a mixture of vibration from the beer-cooler motor and noise from a humming electric sign. The sign was hanging from a brass chain over the bar top; it consisted of a lighted rotating disk inside a clear plastic ball. One side of the disk contained the script Schlitz logo. On the opposite face was a scene of a too-handsome guy and a too-pretty blond grinning into each other's eyes with a gorgeous blue waterfall in the background, its base flecked with white foam. The couple looked like they were having a lot more fun than Bino was having right now.

A cloud cover had moved in, so it didn't take long for Bino's vision to get accustomed to the dimness of the Hidden Door's interior. The place was a couple of blocks from the busy traffic on Lemmon Avenue and sat across the street from some redbrick apartments that had seen a lot better days. Most of the residents were retird, and Bino guessed that he was now looking at three of them, seated at the bar. There were two women and a man, all in their fifties or sixties, completely gray or getting that way fast. They kept each other company with a bottle of beer and a glass in front of each of them, taking occasional sips and watching themselves in the mirror that ran the length of the back wall. None of the three glanced in Bino's direction when he came in. He found an empty table near the back and next to the silent jukebox, where he could watch the entryway. He thought about playing the juke but changed his mind. The other customers didn't look as though they liked music.

A waitress came from behind the bar, wiping her hands with a damp towel. She had straight hair that looked jet black in the dimness and hung to her waist in a single braid, and her trim figure did a pretty good job of filling green slacks and a white long-sleeved sweater. As she came closer Bino thought the darkness was probably kind to her; she was a lot older than she looked at a distance.

She said, "Help ya?"

"I don't guess you serve Perrier in here."

"Nope. We got two locals, Lone Star and Pearl, Schlitz in a bottle, and Bud on tap." She was chewing gum, her lower jaw working in slow rhythm.

Bino said, "Perrier's—skip it. I'll have plain soda, twist of lime. I'm waiting for a guy."

She didn't have anything to say to that, just shrugged and brought a glass of ice and a bottle of Canada Dry. A slice of lime was impaled on the glass's edge.

Hardy Cole walked into the Hidden Door and blinked and looked around just as Bino was letting the fizz subside in his drink. Bino watched him and didn't say anything, figuring it would take about fifteen seconds for Hardy to get used to the dark and see him. It was more like twenty seconds. Hardy recognized Bino, raised a hand in greeting, and sauntered over to join him.

Bino really didn't have any reason not to like Hardy Cole, nor to like him. The county investigator was thin, close to frail, but he talked tough as a boot and Bino suspected that Hardy could take care of himself. He was pretty sure that Hardy felt the same way about Bino. As a cop Hardy had been around and knew the ropes. If the case was a biggie, suspect with money, Hardy toed the line with searches and warrants. But like all cops Bino knew, if the defendant was a broke living in the ghetto, Hardy would kick in the door and worry about the warrant later. Bino didn't know of any payoffs that Hardy was taking, which meant that if he was taking payoffs he was careful about it.

When the waitress came, Bino said, "Don't ask for Perrier, Hardy." Hardy looked puzzled and got a draft beer. The cop was in brown slacks, tweed coat, light shirt, and dark tie.

Hardy took a sip, set the glass down, and smacked his lips. "I ain't wired, Bino. This meeting, I should worry about you being wired, not the other way around." He glanced toward the bar. The three customers were still occupied by the mirror.

Bino shrugged, not saying anything. He thought, Helluva way to go through life, wondering if everybody you talk to is wired or not and never knowing if your case will get shot down by somebody playing a tape that shows a certain conversation didn't go exactly the way you'd just testified that it did.

Hardy bent his thin, angular head over the table as he went on. " 'Course I'm going to tell you up-front that it doesn't make any difference if you're wired or not, Bino. There's nothing I'm gonna say to you that I got firsthand—it's all something somebody else told me. You see?"

Bino did. As long as Hardy gave only secondhand info, Bino's testimony about what Hardy told him wouldn't be admissible in court. Which explained why Mac Strange wasn't here.

"Yeah, I see," said Bino. "Anything you tell me's hearsay. So what do you want, Hardy?"

Hardy frowned, looked thoughtful, and took another pull from his draft, like a guy with a load on his chest that he wasn't quite sure how to get rid of. Finally he said, "I'm not going to give you the standard bullshit, Bino. Mac wanted me to, but I ain't. I'm supposed to tell you that without Longley we got no case. But that's not true, and if I try to tell you that, you'll know better." He looked expectant, like he was waiting for Bino to say something. Over Hardy's left shoulder, the bar sign was revolving to show the guy, the girl, and the waterfall.

Bino wasn't sure what this was supposed to be his cue to say, but if Hardy thought that Bino was going to act grateful for being told the truth, the county investigator was sadly mistaken. Bino blinked his eyes once or twice, not changing expression. He said, "Okay. So I'd know if you fed me a line of shit. That still doesn't tell me what you want."

The bluntness surprised Hardy, Bino could tell. Hardy shifted in his chair and squared his shoulders before saying, "Well, the bottom line is that the Bigelow case is over. The official word to the press is going to be that Longley confessed that he and the other two punks did the killing, and then he committed suicide in jail before he told us anything else. That's the way the Feds want it, and that's the way it's going to be."

Bino felt a burn coming on and forced himself to think about what he was going to say next. But he couldn't keep the anger out of his voice. "This is county business, Hardy, not just federal. Yeah, I know Goldman and his bunch. I've had some time to think about them. They don't want Winnie Anspacher to go down on this thing, not with the election coming on and Winnie being Art Stammer's main man. If Art Stammer was to stub his toe and get beat, there might be somebody get into office that's got some sense. Somebody who'd give them as much trouble as Richard Bigelow was going to, make the public aware of what's going on. Aware that these silly Feds are blowing millions stacked on millions of the taxpayers' dough running around jousting windmills like a pack of Don Quixotes. Acting like they're fighting drugs when all they're really doing is letting the hardcore dealers sell all the drugs they want to as long as they'll set somebody else up as the patsy and snitch them off. Prosecuting bankers who haven't done a damn thing except have a few loans go bad on them, just so the F.D.I.C. can collect off the poor guys' bonding companies. Blowing millions on a bunch of F.B.I.'s and prosecutors that they need like they need a second asshole, then telling them to go dream up a case on somebody so it'll look like they're doing something.

"Yeah, Hardy, I can see Goldman's angle. But yours? Jesus Christ, Hardy, we're talking cold-blooded murder here. For a payoff. I got to tell you that I've always had a lot more respect for the way the state does things than I do the Feds. At least the state is going after *criminals,* Hardy, real stickup men and rapists and whatnot. But now you're telling me that you're going to sweep murder under the rug, just because *Goldman* says to? Jesus Christ. The whole bunch of you make me want to go to the nearest gutter and puke in it." Bino's voice had risen an octave, and one of the old women at the bar turned and glared at him. He stopped to catch his breath.

Hardy kept his gaze riveted on the glass of beer in front of him and his face deadpan as he said, "Okay, Bino, you've made you a speech. Now I'm going to make one. We don't know who knocked off Longley in jail, I swear to God. It could have been Tirelli, probably was. But it doesn't have to be him, see. That's how bad the Feds want this one hushed up. And you can bet your ass that the orders came from a lot higher up than Marvin Fucking Goldman. Goldman's just the errand boy in this, the runner.

"Now me and Mac, we talked this over a lot. Yeah, we want to move on it. If Winnie Anspacher did what it looks like he did, then he ought to be on death row with the rest of the killers. No question about it."

Hardy raised his eyes slowly to look straight at Bino before he went on. "But what do you think's going to happen if we do push it, huh? Jesus, Bino, of all the people in the world I shouldn't have to tell *you.* We prosecute, and the next thing you know there's going to be a federal investigation on *us,* the county. There'll be a bunch of shit in the papers about me taking payoffs, probably Mac Strange, too. Doesn't make any difference if we did or not, the papers'll say we did. Then there'll be indictments and they'll cart us both off to the federal joint. It's the way they do things, Bino. Shit, you know that. One of their own judges, out in Vegas—what's his name, Claiborne? All he was doing was making the Feds toe the mark in court, give a fair trial. So they framed him for income tax, sent him away. My God, Bino, if a *federal judge* can't beat 'em, what do you think they'd do to Mac and me? I'm sorry, Bino, but that's the way it is. They're too damned powerful and we're not fucking with them. And I'd lay off, too, if I were you, buddy. They'll put your ass away if you don't."

Bino thought, Yeah, they probably will. Me and Hardy Cole and Mac Strange along with anybody else who gets in their way. Hardy wasn't putting him on, either. Under normal circumstances Mac would jump at the chance to prosecute Tirelli—or Winnie Anspacher. Mac was scared to death. So was Hardy Cole, and they had plenty of reason to be. Come to think about it, so did Bino Phillips.

He said, "Where's Winnie Anspacher, Hardy? I don't guess there's any reason for the Feds to want to get him out of town, is there? They've already got the girl agent, Karen Allen, in cold storage. With her out of the way there's no way for anybody to prove that Goldman knows nothing from nothing. I mean, anything that Goldman is aware of, she had to be the one to tell him about it."

Hardy shrugged and shook his head. "Naw. There ain't. Mac got the call from the jail about Longley being dead last night around nine. Now he knew all along where Winnie Anspacher was supposed to be, Goldman told him. So Mac puts in a call to the motel. And guess what? They were already gone, Bino, the F.B.I., Anspacher, all of them. That means that the Feds knew about Longley even before *Mac* did. And you're right about Miss Allen. She'll turn up somewhere else, probably working in a foreign office. Wherever they put her, you can bet your ass nobody's going to be able to put her on a witness stand and swear her in. It's over, Bino. Finished. Winnie Anspacher can go around any way he feels like it and nobody's gonna lay a finger on him. He's off the hook, scot-free."

Bino thought, Not quite. Sarah Anspacher knows about it all, and that's going to make things tougher on Winnie. Not as tough as they ought to be, but tougher.

He said, "Yeah, Hardy, I guess you're right. I don't like it, you don't like it. But that's the way things work out sometimes." He checked the wall clock behind the bar. "I guess we'd both better be going. I don't know about you, Hardy, but I'm gonna do something to put this out of my mind. Maybe take a week off, go hide out in Mesquite. Get drunk, who knows?"

"I'll leave the tip." Hardy fished in his pocket and brought out a dollar bill. "Oh, and Bino. Just so you'll know it. Fifteen, twenty years ago Mac and I would have gone after 'em like gangbusters, Feds or no. But we're too old and too much has happened. Things just don't seem to matter like they used to."

Bino was thinking about that one as he left. The old folks at the bar were still drinking. Not much seemed to matter to them, either.

Dodie's posture in the chair said that she didn't like Bino giving up so easily. Her elbows were on the armrests, her shoulders slightly hunched, and her gaze was directed over Bino's shoulder, not directly at him.

She licked her upper lip. "Well, what are you going to do, boss?"

Bino leaned back in his swivel chair and put his feet on the desk, hands clasped behind his head. "I don't know, Dode. I really don't. I'll be back here in a couple of weeks, maybe less. By then I'll know. For right now you're paid for a month, longer if you need it. You sure don't have to work for me, Dodie. There isn't a lawyer in this town who wouldn't hire you in a minute."

She dropped her hands into her lap and watched them. When she looked back up her eyes were misting. "That isn't it, Bino. It's not me I'm worried about, it's you. You don't need the law near so much as it needs you. I've been around. And I've had other offers. But there aren't many lawyers around that I know who care what's right and what's wrong. You do, and that means something. You're down right now, but you'll get it back. I know you will."

It was Dodie's caring look and it got to him. He had to clear his throat before saying, 'Thanks for the vote, Dodie. I need it. I'm not going to make a decision as yet, but I'm—"

He stopped because the phone was ringing. Dodie reached across his desk and picked it up. She said, "Lawyer's office," then, "One moment, please," and put the caller on hold. "It's for you. Mrs. Anspacher."

Bino was frowning as he got on the line. "Sarah?"

It was the steady, calm voice. There was a slight tremor in it, but it was hard to pick up on. "I'm afraid I need a lawyer, Bino. I've just shot Winnie. He's dead, I think. Isn't that what I'm supposed to do, call a lawyer, then the police?"

A few seconds passed before it sank in. "I've shot Winnie," in the same even tone she'd used on Saturday night saying, "There's nothing I wouldn't do to protect them. Nothing."

Bino said, "Don't do anything else, Sarah. Sit down and try to stay relaxed until I get there. Have a stiff drink."

"Why, whatever is left for me to get excited about? But I will have the drink, I think. Make it soon please, Bino." She hung up.

As Bino hustled out of the office, Dodie said, "Well, my goodness. Aren't you going to tell me what's happening? Today's the day you're supposed to meet with Judge Sanderson. It's close to one o'clock, Bino." Her blue eyes were wide, expectant.

Bino paused at the door. "It's a good friend, Dodie. She's in trouble. As for the judge—well, she's a Fed. She can go butt her head against a stump, for all I care."

As he went out in the hall Dodie said, "I'll tell her, Bino. Be glad to."

Funny, but this wasn't the way that Bino would have pictured Winnie Anspacher's study. It was close to the rear of the second floor of the big home and had one small window that overlooked a garden with a creeping vine nearly obliterating a white wooden trellis. The garden was perfectly shaped, trimmed, and manicured. Of course it was. Sarah Anspacher wouldn't have allowed it any other way.

Bino had imagined that a man like Winnie Anspacher would have his library full of Federal Seconds and Southwestern Reporters and all sorts of books that would tell you about the latest court decisions and the best way to use them to screw the other guy. But Winnie's bookshelves were filled mostly with fiction. Modern fiction, Robert B. Parker, Elmore Leonard. Jesus, even a couple by Stephen King. Being careful not to touch anything, Bino leaned over to study the jacket on a Raymond Chandler Omnibus. *The Big Sleep. The Lady in the Lake.* Winnie had a lot better taste than Bino would ever have thought he did.

The next-door neighbors lived in a rambling one-story, whose gray-shingled roof was below the level of Winnie's study window. Nobody over there could see in over here. Bino thought, That's good, then sat down in a wicker chair and studied Winnie.

Winnie was behind a dark polished desk that was about half the size of the one in his office downtown, his chin resting on his breastbone. His glasses had slid down to the end of his nose and perched there. The .22 had made a small, round hole in his left temple that was an ugly purple around the edges. His mouth was open like a flytrap. He didn't look very pretty. He still was short.

Bino couldn't see the bullet's exit wound from where he sat now, but he'd studied it pretty closely a few moments ago. He'd been surprised at how small it was, maybe half again the size of the hole in the front of Winnie's head. And there was a lot less blood than one would expect, most of it splattered on the chair's leather headrest, where it would be pretty easy to clean with a damp towel. Bino wished that Karen Allen had shot John-boy with a .22 instead of the Walther PPK. The hole in the chairback was bigger than the exit wound, the hole that Bino had enlarged while he was digging with a pocketknife. The spent .22 slug was now in Bino's coat pocket, along with the brass casing that he'd found on the carpet. Bino carefully wiped the desk telephone that he'd used one last time with his handkerchief, gave the room another visual once-over, and went downstairs.

Sarah hadn't moved. She was still in the vast living room where Art Stammer's fund-raiser had been, sitting on a high wrought-iron stool at the bar. Bino'd never seen her in slacks before. They were a modestly cut brown, and she looked fine in them. The snifter of brandy that Bino had poured for her might have had a couple of swallows gone, no more. Bino eyed her manicured hands. They weren't trembling.

Bino said, "Are you sure that he didn't call anybody else? That nobody knew he was at home?"

There was a dull glaze over Sarah's eyes. She might

go berserk in private, but nobody was going to watch her make a scene. Calmly, she said, "No. He was supposed to be on his way to the club. I've already checked it out with the secretaries in his office. They think he's playing golf right now. And that may be where he was going, I don't know. He just came by here to make his"—her upper lip curled slightly—"his damned phone call."

"And he didn't know that you were here?"

She took the brandy in both hands and sipped, then shook her head slowly. "Monday is supposed to be a meeting day for me—some ghastly charity or other. I didn't feel like going after what's happened lately. I was in my room lying down when I heard him come in. I just took the pistol with me to show it to him, that I had it. That's when I heard him on the phone. God, Bino he was *laughing* about it." She set the glass down and hugged herself, like she was suddenly cold.

Bino moved around behind the bar so that he was facing Sarah and leaned slightly toward her. "I want you to think now, Sarah. You don't know who it was that he was talking to, you've told me that. But did he tell the person on the other end where he was calling from?"

Behind Sarah lay the big den with its mile-long divans and stuffed chairs. It hadn't seemed this large the other night. Empty now, it looked to be the size of the Astrodome.

She said, "It was some trollop, is all I know. No, he didn't say where he was calling from. That much I'm sure of, and I heard the whole conversation from the hall outside the study. Probably didn't even want her to know he had a wife and children. God, I wish I hadn't taken the gun with me—then I'd probably have just kicked him out. Whatever's going to happen to me, Bino?" She was starting to break down.

Bino thought, Nothing if I have anything to say about it. He said, "What time do your kids get home from school, Sarah?" He'd noticed their pictures in Winnie's study. Good-looking pair.

"Around four. In a couple of hours. Why?"

"I saw Winnie's Caddy parked out in front. The keys were upstairs in his pocket." Bino pulled a set of jingling keys up and showed them to her. "You're coming through like a champ, Sarah. Think you can drive?"

Her lips parted in surprise. "Why, yes, Bino. I suppose so. What are you–?"

"Don't give me time to think about this, Sarah. I'll probably chicken out if you do. But I'm going to try to do the only decent thing that's been done in this whole stinking mess. There's a guy on his way over here right now that's going to help me. I'm going upstairs again, and I want you to drive Winnie's car up the slope into the garage. Shut the door to the garage and pop the trunklid open."

She was staring openmouthed. Both of her hands were on the brandy snifter.

Bino winked at her. "Get going, Sarah. This is the easy part."

Barney Dalton stood in the aggregate circular drive about halfway between the street and the garage. His hands were spread apart, palms up. "You're shitting me, Bino. He's in the trunk?"

Bino was on the slope of the drive, about five feet closer to the house, Barney's head on a level with his belt buckle. It was overcast and chilly, and Barney's Crooked River windbreaker was dark green. Bino'd shed his coat and was in shirtsleeves. Despite the weather he was still perspiring from lugging Winnie. The soreness in his pectorals had seemed a lot better this morning, but now they'd started to ache again.

The butt of Winnie's tan Seville was visible where the driveway flattened out to enter the open garage. Sarah stood next to the car with her arms folded. She'd thrown a white sweater around her shoulders. Barney's blue Monte Carlo was far below them on the street, smoke curling upward from its exhausts.

Bino said, "Trust me, Barney. When they find him there's not even going to be much of an investigation."

"Naw, Bino. There ain't. What's to investigate? They'll just pick you and me up and give us about thirty years apiece."

Bino laughed. "They can't afford to. Not with the Feds trying to cover up—Look, Barney, I don't have time to go into a long song and dance about it. But believe me, it'll go down as a suicide. Tell you what, Barney. If it ever comes up, nobody's even going to know you went with me. But somebody's going to have to follow along to pick me up. Come on, Barney."

Barney looked skeptical. "I don't know, Bino. You're the lawyer and all, but—"

"Besides," said Bino. "You owe me one. Remember Dupard?"

"Jesus Christ, Bino, so next time I'll get better info. You're crazy, you know that? Absolutely fucking—" He stopped, looked up to where Sarah was standing. Then he turned and began to plod back down the driveway to his car, talking to Bino over his shoulder. "One time, Bino. Just this once. I always wondered what the penitentiary was like, anyway. Hurry up, Bino. Before I change my mind."

When Bino was standing in the garage next to the Seville, he said to Sarah, "Have you got the gun?"

She handed it to him, a faraway look in her eyes.

"You shouldn't be doing this, Bino. I ought—well, I ought to just take my medicine."

He felt tears stinging the backs of his eyelids. "Hush, Sarah. You've already had plenty of medicine. Now you get upstairs and clean up that study like I told you to. And Sarah—"

Impulsively, he leaned over and kissed her on the forehead.

"You go raise some good kids, Sarah," he said. "Just like you."

After Bino'd parked the Caddy on South County river bottom land and Barney had helped him wrestle Winnie Anspacher into a sitting position behind the steering wheel, there was one more problem. It occurred to Bino just as he was about to drop the .22 onto the floorboard of the Seville.

Bino murmured, "Powder burns."

Barney said, "Huh?"

"I'm going to have to shoot him, Barney."

"Shit, Bino, he's already shot. I *thought* you were crazy. Next thing you'll be shooting me."

Bino put the barrel of the pistol over the hole in Winnie's forehead, aimed it in the direction of the exit wound, and pulled the trigger. The report was like a Chinese firecracker, echoing over silent fields of brown weeds and muddy-banked creeks. Winnie jerked once, violently, then was still.

Bino wiped the gun down for fingerprints. Thinking about Goldman, Mac Strange, and Hardy Cole, he wasn't too careful about it. He halfway hoped they'd know who'd done it.

The office lights were turned off when Bino got back. Darkness was falling. He had to show his I.D. to the chubby kid in the lobby, sign in, and drive himself upstairs on the elevator. Teresa Valdez's elevator.

He groped for the switch just inside the door to his suite and turned on the overhead. Dodie's chair was pushed up to where its cushioned back touched the edge of her desk. Every pen, glass paperweight, and piece of paper was in perfect alignment on and around her blotter.

He started to turn on Half-a-Point's light, then decided that there was enough illumination from the outer room for him to see. Half's wooden swivel chair squeaked in protest as Bino sat down. Half's belongings were as jumbled as Dodie's were organized, so Bino had a little trouble finding an envelope. The black phone rang a partial ring, then was silent. It was "Monday Night Football" tonight and the calls were being forwarded to Pop's.

Bino finally located a white business envelope and slipped five hundreds and a fifty inside. He sealed the flap, wrote "10–7, Texas. Barney says he'll see you Wednesday" on the back, and put the envelope in the top drawer.

He gazed out the window for a while. On Main Street, headlights were beginning to come on. South I-45 was a twinkling ribbon on the horizon. Half's office had the only view that wasn't blocked by a structure taller than the Davis Building.

Bino hoped that when Winnie's body was discovered it would somehow cause Art Stammer to lose the election. But it wouldn't. Winnie's apparent suicide would be glossed over, and somebody else would take up Stammer's campaign where Winnie'd left off. And the conservatives would keep running the show, and the voter would keep thinking he had a good deal. Right up until the voter needed some constitutional rights of his own. Then it would be too late. Bino thought briefly about dropping a bug in the ear of some investigative reporter—someone like Skip the Scoop. But he'd never do that to Sarah.

No, it was over, and Bino'd done about everything that he could do. He got up and headed for his own office. He wanted to pack a few things.

He stopped halfway there. There was a note in Dodie's typewriter that he hadn't noticed before, a note with his name at the top. He rolled the platen, took the paper out, began to read. And grinned.

The note said:

Bino,

There are a number of reasons why you should keep on practicing law. A few of them are

Someone has to support Cecil.

Someone has to defend Half when he gets busted.

People like Wimpy need help.

White-haired lawyers are cute.

Call me when you get here and I'll give you some more.

D.

He flopped down at her desk and called her home number. She answered breathlessly. "Bino?"

He leaned back. "Yeah, Dodie. It's me."

"Wow, I was in the shower. I was scared to death I'd miss you. Listen, Bino. It's me, too. I don't want to work for anybody else. It just—"

"Now hold on, Dode. I—"

"—wouldn't be the same. Nobody else is going to be such an inspiration to me, and—"

"—don't know if I'm going to—"

"—besides, you're just tired is all, and I know just what you need."

"—quit or—What I need? What's that, Dodie?" He sat up.

She was silent for a moment. Then a loud jangling started in the background and she said, "Hear that? You know what that is? I've got it wound up tight, and if you can get over here before it runs down I'll—"

Bino'd already set down the receiver and was halfway out into the hall. It was silly to even think he might have a chance to get all the way to Dodie's apartment before the old drugstore alarm clock stopped ringing. But he was going to try like hell.

About the Author

A. W. Gray has played poker at Binnion's World Championship and driven to South America with golf star Lee Trevino. He has lived in Memphis, Los Angeles, and New Orleans, and currently makes his home in Fort Worth, Texas.